ID0439995

The Battle of Jericho

ALSO BY SHARON M. DRAPER

Copper Sun
Double Dutch
Out of My Mind
Panic
Romiette & Julio
Stella by Starlight

The Jericho Trilogy:
The Battle of Jericho
November Blues
Just Another Hero

The Hazelwood High Trilogy:
Tears of a Tiger
Forged by Fire
Darkness Before Dawn

Clubhouse Mysteries
The Buried Bones Mystery
Lost in the Tunnel of Time
Shadows of Caesar's Creek
The Space Mission Adventure
The Backyard Animal Show
Stars and Sparks on Stage

THE JERICHO TRILOGY #1

The Battle of Jericho

SHARON M. DRAPER

atheneum

A Caitlyn Dlouhy Book

NEW YORK LONDON TORONTO SYDNEY NEW DELHI

An imprint of Simon & Schuster Children's Publishing Division | 1230 Avenue of the Americas, New York, New York 10020 | This book is a work of fiction. Any references to historical events, real people, or real places are used fictitiously. Other names, characters, places, and events are products of the author's imagination, and any resemblance to actual events or places or persons, living or dead, is entirely coincidental. | Text copyright © 2003 by Sharon M. Draper | Cover illustration copyright © 2017 by Edel Rodriguez | All rights reserved, including the right of reproduction in whole or in part in any form. | Atheneum logo is a trademark of Simon & Schuster, Inc. | For information about special discounts for bulk purchases, please contact Simon & Schuster Special Sales at 1-866-506-1949 or business@simonandschuster.com. | The Simon & Schuster Speakers Bureau can bring authors to your live event. For more information or to book an event, contact the Simon & Schuster Speakers Bureau at 1-866-248-3049 or visit our website at www.simonspeakers.com. | Also available in an Atheneum hardcover edition | Book design by Debra Sfetsios-Conover | The text for this book was set in Trade Gothic. | Manufactured in the United States of America | First Atheneum paperback edition July 2017 | 10 9 8 7 6 5 4 3 2 1 | The Library of Congress has cataloged the hardcover edition as follows: | Draper, Sharon M. (Sharon Mills) | The Battle of Jericho / Sharon M. Draper | p. cm. | Summary: A high school junior and his cousin suffer the ramifications of joining what seems to be a "reputable" school club. | ISBN 978-0-689-84232-0 (hc) | ISBN 978-1-4814-9029-0 (pbk) | ISBN 978-1-4391-1520-6 (eBook) | [1. Clubs—Fiction. 2. High schools—Fiction. 3. Schools—Fiction. 4. Cousins—Fiction. 5. Death—Fiction.] I. Title. | PZ7.D78325 Bat 2003 | [Fic]—dc21 2002008612

For Larry,
who understands it all

THE BEGINNING OF THE END: JANUARY 28

THE PLEDGE MASTERS MARCHED THE FIFTEEN *pledges to the middle of the soggy yard. The ground was muddy and squished as they walked, and the frigid air whipped across the pledges' wet T-shirts. Sharp needles of rain stung them as they stood there silently waiting for instructions.*

"Kneel!" Rick Sharp shouted to Jericho.

Jericho wanted to disobey, but instead he knelt immediately. Cold mud soaked through his jeans in seconds.

"Take off my boot, Pledge Slime!" the six-foot, broad-shouldered senior shouted to Jericho over the noise of the pouring rain. He glanced down at Jericho, who huddled at his feet.

Jericho shivered as the rain came down harder and made him sink deeper into the mud of the desolate warehouse yard. His fingers were wet and stiff, but he reached for Sharp's big, black army boot and slowly began to untie the laces.

"Hurry up, Pledge Slime!" Sharp shouted. Jericho dejectedly struggled to untie the wet lace of the pledge master's boot, his fingers aching. He wasn't sure what to do when he finished. He had no idea how to get the boot off Rick's foot.

He glanced over to see, if he could, the line of the other pledges, also kneeling in the mud at the feet of their pledge masters. But the rain and the darkness made it difficult to see very much. Jericho could barely even see Josh, who was closest to him in the line, but he could hear Mad Madison shouting at him in the darkness. Jericho couldn't see Kofi or Dana at all.

"All of us have been where you are tonight," Sharp told Jericho. *"A Warrior of Distinction is not afraid to lower himself for his brother. A Warrior of Distinction does not show fear. Are you afraid, Pledge Slime?"*

"No, sir," Jericho replied. *"I'm not afraid."*

"Then get busy! The rest of your pledge class, slimy and disgusting as they are, seem to be doing fine. Do you want to let them down?"

Jericho inhaled slowly. It was all of them or none of them. *"Can you lift your foot, Master Senior Sharp, sir?"* Jericho asked timidly. As he raised his face to look at Sharp, he gasped as the icy rain stung his eyes.

"Did I give you permission to speak, Pledge Slime?" Sharp snarled. Jericho said nothing, but Rick lifted his right foot, using Jericho's head to balance himself.

Jericho pulled the boot off with difficulty. He was afraid that he would fall or would make Rick fall as he tugged at the boot. Either would have been disastrous, but he managed to get the boot off smoothly. The stench of Rick Sharp's foot was enough to make Jericho choke.

"Now take off the sock," Rick barked.

Jericho hesitated and hoped they would be able to go home soon. He slowly peeled off Rick's sock. Rick's foot reeked of sweat.

"Place the sock on the ground, then set my foot down on it. Make sure not a speck of mud touches my foot," he commanded.

Jericho did as he was told and Rick Sharp removed his hand from Jericho's head as he lowered his foot to the ground. Then he bent down and whispered into Jericho's ear, "You havin' fun yet?"

Jericho didn't dare tell the truth—that he had stopped having fun long ago.

"You really want to be a Warrior of Distinction?" Rick asked.

Jericho nodded. He thought of the prestige of having one of those black silk jackets, the admiring glances in the halls at school, but mostly he thought of Arielle. He tried not to think of the rain and the mud and the stink of Rick's feet.

"Are you willing to do anything to be a Warrior of Distinction?" Rick demanded. "You have permission to answer."

"Yes, sir! Yes, Master Senior Sharp, sir! I am willing to do anything to be a Warrior of Distinction, sir!" Jericho repeated the words that he and the other pledges had been chanting automatically since the whole process began. But he wasn't sure if he meant them anymore.

"Are you willing to do anything to help the others become Warriors of Distinction?" Rick demanded.

"Anything, sir." Jericho just wanted it to be over.

"Then suck my big toe."

"Sir?" Jericho wasn't sure if he had heard correctly.

"If you want to be a Warrior of Distinction, you must suck my big toe. Now!"

Jericho looked around desperately; he had no idea what the others were being forced to do. As he lowered his head close to the mud and closer to Rick Sharp's foot, Jericho wondered miserably how he could have sunk so low.

THE BEGINNING:
THE FIRST WEEK OF DECEMBER—
THURSDAY, DECEMBER 4

"HEY JOSH, WHAT YOU GETTING YOUR GIRL
November for Christmas?" Jericho asked
as the two headed for a table in the hot,
crowded cafeteria. The lunchroom, stuffy
with the odors of pizza, salsa, and sweat, was
especially full today because the weather was
cold and blustery, and nobody chose to eat outside.

Josh laughed as he squeezed his long legs
under the cafeteria table. "Oh, you know, the
usual—diamonds and gold jewelry!"

"So I see you plan to shop at the dollar store
again this year!" Jericho teased his cousin. "I don't
see how November puts up with you." Jericho's hefty
body barely fit in the small cafeteria seat. He hated
feeling squeezed in—he liked his jeans baggy and his
T-shirts extra large.

Josh grinned. "She knows she's lucky. She gets to walk
in the glow of my light. She's thanked me every day since

ninth grade when I first let her hook up with me!"

"That Rice Krispies–colored hair you got does make you kinda look like a lamp on top," Jericho joked.

"November loves it—that's all that matters. She clicks my switch and turns me on. And then I let her walk down the halls with me so she can share in my glorious light!"

"You better not let her hear you talk about her like that, or she may put your lights out!" Jericho warned as he ate his cafeteria pizza. "November's like a deep lake, and you're a bowl of goldfish water!"

"How you figure?" Josh asked.

"When's the last time you volunteered to work with little kids at a hospital?" Jericho continued to eat the pizza, even though he thought it tasted like cardboard covered with red sauce.

"I used to *be* a little kid," Josh replied. "Does that count?"

Jericho laughed. "Maybe that's why she hangs with you—you're just another project for her to work on."

"She can work on me all night long!" Josh answered with a grin.

"You know, this pizza tastes more like the plastic they wrap it in than real pizza." He licked the plastic just to make sure. Even though he didn't like the pizza, he ate four pieces.

"I don't know how you can eat that stuff, Jericho," Josh commented as he bit into a cold Big Mac that he had bought the night before.

"Look who's talkin'!" laughed Jericho. "At least I don't

go with a girl whose mama named her for one of the coldest months of the year!"

"At least I got a girl!" Josh shot back as he stuffed the rest of the burger into his mouth. "She was born on Thanksgiving Day. I'm just glad her mama wasn't drunk that day. She coulda named her Turkey!"

A tall, thin boy wearing wire-rim glasses sat down with them. "Hey, whassup, Kofi?" Jericho greeted him. Kofi Freeman's face was covered with the zits and scars of an ongoing battle with acne, but Jericho noticed that he never seemed to have a problem talking to girls. "What took you so long?"

"Long line." For lunch Kofi had purchased a large bag of french fries and a Coke. He dipped each fry into his drink before he ate it.

"Now *that's* disgusting!" Josh hooted, shaking his head. "You both still coming over my house on Saturday?"

"Yeah, I ain't got nothin' better to do," Kofi replied as he sucked a french fry dry.

"You gonna bring Dana the Wolf?" Jericho asked Kofi. "You sure you're tough enough to handle her?"

"Yeah, probably. Strong, tall women turn me on!" Kofi answered with a laugh.

"Hey Jericho, speaking of women, here comes your girl Arielle," Kofi whispered as she walked toward them carrying her tray. Arielle wore a blue-and-white Douglass High sweatshirt, blue jeans that hugged her hips, and clean white tennis shoes. She wore her hair swept back from her face, with three small silver earrings in each ear. Jericho could feel his underarms getting clammy as she approached. "I heard she liked her men large and sloppy, with messed-up trumpet-playin' lips, so you just may have a chance!" Kofi said, giving his friend a shove.

Josh added, "Yeah, my cuz here knows how to kiss a trumpet and make it sing, but he may have some trouble with a girl like Arielle!"

"If she was shaped like a trumpet, Jericho would know just what to do," Kofi teased. "A trumpet he can handle—it doesn't talk back like a girl does!"

Josh laughed, "Arielle is all that *and* a bag of chips! That girl can talk and walk better than any trumpet Jericho has ever seen!"

Kofi chuckled as he worked on his Coke-soaked french fries. "You better go ahead and talk to her, Jericho, before all that good stuff is gone!"

Jericho didn't really mind the teasing—he just wished he could be as comfortable with girls as Josh and Kofi were. "Shut up, man," Jericho whispered, "before she hears you. You know I been tryin' to talk to her since school started." He couldn't figure out how he managed to feel so completely stupid around a girl like Arielle.

"So talk! Here's your chance," Josh replied.

"I can't—she's got Dana the Wolf with her." Dana Wolfe had a reputation of being tough. She had been the first girl to get a tattoo, the first to get her eyebrow pierced, and could be depended on to be the first to jump into a fight to defend her friends. And she could outshoot in basketball and outrun on the track many of the boys in the junior class.

Arielle and Dana whispered something to each other and laughed just before they reached the table where Jericho, Kofi, and Josh sat.

"Whassup, Kofi?" Dana said, clearly ignoring Jericho and Josh. Wearing tall black boots, a suede skirt, and a soft green sweater, she carried her five-foot-ten-inches regally. She was almost as tall as Kofi.

Kofi grinned and replied, "Just you, Dana. Did I ever tell you I was a wolf in a former life? Maybe that means we were meant to be together!"

"Yeah, and maybe that means you've got some serious mental problems!" she replied with a smirk.

"Ooh, she got you, man!" Josh hooted.

"Don't get me started on you," she warned Josh with a grin, "or I may have to chase you home from school, so you can run to your mama for protection!"

They all cracked up then. Arielle said very little, and even though she laughed at Kofi and Josh with the rest of them, she looked bored and impatient. She barely glanced at Jericho. He had stopped eating when the girls got to their table. He didn't want to say something to Arielle with pepperoni stuck in his teeth, and he couldn't think of anything clever to say anyway. Just as Jericho figured out that he'd ask Arielle about the biology homework, she and Dana saw three other girls they knew and went to sit at their table. It seemed to Jericho that the air where she had been standing was suddenly chillier when she left. Why did he feel like such an idiot whenever she was around?

The three boys had almost finished lunch when two seniors sauntered across the crowded cafeteria. They wore black silk jackets, black jeans, and the very latest, most expensive Nike shoes. Jericho recognized them immediately—everyone in the school knew the Warriors of Distinction.

Whispers and rumors surrounded the club. It was common knowledge that the Warriors all wore the latest shoes and clothes—every single day. They had a reputation of giving the very best parties—you had to know somebody just to get an invitation. Kids who had been to these functions came back boasting about the live entertainment, the upscale houses where the parties had been held, and the easy access to kegs and smokes.

But the Warriors also had a positive reputation with adults. The club was well known for collecting and distributing books to kids in the summer and toys in the winter. Many fathers of current Douglass students, and lots of men in town as well, had been members of the Warriors when they were students. They kept up with each other at annual meetings, and rumors of fixed parking tickets or lower rates for car loans buzzed around.

Jericho wondered whose table the boys were heading to as they walked confidently across the room. A club like that was just plain tight. His heart thudded as they seemed to be heading directly toward them. Jericho, Josh, and Kofi looked up with disbelief as the Warriors stopped abruptly at their table. Kofi dropped his french fry into his Coke.

"Kofi Freeman? Jericho Prescott? Joshua Prescott?"

"Yeah, that's us," Jericho answered.

"Are you two brothers?" one of the Warriors asked Jericho and Josh.

"No, cousins," they answered together. They were used to the question; people had been asking them that since they were kids.

"We've been observing the three of you," the taller of the Warriors began, "and we think you have potential."

"Us?" Jericho asked. He couldn't believe that anyone had bothered to notice him at all.

The two members of the club stared at Josh, Jericho, and Kofi with stony eyes. They turned as if they were going to walk away. Jericho gasped silently. Then the two seniors looked at each other, faced the three friends once more, and crossed their arms in unison. The taller one cleared his throat and said finally, "The Warriors of Distinction want to know if you would like to help us this year with our holiday toy drive. It's hard work and there is no pay. But underprivileged children all over the city will thank you."

Josh spoke first. "Yeah, I'll help."

"Me too," Kofi added.

"Sign me up," Jericho said quickly, just in case they might think he wasn't interested.

"We'll meet at five P.M. Eddie Mahoney's place on Gilbert Avenue. Here are the directions. Don't be late." With that, the two Warriors of Distinction turned and left the cafeteria. They spoke to no one else, although Jericho noticed that every girl in the lunchroom watched them as they made their way out of the door and into the hall.

Jericho and Josh looked at each other and grinned. "You know what this means?" Josh said. "It means we're on the list to be Warriors!"

"Not necessarily," Jericho countered. "I knew a dude

last year that got asked to do the Christmas thing and he didn't get asked to pledge."

"Well, there's lots of things they check, you know," Kofi reminded them. "Like grades, stuff you do around the school, and who you hang with." He had pulled the dropped french fry out of the soda.

"And how you eat your french fries?" laughed Josh.

"Who knows what they check? Who cares! All I know is the first step to getting in is being asked to help out at the toy drive, and we just got there!" Jericho said exultantly.

"What's the real deal with Warriors of Distinction and the school?" Kofi whispered, looking around to make sure that no Warriors were close enough to hear him.

"Well, it's not officially school sponsored anymore—some business in the community decided to sponsor them a few years back, I heard," Jericho explained. "But only Douglass kids are members, and they always get a Douglass teacher to help them out."

"Doesn't matter," Josh declared breezily. "They've been around for like a million years—almost as long as this old, rusty school has been here."

"So how do they get over with the principal and teachers if they're not really a school club?" Kofi continued.

"I've seen the principal, Mr. Zucker, wear his old Warrior jacket to school sometimes, so I know he was a member of the Warriors when he went to school here—several of the teachers, too," Josh offered. "Even my dad was a Warrior!"

"Yeah, yeah, we know." Jericho then said thoughtfully, "I've seen the Warriors around at school stuff, at Open House and Homecoming and Teacher Appreciation Day.

They show up and look good, doing stuff for the school like showing parents around or passing out apples to the teachers, and the school has always given them perks."

"Like what?" Kofi asked.

"Like they get their schedules fixed so they have no afternoon classes. And they get trusted with keys to things that no other student has access to—the faculty lounge, the student store, the supply room. And who ends up working in the office in the computer room where report card records are kept? Warriors of Distinction!" Then he lowered his voice. "I've heard kids talkin' about grades being changed. I don't know how they do it, but I'd love to have that kind of power."

"I heard they've got the answers to every teacher's final exam!" Josh exclaimed.

"Is that, like, possible?" Kofi asked.

"And did you ever notice the hottest girls in school seem to hang with the Warriors?" Jericho asked, thinking of Arielle.

"Well, sign me up, dude!" Josh declared cheerily.

"You ever been to one of their parties?" Kofi asked in a whisper.

"Not hardly. I know some kids who did, though," Jericho told them. "All the way live!"

Josh finished the last of his chocolate-chip cookies. "Where you think they get those jackets, man? They wear the silk ones when they want to look slick, and the leather ones when they want to look tight. Either way, I'd look *too* good in one of those!"

"I hear they got connections. Goes way back, I hear,"

Jericho answered vaguely. Since everybody at school talked about the Warriors all the time, it was hard to tell what was real and what was made up. Not all the whispers about the Warriors were good.

"Aw, you can't believe everything you hear, man," Kofi told them. "But I'd take that kinda hookup if it's for real."

"I can see how they'd ask you two—Kofi, you're the computer genius, and Josh, you're good at sports and just about everything else, but I can't believe they asked me, too," Jericho admitted quietly.

"Aw, quit dissin' yourself," Kofi told him. "The Warriors know who's got it together. And I bet Arielle figures it out too!"

"For real, though, the only way I can get a girl like Arielle to speak to me is if I need to borrow a pencil in class."

"Relax, man. I bet she'll be sharpening your pencils before you know it," Josh said with a chuckle. "This is so awesome! I can't wait to tell Dad."

"Yeah," Kofi said. "He'll think it's pretty cool that his pinhead son finally did something right! Hey Jericho, didn't your dad go to school here too? How come he wasn't a Warrior?"

Josh's father, Brock, and Jericho's father, whose name was Cedric, were brothers and had both attended Frederick Douglass High. However, Cedric, the older of the two, had never been asked to pledge. Brock, three years younger, had pledged and boasted about it ever since. Jericho wasn't sure if his father regretted not being a Warrior or not. But he told Kofi, "Aw, my dad ran the school when he was here—he didn't have time to be a Warrior!"

"You think he'll be glad you might be in it?" Kofi asked.

"Probably." Jericho bit into his second ice cream sandwich. "He don't stress me about that kind of stuff."

"You think they make those Warrior jackets big enough for you, Jericho?" Josh asked with a grin.

Jericho had actually wondered the same thing, but he said, "You just jealous 'cause when the girls try to put their arms around you, they think they're grabbing a skinny old pencil instead!"

"I'd rather look like a pencil than a bowl of oatmeal!" Josh countered.

"Well, at least my hair doesn't *look* like oatmeal!" Jericho zapped back at him.

The three of them laughed as the bell rang and they picked up their lunch trays. "We're gonna be Warriors of Distinction!" Josh declared as he did his own little dance of joy across the cafeteria floor.

As they left the lunchroom, Jericho glanced over to Arielle's table. She had gathered her books, and she seemed to be looking directly at him. The faintest hint of a smile touched her lips.

"JERICHO, MAY I SEE YOU A MOMENT?"
Mr. Tambori called as Jericho was packing his book bag after school. Jericho frowned momentarily and glanced at his watch. He was in a hurry to get out of school on time today. But Mr. Tambori was his favorite teacher, his music teacher.

"Sure, what's up, Mr. T?"

"You know the citywide instrumental competitions are very soon—the last week of January," Mr. Tambori began. "Your trumpet solo will be the highlight of the evening."

"Yeah, I know—a Thursday, right? Talk about pressure! I've been practicing every night. I'm at the place where I dream the music," Jericho replied, smiling.

"Good. A colleague of mine who lives in New York will be there. He is a professor in the music department at Juilliard. This could be the ticket to the rest of your life, Jericho," he said seriously.

Jericho fidgeted with the buckle on his book bag. "Can I just get a ticket for the rest of this week first? I don't want to think that far ahead. Maybe I'd rather play football."

Mr. Tambori looked at Jericho intently. "Are you serious? You have a talent that is rare and wonderful."

Jericho shrugged. "Coach says I'm pretty good as a fullback."

"How many fullbacks were asked to play 'The Star-Spangled Banner' at the opening day of the Bengals game last year?"

"Look, Mr. T. That was really cool—my dad was so proud of me. Even some of the girls around here thought I had it all together when I was asked to do that. But I got to watch the game while I was there, and the football players saw more action, got more attention, and got paid more than any trumpet player I ever met!"

"Have you ever met Wynton Marsalis?"

"I wish." Jericho smiled wistfully. "But don't worry, Mr. T. I'm not gonna blow this off. Don't get me wrong—I love my trumpet. And playing it makes me really mellow. But it's hard to decide about the rest of my life in the next five minutes or five days. I can't even decide whether I want pepperoni on my pizza or not. Give me a little space about the big stuff, okay?"

Mr. Tambori smiled. "Okay, Jericho. Take your time. Just keep on practicing. And don't be afraid to dream beyond where you can see."

Jericho wasn't sure what that meant, but he thanked Mr. Tambori and hurried to the main hall. He knew he had missed his bus.

Then he saw Josh at the end of the hallway. "Hey, Jericho, want a ride?" Josh yelled. "I called my dad and he's on his way to pick me and Kofi up."

"Yeah, man, thanks. Will he drop us by Eddie's house?"

"That's the plan, my man!" Josh had taken off his shoes and was sliding down the slick hall in his socks. Kofi walked behind him, shaking his head.

"You're in a good mood, Cuz," Jericho said cheerfully.

"No, he's just crazy," Kofi explained as he caught up with Josh.

"Dad is gonna be so excited," Josh said as he put his shoes back on. "I'm finally doing something he'll be proud of."

"I know what you mean," Jericho admitted. "Geneva sweats me all the time about my grades and my weight and the clothes I wear and stuff. Maybe she'll think this is cool."

"Hah! My folks *never* sweat me!" Kofi bragged. "I don't even have a curfew!" But he turned to the door and added in a quieter tone, "They don't really care what I do."

"Don't you like not having a curfew?" Jericho tried to sound encouraging.

Kofi picked at a button on his coat. "Hey, no curfew means I'm never late, man. It's cool with me."

They hovered just inside the front doors. The early December winds were frigid—the temperature was barely in the teens. Jericho shivered a little, thinking of what Kofi had just said.

Just then, Eric Bell, another junior, rolled into the main hall in his motorized wheelchair. His feet, strapped into the foot pads of the chair, were motionless. Jericho wondered what it felt like never to be able to walk. He had heard that Eric had been injured in some kind of swimming accident a few years ago. Eric's tennis shoes carried none of the scuffs that everyone else's shoes had; they looked brand-new. He had his book bag slung around the wheelchair's back, and he controlled the movement of the chair with a lever on the right arm rest. "Did my bus come yet?" he asked.

Kofi glanced out the door. "No, man, not since we been standing here." He looked at Eric's wheelchair and asked, "Hey, Eric, how do you manage that thing on the ramp in the ice and snow?"

Eric spun the chair around with skill. "Sometimes it gets pretty rough, but I'm used to it. I've been doing this since I was twelve. I remember one time I slid backward down a ramp, flipped my chair over a couple of times, and landed like a turtle on its shell, kicking and cursing!"

"I don't think I've ever heard a turtle curse," Jericho said, not sure if he should laugh or not.

"I don't think I'd want to," added Josh.

"What are you guys doing here so late?" Eric asked. "Detentions?"

Jericho chuckled. "I've done my share of detentions, man, but today we're just waiting for Josh's dad to pick us up. I hope he's not late, because we have to get to a meeting called by the Warriors of Distinction," he asserted proudly. "For the toy drive," he added.

"Oh, is that meeting today? I hadn't heard." Eric looked down and fumbled with one of the straps on his chair. Jericho didn't know what to say.

"Here's your bus, Eric," Kofi said finally. "You need some help?"

"No, I got it. Just hold the door for me." Eric wheeled out into the cold, down the wheelchair ramp to the left of the front steps—the ramp that many of the students used for skateboarding—and over to the electric lift of his waiting bus. He did not look back at Kofi, Jericho, and Josh, who somehow could not look at each other, either.

"So, who do you think is going to the Super Bowl?" Jericho broke the awkward silence that remained after Eric's bus took off.

"Too soon to tell, man," Kofi replied.

"Hey, here's my dad—finally," Josh said with relief. "Let's get out of here." They dashed from the warmth of the school building into the cold December air, tossed their book bags and Jericho's trumpet into the trunk, and sank into the soft leather seats of Mr. Prescott's car. Jericho always enjoyed it when it was his Uncle Brock's turn to pick them up from school or games or rehearsals. He was a lawyer in a big firm downtown, and he drove a loaded, late-model Lexus.

"How was school today, guys?" Josh's dad asked as he adjusted the climate control.

"Boring as usual," Kofi began.

"Till lunchtime," Jericho continued.

"So what happened then? Somebody throw a stink bomb in the hall? We did that once when I was your age," he chuckled.

"No, Dad, we don't do old-fashioned, juvenile stunts like that," Josh replied, rolling his eyes at Jericho. "Today at lunch we got asked to come to a meeting of the Warriors of Distinction to help with the Christmas toy drive!"

"Hey, that's great! Is it that time of the year already? Yep, the first week of December. I had almost forgotten."

"Can you drop us off, Dad?" Josh asked. "Here's the address."

"Of course. I'd be glad to. I am so proud of you, son— and you two as well," he added. "This brings back such strong memories. It will make you a man, son. It will make all of you better people!"

"So what happens after the toy drive, Dad?" Josh asked.

"Oh, I couldn't tell you that," his father replied. "A Warrior of Distinction never breaks the code of silence." Jericho and Kofi, sitting in the backseat, looked at each other and frowned. "Besides," he continued, "it would spoil all the fun if I told you anything. Just do your best as you work the toy drive and everything will be revealed as it should."

"Hey, Uncle Brock," Jericho began, "has there ever been a Warrior of Distinction with, like, a disability, or in a wheelchair?"

Brock Prescott was silent for a moment. "I don't think so, Jericho. Why do you ask?"

"No reason—I just wondered."

EDDIE DIDN'T LIVE FAR FROM THE SCHOOL. Jericho, Josh, and Kofi drove in silence for a few minutes, then Josh's dad pulled into the lot of a huge, old, brown apartment building. The building, with seemingly endless rows of windows and walls, was depressing-looking, Jericho thought.

"Where are we supposed to go?" Kofi asked quietly.

"It says go to the recreation room on the first floor," Jericho replied, looking down at the invitation in his sweaty hands. He was surprised at how nervous he felt.

"Do you guys want me to pick you up?" Josh's dad asked as they climbed out of the car.

"Naw, we'll get the bus," Jericho replied. "But Uncle Brock, could you call Geneva and tell her where I am so she won't be sweatin' me when I get home?"

"Sure, Jericho. Kofi, do you need for me to call your folks?"

"They're not home, so I'm cool. But thanks anyway," Kofi replied quietly.

Josh's dad drove off and the three friends stood hesitantly at the door of the apartment building, not sure which of the dozens of doorbells to push to get in. Jericho closed his eyes and picked one. A buzzer bleated from within, and the heavy, battered door swung open.

They found themselves in a dim hallway. Irregular, dirty tiles lined the floor, and the walls were painted a faded gray. A single sheet of typing paper was stuck to the wall with a piece of tape. It read, "Warriors meeting—Second door on the right."

Jericho, Josh, and Kofi said nothing, but turned right and entered what looked to be a general meeting room for the apartment complex. A soda machine and a snack machine decorated one wall. A stack of well-used board games and puzzles sat on a shelf in the back. The rest of room contained about a dozen card tables with metal folding chairs surrounding each. The room looked bleak and cheerless, Jericho thought as he looked around. Then he noticed the other people in the room—a nervous cluster of boys waiting for the meeting to start, and confident Warriors, whispering and laughing with one another.

Jericho recognized Eddie Mahoney standing near the door, checking off names on a clipboard. He looked more fierce than welcoming and wore his black silk Warrior jacket tied around his waist by the arms. He wore his T-shirt so tight that his well-developed biceps and triceps bulged menacingly. It was clear he worked out regularly. He was short and rarely smiled. Jericho had heard that girls would only go out with Eddie one time—he had a reputation at school of being mean.

He was surprised to see Mr. Culligan, wearing not the lab coat that he usually wore when he taught chemistry at school, but an old-fashioned-looking black Warriors of Distinction jacket very similar to the ones worn by the young men standing around the room. A few more anxious-looking boys hurried into the room as Jericho, Kofi, and Josh sat and waited quietly on the uncomfortable folding chairs. When it seemed that everyone who had been invited had arrived, Mr. Culligan called the meeting to order.

Josh whispered to Jericho, "Everybody looks pretty nervous."

Kofi added, "They know what a big deal this might be." Jericho nodded in agreement.

"Welcome, gentlemen," Mr. Culligan began. "You have been asked here today for only one reason: to help in our holiday drive for underprivileged children. Nothing else. We choose the best and the brightest in our school to help us out on these occasions. The holiday toy drive has been one of the traditions of the Warriors of Distinction for almost fifty years. We take this very seriously and we expect you to do so also. I'm only the unofficial sponsor of the club; it runs pretty well under the leadership of the seniors. I'm going to turn the meeting over now to one of those seniors, Rick Sharp, truly a man of distinction. Rick?"

Rick, looking relaxed and comfortable in his Warrior jacket, smiled at them. "Welcome," he said. "First we'd like to tell you a little about the Warriors of Distinction. Believe it or not, this is our fiftieth year in existence. Basically, we work out of Frederick Douglass High School, which, as you know, was built when dinosaurs roamed the Earth!" Everyone laughed a little, easing some of the tension.

"I know that's kind of amazing—that a club could last so long—but I think it's because of the kind of members we have and because of the good things we do," Rick continued. "We began as a service organization, and that continues to be our main focus. We have other activities on our agenda as well, and those will be revealed in time. We do not discriminate—as you can see by looking around at the members, all races, religions, and ethnic backgrounds are welcome. All of us work together for our common goals."

Jericho noted the rainbow of faces around him, especially notable coming from a school like Douglass where the largest number of students were African-American. He also noticed that there were no girls in the room, but after all, he reasoned, the name of the club was the *Warriors* of Distinction.

Without warning, the door of the recreation room burst open and smashed loudly into the wall. Everyone looked over, startled. A short, wiry man with a bald head and red-rimmed eyes stumbled into the room. He carried a small brown paper bag with a green bottle sticking out of the top of the bag. The smell was overpowering and the man was obviously quite drunk. Everything stopped.

"Where's dat stubby little punk?" he yelled. No one

answered. "I'll teach him to lock me out! I'll kick his a . . ." Before he could finish, he spotted Eddie, who had turned his face to the wall. "Eddie, my boy! Who's all these delinquents you got in here? Get over here and come unlock the door of our 'partment. I know your game, but you can't outsmart yo daddy, you little piss ant!"

Eddie grabbed the man fiercely by the arm and pulled him out of the room. The door slammed behind them and the silence that followed was deafening. Eddie had to be embarrassed, Jericho thought.

Mr. Culligan loudly cleared his throat. "Well, we've gone over the preliminaries. Are there any questions?" No one said anything at first.

Then a wiry basketball player named Rudy finally asked, "Is this an official school club?"

"Basically, the school ignores us. Officially, they have to. We're an off-campus club. But we've forged a real close connection over the years. We take care of the school, and the school takes care of us," Rick replied cryptically.

"I heard the Warriors give live parties," a sophomore said jokingly.

Rick laughed and told him, "You're right, but remember that everything we do is better than the rest. We take great pride in the power of our brotherhood."

Jericho wasn't sure what that meant—but he liked their bold attitude.

"Anything else you want to know about the holiday service project?" Mr. Culligan prompted.

"How much time will this take? I have a job," asked a junior seated in the back of the room.

THE BATTLE OF JERICHO

"Each of you will work every day after school, or in the evening, for four hours. You choose your time slot. The week before Christmas we work until every package is delivered. Sometimes we work all night."

The room was silent for a moment. Then another hand was raised. "Does being called to this meeting mean we're on the list to be Warriors of Distinction?" a boy from the baseball team asked.

"It means you have been asked to work hard. The young men standing here wearing the Warrior jackets have proven themselves to be Warriors of Distinction. None of you has done that yet."

"Can you tell us about when you were a Warrior, Mr. Culligan?" Jericho asked timidly.

"It made me who I am today. It wasn't easy, and I had to learn to make difficult decisions." Mr. Culligan allowed himself a slight smile. "And it all started with the holiday toy drive. So if you are interested in being a part of this service project, there are sign-up sheets on the front table. Be sure to include your home phone number. We will be in touch."

Every single boy in the room rushed to the front to sign up. Eddie never returned to the meeting.

IT WAS DARK BY THE TIME JERICHO GOT HOME.
Even though he was still tingling with
excitement about the Warriors, he sighed
as he walked into the house he shared with
his father, stepmother, and her two sons. It
was Geneva's house—Jericho and his dad had
moved in after the divorce, about five years
ago—and Jericho still couldn't get used to
her dullness. She had no taste in decorating or
style or even clothes. Everything in the house was
brown—the carpet, the drapes, even the wallpaper.
She dressed in drab brown dresses, drove a faded
brown car, and even had the nerve to have a dumb
brown dog.

But he had to admit that in her own way she did try
to make him feel welcome in her muddy-looking house.
She had helped him to decorate his room, made sure he
had spending money, and she let him call his mother,
which was a long-distance call to Alaska, whenever he

needed to talk to her. An edge existed between them, however, usually unspoken, but he knew it was there. It could
be because Jericho looked so much like his mother, who
was round and dimpled and always laughing. She lived in
Anchorage with her new husband and his six kids. Jericho
visited her every summer and even though he missed her
terribly, he was always glad he didn't live there in that
crowded house with them.

Geneva was a great cook, however, and the smell of
fried chicken pulled Jericho to the back of the house. He
tossed his bag into a corner and headed to the kitchen.
Rory, who was nine, and Todd, who had just turned eleven,
were doing homework at the kitchen table.

"Hey, Jericho," Rory called out.

"What's up, Shorty," Jericho replied. "You break any
hearts today?"

Rory giggled, as he did every day when Jericho asked
him that. "Not yet, but I'm working on it! How about you?"

Jericho tousled Rory's curly black hair and tickled him,
making him laugh even more. "Just my usual thirty or forty
girls. It was a slow day today." But Jericho's smile faded as
he thought about how far from the truth that was. His
friends seemed to be able to collect girls like baseball
cards, while he couldn't even say one intelligent word to
Arielle Gresham.

"Whassup, Jericho," Todd piped up.

"Nothin' much. How's it going, Todd?" Jericho asked
the older boy.

Todd, who wore an old Cleveland Browns sweatshirt that
Jericho had given him, looked up from his math homework

and smiled at Jericho. "We had track signups today. I'm gonna run this spring," he said.

"Looks like we got an Olympic star at the kitchen table, Geneva," Jericho said to his stepmother as she came into the kitchen to turn the chicken. "Better give him extra mashed potatoes. While you're at it, since I'm gonna be his trainer, better give me extras too!" Jericho was starving—he hadn't eaten since lunch.

"When did you get home?" she asked. "Don't you think you ought to say hello or something when you get in?"

Jericho could feel his good mood fading. Geneva could always find a way to put just a little edge to her voice, with just the slightest touch of disapproval or displeasure. "Just a few minutes ago," Jericho replied. "Didn't Uncle Brock call you?"

"Yes, he called," she replied without comment.

"I came in here to say hello to everybody, but all I found were these two jokers," Jericho said, trying to remain cheerful. Rory and Todd grinned at him.

"Well, you're just in time. Wash your hands for supper," Geneva said without looking at him. "Boys, clear this stuff off and set the table for me," she told Todd and Rory.

Jericho refused to let Geneva spoil his good mood, nor did he intend to tell her about the invitation from the Warriors of Distinction. He was sure she'd find a way to make it somehow seem less important. So he helped the boys set the table and he smiled to himself all through dinner. He knew that Geneva liked the way he treated his stepbrothers—he gave them football jerseys and played base-

ball with them and helped them with their homework when
his dad was busy. Jericho could tell the boys adored their
built-in big brother.

"What time is Dad coming home?" Jericho asked
Geneva.

"He called and said he'd be late again," she replied. "A
couple of the officers are out sick with this flu, and he's
doing overtime. With Christmas coming, it can't hurt."

"Cops aren't s'posed to get sick," Rory reasoned. "Suppose I call nine-one-one and a recording says, 'Sorry, but
the officers had to go blow their noses, so tell the burglar
to take whatever he wants.'"

Todd laughed at his brother, and turned to his mother
with a mouth full of mashed potatoes. "Hey Mom, can I
get that new video game player for Christmas?"

Not to be outdone, Rory demanded, "I want a CD
player! My old tape player is history!"

"We'll see," she said mildly. But Jericho knew without a
doubt that she'd get them whatever they asked for.

"What about you, Jericho?" Rory asked. "What do you
want for Christmas? Let me guess—a brand-new SUV! You
got your driver's license now."

"Yes, but that's just a piece of paper. An SUV costs too
much money, Rory. Maybe I can get a car for my birthday,"
Jericho replied quietly. "I think I'd just like some clothes
for Christmas." He glanced at Geneva, who said nothing.
"May I be excused?" he asked. "I have some homework to
do, and I want to practice my trumpet."

"You don't want any apple pie, do you?" Geneva asked,

in a way that made Jericho think she wanted him to say no. He didn't need it anyway, he thought. A Warrior of Distinction should look good.

"Maybe later, but thanks," Jericho told her as he headed up to his room.

"Don't play that trumpet too loudly," she called up the steps to him. "You know it gives me a headache."

Jericho didn't reply. Geneva hadn't even come to the Bengals game for which he'd been asked to play. Todd and Rory and his father had been thrilled to go, but she'd said something about not being able to get off from her job as a nurse. He knew she could have managed if she had really wanted to. He could hear the boys arguing over who got the biggest piece of pie as he shut his door and finally let himself relax.

He had tacked posters, mostly of the Cleveland Browns, the Cincinnati Bengals, and a few of his favorite jazz players, all over the brown walls of his bedroom, which added quite a bit of color. He turned on his CD player, popped in a piece by Miles Davis, and sighed in satisfaction. He flopped on his bed and let the music take him away.

He couldn't help but think of the Warriors of Distinction, and how good he would look in one of those jackets. He knew his dad would be very proud of him. He was always sweatin' him about getting involved with stuff that would look good on a college-bound transcript—especially to Juilliard. The Warriors of Distinction was a good start. He wondered why the club carried a name that sounded like they were soldiers or fighters. From what he could tell, they were a bunch of do-gooders who knew how to play the game of pleasing the school administration. He thought briefly of Eddie and how rough his home life must be.

But he let the thought pass as he weighed the value of getting hooked up with such a group. Mr. Tambori was always hounding him to make serious life decisions. Well, this was an easy choice, Jericho thought. Jericho figured maybe even Geneva would be proud that he finally did something exactly right. But as the jazz music swirled around him, it wasn't Geneva he thought about. It was Arielle Gresham—the girl with the skin the color of warm, sweet cocoa, the girl whose walk made him dizzy.

He got out his trumpet then, and played with Miles Davis until the brown house he lived in became a blaze of colors.

THURSDAY, DECEMBER 4—
NIGHT

THE PHONE RANG HALFWAY THROUGH THE CD, jarring Jericho back from the music of his trumpet and thoughts of Arielle to reality. "Hello," he said softly, wishing that it would be Arielle's voice on the other end.

But the strong male voice that answered was one he didn't recognize. "Jericho Prescott? Warriors of Distinction calling here."

"Uh, yes, that's me, I mean I, I mean me." Jericho closed his eyes. *Get it together!* he told himself.

"There's a small warehouse on Reading Road, right down the street from the school. The sign on the front says 'express deliveries,'" the boy on the other end of the line told him.

"Oh, I know where you're talking about. That delivery service went out of business last year. No problem."

"Be there Monday at three-thirty P.M.," the young man

continued. "We will work on the toy drive then. You may bring a guest if you like."

"That's straight! I'll be there."

"And Mr. Prescott?" The voice sounded so serious.

Jericho hesitated. "Yes?"

"Monday night. Midnight. Same place. Bring no one. Tell no one. This is *not* about toys."

"Huh? I don't understand."

"See you on Monday." The caller hung up.

Jericho sat holding the phone a moment. What was *that* about? He dialed Josh's number.

"You get the call from the Warriors, man?" Jericho asked as soon as Josh picked up.

"Yeah, about ten minutes ago. This Warriors of Distinction thing is going to be awesome, I think," Josh replied. "Kofi told me they had just called him, too." Josh was silent for a moment. "Uh, they say anything to you about something at midnight?"

"Uh, yeah, I guess. What's up with that?"

"I guess we'll find out soon enough."

"I'll have to sneak out. No way is Geneva gonna let me out that late."

"Me too, but I really don't care. As long as I get in— that's all that matters," Josh said seriously.

"Why?" Jericho asked.

"Forget it, man," Josh answered, brushing off Jericho's question. "November is so excited. She's already talking about what she's gonna wear to the Warriors of Distinction dance. You better get yourself together and stop acting like a third-grader every time you see Arielle."

With a resolve and confidence he did not feel, Jericho boasted, "Arielle is just another honey. I'm gettin' ready to call her right now."

"Go for it, my man. I'll catch you later."

Josh hung up and Jericho stared at the phone for a full ten minutes before he pushed the first button to dial Arielle's number. He hung up twice, then, before he could change his mind, he quickly dialed Arielle's number. A child's voice answered.

"Hello, may I speak to Arielle?" Jericho said, his heart pounding.

"Arielle! There's some boy on the phone for you!" the kid shouted on the other end.

"Hello?"

"Hey, Arielle. This is Jericho—uh—from school. You sure got a loud little brother!"

Arielle laughed. "That's my little sister, Kiki. They ought to hire her to announce for the Cincinnati Reds!"

"How old is she?"

"Seven, going on seventeen. She thinks she is so grown! Yesterday she asked me to take her shopping for a bra!"

Jericho chuckled. "I got two little stepbrothers underfoot here. They'd both be driving if they could. They can't wait until I get a car so I can drive them to all their games and practices and stuff."

"You getting a car?"

"Not likely. Christmas is coming, but there is no way they'll be squeezing a car under the tree. Money's been a little tight. I'm gonna get me a job so I can buy my own car!" Jericho stated.

"That's a lot of hamburgers to flip."

"You got that right!"

"Hey, Jericho, we saw a couple of the Warriors of Distinction talkin' to you and Kofi and Josh at lunch. What's up with that?"

"Well, that's one reason I called. They asked us to help out in the Christmas toy drive this year."

"That's awesome! Doesn't that mean you get asked to pledge, that you'll be a Warrior? I think the Warriors are, like, off the hook. I mean, they wear really sharp stuff and . . ." She stopped speaking suddenly.

"I know what you're sayin'," Jericho said, delighted that she seemed so interested. "That's what we're hoping. But at this point, they told us, all this means is we get to help with the toy drive." He hesitated, then blurted out before he lost his nerve, "We get to bring a guest to help with the toys. Uh, you feel like wrapping some toys? It's Monday after school." He did not mention the midnight meeting.

She said nothing for a moment. "You know what?" she replied finally. "I'd like that."

Jericho couldn't believe it. She said yes! He felt like he was swimming in deep water now, but he knew he had to ask her one more thing before she hung up the phone. "Hey, Arielle," he added awkwardly, "Josh's having some people over on Saturday, just to mess around. You want to come?" Jericho tried to sound casual, but his heart thudded.

"Yeah! That would be tight," she replied with what

sounded to Jericho like cautious enthusiasm. He was amazed.

"I think Kofi asked Dana, and you know Josh and November are joined at the hip!"

"Joined at the lip is more like it!" Arielle laughed, then added, "I gotta call November and Dana to see what they're wearing."

"Why?" Jericho asked.

"'Cause we have to make sure nobody wears the same outfit, but everybody's outfit complements the others. Like if Dana wears leather, we won't wear it because that's her thing. But if November is wearing jeans, then we'll all wear jeans—as long as we have the right shoes."

Jericho chuckled and shook his head. Girls and how they thought were a mystery to him. "Don't worry. I don't think the fashion police will get you if you wear the wrong shoes."

Arielle replied, only half joking, he thought, "I *am* the fashion police!"

Jericho wasn't sure what to say next. "Uh, yeah," he said finally.

"I guess I'll see you Saturday," Arielle said, with that lilt in her voice that made him grin stupidly.

Jericho tried to think of something else to talk about to keep her on the line, but couldn't, so he just said, "Okay," and she hung up.

He turned the jazz music back up loud, and let it take him beyond his small, brown bedroom. Good things waited for him. He was sure of it.

JOSH'S HOME WAS SUCH A SHARP CONTRAST to his own, Jericho thought as he walked through the front door. He gave his Aunt Marlene a hug, placed his trumpet case with care on the floor next to him, and flopped comfortably on the soft leather sofa in the living room. He sighed with contentment as he looked around. African artifacts from Brock and Marlene's many trips to Ghana and Ethiopia decorated the mantle and bookshelves. A large, carved giraffe stood in one corner, and several beautifully carved masks grinned at him from the walls, which were painted a pale peach color. Turquoise accent pillows, redwood-trimmed furniture, and a golden hand-woven area rug sang harmony and happiness to Jericho. So very different from the bland, brown home he lived in. In the fireplace, orange flames crackled with bright intensity, making the room smell toasty and safe.

Jericho was just as comfortable here as he was in his own home, maybe even more. He envied the closeness of Josh and his aunt and uncle.

He loved to play his trumpet in this room. Sometimes Josh would be downstairs playing video games, his aunt and uncle would be out, and he'd have this wonderful room to himself. The tones seemed to dance off the wall here, sounding fuller and more powerful somehow. He could play like that for hours, but he usually had only a few minutes before Josh interrupted him. Josh couldn't seem to understand how serious the trumpet was to Jericho. Josh bounced from activity to activity, never really settling on anything for very long. But Jericho knew what he loved: his trumpet.

Josh thundered down the steps two at a time, heading for the rec room in the basement. He stopped short when he saw Jericho sitting on the sofa. "When'd you get here, Cuz?" he asked.

"Just a few minutes ago."

"Why you sittin' in the living room like company?"

"Just chillin'. I've always liked this room—makes me think back to when we were kids."

"Yeah, remember when we were playing movie monster and broke that Ethiopian mask Mom liked so much?"

"Yeah," Jericho said laughing. "She busted our butts for that one!"

The doorbell rang then. Josh pulled open the door, letting in November, Dana, and a gust of cold air.

"What you tryin' to do, girl?" he said to November, who, as usual, was carrying her digital planner.

"I figured if I bring the cold in with me, you'll appreciate how warm I am!" she said teasingly. Jericho watched as Josh grinned. He looked like a puppy, performing for a treat from its master.

"Don't you ever go anyplace without that calendar?" Josh asked as he took her coat.

"This is my life!" she replied cheerfully. "I've got everything in here: my volunteer schedule with the kids at Children's Hospital, the three second-graders I tutor in math, the parties I've been invited to—the works! Life gets complicated for a social butterfly like me if I don't write it down."

Dana said nothing, but walked over to the fireplace, warming herself and looking carefully at each of the African artifacts on the mantle.

"What's up?" Jericho said to the girls. He looked out the front window, but there was no sign of Arielle.

"Dana's got the right idea," November said as she joined her in front of the fire. "I don't know how your mother stands it, living up there in Alaska all the time," she said to Jericho.

"I guess you get used to anything after awhile," Jericho said with a shrug. He walked into the kitchen, got a soda from the refrigerator, and drank it down in a couple of gulps. He burped loudly just as November and Dana walked in.

"Yuk!" said November. "Dudes are so gross!"

"You've never burped?" Jericho asked with a grin.

"Not like that!"

He tossed her a can of cola, and said, "I dare you to chug it and then not burp!"

She tossed it back and said, "Grow up!"

"Here, help me take this case of colas downstairs," Jericho said. "I'm gonna make you burp before this night is over!"

November laughed, but she grabbed the sodas and headed down the stairs to Josh's rec room. Dana followed them, carrying a couple of bags of chips. Josh's father had remodeled the basement so that the boys and their friends could dance or play video games or just sit around and watch TV. It was even soundproofed so that their music, which they played as loud as the machine would go, wouldn't bother the adults upstairs.

Jericho heard the doorbell ring again. He hoped it was Arielle, but he didn't have the nerve to go back up and open the door.

"Hey, Cuz, Kofi's here, and so is your girl Arielle!" Josh shouted down the basement steps.

Jericho cringed. November and Dana hooted with laughter. Minutes later, Josh stomped down the steps, followed by Kofi in his heavy-footed army boots, and Arielle. As Jericho watched her come down the steps, she seemed to float, especially after all the noise that Josh and Kofi made.

"Did you bring your CDs?" November asked.

"Yeah, I got some new ones—check this out," Arielle said as she showed the girls her collection. They put a couple in the player and as the music began, Jericho relaxed a little.

"Who wants to order something from Pizza Hut?" Josh asked. "They got a pepperoni special this week."

"Order from LaRosa's instead," November suggested. "For every pizza you buy this month, they're donating five dollars to the Free Store."

"How do you know all this stuff?" Josh asked.

"I make it my business to be well informed about all sorts of serious stuff—from shoe sales to canned-goods drives to pizza specials. And you should too," she added.

"I got you to do that for me, my little pepperoni!" Josh said as he hugged her.

"Some stuff you gotta do for yourself, Josh," November told him seriously.

"I'm a vegetarian," Dana explained, as she nibbled on a corn chip. "Make mine just cheese." Josh nodded as he called in the pizza order.

"I thought you eat raw meat for breakfast!" Kofi teased.

"Why you say that?" she asked.

"'Cause you so bad, girl. I heard you wanted to be a Boy Scout instead of a Girl Scout when you were little. Is that true?"

Dana laughed. "Sort of. I hated those ugly green Girl Scout uniforms—the boys' uniforms looked so much better, and they didn't have to sell those stupid cookies!"

"Speak for yourself, girl," Jericho joked. "Those cookies are sacred to me—they're a whole new food group!"

"That's what I like about you, Dana," Kofi continued. "You think for yourself—you're a trendsetter. Have you noticed the little ninth-grade 'Dana clones' who try to dress like you?"

Dana shrugged. "I can't help it if people copy me. I just do my own thing."

"How's your dad?" Arielle asked her.

Dana sighed. "He's still in the Middle East someplace—he's not allowed to tell us where—but it's always danger-ous over there. We don't know when he'll be home again." Her father, an Air Force lieutenant, was a career military man. "He's, like, my hero, you know. He's always told me to be whatever I wanted to be, and encouraged me to try new things, not to let boundaries stand in my way. He taught me to fly a plane when I was just ten."

"You can fly a plane?" Kofi asked in amazement.

"I've soloed in a single engine, and I could probably handle a bigger plane in an emergency if I had to," she replied, her eyes shining. Josh looked at her with awe.

Jericho didn't care. He was just glad that Arielle was sit-ting with them, looking relaxed and comfortable. He wished he felt the same.

The evening moved softly and easily, Jericho thought. Josh and November danced, caught up in their own little world, Kofi played video games, and Jericho marveled at every moment with Arielle. She laughed at Josh's antics as he demonstrated, in hilarious detail, exactly what his par-ents looked like when they danced, but more importantly, she paid attention to Jericho, seemingly interested in his every word as he talked about school and made jokes about teachers. He was amazed. The pizza arrived, and Jericho, conscious of his weight and nervous around Arielle, found he had very little appetite. He ate only one small piece.

"So what's the big deal about the Warriors of Distinc-tion?" Dana asked suddenly, jarring the easy conversation that had surrounded the music and food. "Why isn't there a group called the Distinguished Women?"

"Maybe there aren't any distinguished women!" Kofi laughed at his own joke.

"I'm serious," Dana continued. "Why aren't there girls in the group?"

"Aw, Dana, quit trying to put salt in the milkshake! It's the way the club has been for fifty years," Josh complained.

"So, in fifty years, nobody ever asked the question? I think it's about time somebody did!" she continued. Jericho noticed that Kofi was frowning.

"It's called the *Warriors,* Dana," Kofi said as if talking to a child. "That doesn't sound much like a club for girls!"

"So there's no such thing as women warriors? Don't get me started, skinny boy!"

Kofi's lips grew tight with anger. He didn't answer her.

"Oh, let the boys have their little club, Dana," Arielle said. "Unlike women, they need stuff like that to help them grow up!"

"Besides," November added, "the Warriors help so many people with that toy drive. Don't mess with what works. I admire their social activism."

"You also admire their jammin' social events," Arielle reminded her.

November grinned. "I gotta admit it. They look so good in those jackets, and they give those sweet formal dances, and Josh takes my breath away when he wears a tuxedo!" Josh grinned at her and took her hand.

Arielle laughed and said, "You two are a mess!"

"Well, I'm opposed to the idea of a club just for dudes," Dana said again. "I just may have to do something about it!"

"You think you're gonna change a tradition that's been around for fifty years?" Josh said with derision. "Some things girls just don't need to be a part of!"

"And who are you to tell me what girls can and cannot do? Who made you king of the world, Mr. Cornflake Head?" Dana's anger was obvious and, judging by her tone of voice, growing stronger.

"And who made you queen?" Kofi answered for him. "You can't change a tradition just because it suits your mood! The world don't work like that!"

"I think she's right!" November said. "People get taken to court for discrimination like that! Not that I want to be in a stupid club named 'Warriors' of anything!"

"If I did decide to join, I ought to be able to!" Dana cried. "The club is way outdated. *Everything* is integrated now, and I'm not talkin' about racial fairness—I'm talkin' male/female stuff."

Josh groaned. "Aw, girls always want what they can't have!"

November frowned at Josh. "I think Dana ought to have that right, if that's what she wants," she said quietly.

Josh ignored her. "Every time we get something that's just for us dudes, girls want a piece of it—like the lady sportscasters on ESPN runnin' around the locker rooms after a game. You know they just want to see naked men in the shower!"

Dana threw her shoe at him. Luckily he ducked. "Girls ought to be able to do anything they want and be in any club they want to be in," she proclaimed. "Who made men the kings of the world?"

"Other men, of course!" November replied without smiling. The room was filled with hot, tense anger.

"HEY, ARIELLE," JERICHO SHOUTED OVER
the accelerating noise of the argument,
"come upstairs and let me show you something!"

"Good thinking," she said as the discussion in the basement got louder and she hurried with him upstairs. "I wasn't ready to dive
into that."

"Me neither. I'm a lover, not a fighter," Jericho
said with a grin.

"Is that what you called me up here for?" she
asked, as she grinned and smoothed the wrinkles
from her hip-hugger slacks.

"No. I want you to meet my best friend."

Arielle looked confused. "I didn't hear anyone else
come in."

Jericho smiled again. "She's right here, always waiting
for me, always ready to take me to another place, a better
place."

"She?" Arielle asked.

Jericho was enjoying this. And he was enjoying the fact that somehow all his shyness had disappeared. "Yeah, my best girl. Zora." He picked up the leather trumpet case and slowly unzipped it. He removed the trumpet with care, then carefully wiped its smooth, shiny bell with the soft cloth he kept just for that purpose. "Arielle, I want you to meet Zora."

Arielle smiled and reached out to touch it. The fire still flickered, and its reds and oranges reflected off the trumpet's metallic body. "She's beautiful, Jericho," Arielle whispered.

"Most people think I'm stupid to name my trumpet, but somehow I knew you'd understand." He deftly tapped the finger buttons, listening with an experienced ear to the muffled sound of the valves inside the casing of the trumpet.

"How long have you been playing?" she asked as he attached the mouthpiece.

"Since third grade."

"I heard about you getting asked to play at the Bengals game. That must have been awesome."

"It was the most exciting thing I've ever done in my life. All those people. The lights. Just me and Zora. If I had been by myself I would have been nervous. But I'm never scared when I have my trumpet with me. She's like my best friend. Does that sound stupid?" he asked suddenly.

"Not at all. I know where you're comin' from. Did you love it like this from the very beginning—like love at first sight?" She giggled.

"Actually, I didn't like it at first. I wanted to play the violin. But I was late turning in my instrument money, all the other kids had picked the cool instruments, and all they had left was a trumpet."

"That's really funny!" Arielle said.

Jericho just smiled. "But as soon as I started playing it, I fell in love. It talks for me, speaks to me, sings my songs. I'm never completely alone or unhappy when I'm playing. It's like part of me, part of who I am."

"That's deep," Arielle whispered. "Can you play something for me?"

Jericho shrugged but then, placing his fingertips on the three pearl finger buttons, put the trumpet against his lips and let it speak the words he could never say to Arielle. He closed his eyes and the fireplace faded, then the walls, and finally the rest of the world became the golden notes he felt inside. Arielle sat on the sofa, listening breathlessly.

"Zora is amazing," she said when he finished. Then she blushed. "Where did you come up with that name?"

"In sixth grade our teacher read us a story by Zora Neale Hurston. She's one of my favorite writers now. But at the time I just thought she had a cool name."

"It fits," Arielle said, "because your Zora-trumpet certainly tells a tale when you play her. It's like I can imagine stuff while you're playing."

Jericho felt his heart pounding—she understood! He picked up the trumpet and let Zora speak again. This time he played a quick tune with lots of trills and leaps and rapid repetitions. It was a tale of confusion and anger, and ended suddenly, in a minor key. "That's how I feel most of the time," he told Arielle, "but not tonight. This has been different. I'm glad you decided to come."

"Me too," she said quietly.

"I've got a big trumpet competition comin' up the last Thursday of January," he told her suddenly. "Maybe you can come and give me good luck." He was suddenly embarrassed. "But maybe you won't want to sit through dozens of kids playing their instruments one at a time. It's kinda boring sometimes—like a track meet—you wait for hours for your three minutes on the track."

"But I bet those three minutes that you're up there playing are dynamite!" she told him. "Maybe I will come. Who knows? That's not till next month."

Jericho couldn't believe how nice she was. He felt like he didn't deserve it for some reason. "I don't hear them arguing downstairs anymore. We'd better go check and make sure everybody is still alive," he suggested. He headed with Arielle toward the basement.

"Nice playing down there, Jericho!" Josh's mother yelled from an upstairs bedroom. "You must have some new inspiration with you tonight!"

"Thanks, Aunt Marlene!" Jericho yelled back. He didn't answer the second part.

When they got downstairs, Josh and November were cuddled together on the sofa, obviously no longer angry with each other. Dana sat by the CD player in one corner, earphones on her head, pointedly ignoring Kofi, who sat in the farthest corner of the basement, playing a video game with unnecessary fierceness.

"I better get home, Dana," Arielle said, tapping her on the shoulder. "Can you drop me off at my house?"

"Yeah, let's raise up out of here. I've had enough of these little boys."

"I had a good time," Arielle said quietly, glancing at Jericho as she said it.

Kofi never stopped playing the video game, never even acknowledged that anyone else was in the room. Dana continued to ignore him as well.

After Dana and Arielle left, Jericho called his dad to pick him up, and asked if he could take Kofi and November home too. Then he went back upstairs and played a series of soft, sweet melodies on his trumpet in the living room while the fire died in the fireplace.

THE SCHOOL DAY ON MONDAY SEEMED TO drag on forever. Jericho kept checking the time, hoping the loud clicking of the classroom clocks and droning voices of his teachers would move into fast forward. When the last bell finally rang at three o'clock, Jericho grabbed his book bag, hurried to where he knew Arielle's locker was located, and grinned as she looked at him with pleasant expectation. They walked quickly to the warehouse, which was only a couple of blocks from the school. Jericho shivered a bit—partly from the excitement, partly from the weather, and partly because Arielle was walking so close to him.

Jericho knocked and the door opened immediately. Michael Madison, one of the Warriors who had come to their table last week, smiled and offered his hand. No one ever called him Michael. He was called simply "Madison" by students and teachers alike, "Mad Madison" behind his back because he always looked angry. But he didn't look angry now.

"Welcome!" he said. "Let me introduce you to everyone." Madison's head was shaved completely bald, which made him look stark and serious, but he seemed to be trying to make everyone feel welcome.

Josh and November arrived a few minutes later, followed by Kofi, who came alone. From what Jericho could tell, about ten of the people in the room were members of the Warriors of Distinction. Another ten were guys he recognized from the meeting last week, and he guessed the girls who were with them were their guests. Mr. Culligan hovered in the background; the Warriors seemed to know what they were doing.

When everyone had arrived, Madison climbed on a table and spoke to the group. "We're glad you're here. This afternoon, and the rest of the days we meet here until Christmas, we'll be sorting, wrapping, and later, delivering these toys." He pointed to what seemed like a mountain of toys behind him.

In one corner of the room a scraggly Christmas tree leaned against a wall. "Over there," Madison explained, "is the tree we will be giving to an orphanage. All the ornaments are donated." He laughed for no apparent reason then, and the other members of the Warriors laughed with him. Jericho couldn't see what was so funny.

Just then Dana walked in, dressed in black leather pants and jacket, and leaned against a wall. She did not look at Kofi and she spoke to no one.

Madison nodded at her and continued. "We've been collecting this stuff all year. If you check the charts posted on the walls, you'll see where you'll be working. Any questions?"

Dana raised her hand at that point. Jericho was sure she was going to ask why there were no girls in the club. He glanced at Kofi, who looked angry. "Is this just a Christmas project or do we include Hanukkah and Kwanzaa?" Dana asked. Jericho sighed with relief. He wanted to get in this club before Dana started causing trouble.

"Good question. We have a large list of families that we serve. If our records indicate that a family's Jewish, we provide enough gifts for each night of Hanukkah. If we know that the family celebrates Kwanzaa instead of Christmas, we again provide multiple gifts, ones that agree with the seven principles. We try to provide whatever the family needs."

"I have another question," Dana continued. Jericho knew what was coming. He tensed. "Why are there no girls in this club? I'd like to be considered for membership, and I want to know why I wasn't asked to join."

Madison looked bewildered. "Uh, no one has been asked to join yet. We're just working on the toy drive today."

"Good," Dana replied. "Then there's still time." The members of the Warriors looked at each other in consternation. Clearly, this had never happened before.

Jericho noticed Eddie Mahoney then, standing at the far end of the warehouse. His face looked tight as he glared at Dana.

"Well, let's get started!" Jericho said quickly. He was

hoping Dana wouldn't ask another question—for her sake and for theirs. He didn't like the look he saw on Eddie's face.

"Good idea," Madison agreed. "There's plenty of chips and soda on the table at your left, bathrooms are down the hall to your right, and the music is loud and sweet and starts right now!" He turned on the CD player.

"Good choice of tunes," Jericho murmured to Arielle, who didn't answer. She seemed to be taking it all in—the scrape of boxes across the concrete floor, the crackle of wrapping paper, the soft laughter and conversation, and the dominant figures of the Warriors of Distinction.

As the activities began to fall into place and everyone began to figure out what they were to do, the members of the Warriors—dressed in black-and-red Warrior sweat-shirts—mingled, assisted, and observed. Jericho noticed a couple of the Warriors with clipboards and notepads. They didn't seem to be checking on the progress of the toys, however; they seemed to be checking on the people. They watched the new volunteers, their interaction with the members, even the actions of the girls who had been brought as guests. They especially watched Dana, who worked swiftly and efficiently. And Jericho noticed that Eddie never took his eyes off Dana.

Jericho found his name on the poster on the wall and headed to the first station—sorting. Rick Sharp, another Warrior, had already started on the pile in front of them. Rick was wide and broad-shouldered. He had a short, stubby neck—so short that his round head seemed to balance on his shoulders like a bowling ball.

"He looks like he's wearing shoulder pads," Jericho whispered to Arielle as they approached him. "And where's his neck?" He stifled a laugh. He liked whispering in her ear—her hair smelled good.

"I'd hate to meet him in a dark alley," she whispered back. But Jericho noticed that she looked more excited than intimidated.

Rick grabbed both their hands and shook them firmly when they got to the sorting table. "Okay, we sort the pile into gifts for girls, gifts for boys, gifts for either. Sometimes girls want footballs and boys want dolls. That's cool too—we try to give them what they ask for."

"Sounds pretty simple," Jericho said, taking a step back to observe the huge mountain of toys.

"It's not hard—it's just so much!" answered Rick. "We work all through the summer asking companies for donations. They know us here in town, so they get more generous every year."

"I'll do the girl stuff," Arielle offered. She started pulling packages out of the pile.

"I had a truck like this when I was five," Jericho mused as he picked up a large yellow truck. "That was a great Christmas that year. Mom and Dad were still together, and my world was toy trucks and motorcycles." He sighed.

Josh and November worked on wrapping and stacking with Madison, while Dana sorted toys with an honor society member named Demetrius Stanford. Jericho noticed that Kofi kept glancing at her, looking pained as she joked with Demetrius while they worked. Kofi and a kid named Rudy seemed to be trying to match wrapped, labeled toys with lists of families. They worked with Eddie Mahoney, who never once cracked a smile.

Jericho asked Arielle, "What's up with Dana and Eddie? He keeps lookin' at her like she slapped his mother or something."

"The way I hear it, Eddie's father does a pretty good job of slapping his mother around."

Jericho remembered the scene at Eddie's apartment building. "Eddie's got some really serious issues," he told Arielle.

Arielle nodded. "Dana told me that Eddie used to ask her out all the time when we were in ninth and tenth grade. She didn't really like him, and he was way too short for her, so she kept blowing him off. You know, Dana will probably fight somebody for what she believes in, and break rules just to make a point, but she won't play games."

"So what happened?"

"He had tickets to some concert last year, so one day in the cafeteria, in front of all his Warrior brothers, dressed in his cool-looking Warrior jacket, he asked her to go. I guess he figured she couldn't turn him down with all that support behind him."

"What did she do?"

"She laughed at him—told him to take his short little carcass out of her face!"

"Man, that's cold."

"I don't know if I would have turned him down," Arielle mused. "Not with all those Warriors standing there."

Jericho looked at her oddly, but made no comment. "So why is she here today?" he asked her.

"I don't know. Kofi probably asked her to come before they got in that fight at Josh's house. Maybe she wants to show she's bigger than he is."

"Well, she's taller for sure!" Jericho laughed.

"Tougher, too," Arielle said with admiration. "She's not scared of anything!"

"What are you scared of, Arielle?" Jericho asked suddenly.

"Me? I don't know. I'm scared of the dark when I'm at home alone, and I'm scared of flying on airplanes these days, but nothing like bugs or snakes. What about you?" She handed him a stack of board games and puzzles.

Jericho thought for a moment. "Guys aren't supposed to be scared of anything. But I guess I'm afraid of doing something stupid in front of other people." He was surprised that he had admitted that to her. "And I hate spiders," he added quickly, "and roller coasters."

"Roller coasters? Really? What do you ride on when you go to King's Island?"

Jericho grinned sheepishly. "The merry-go-round. The race cars. I just hate the feeling of falling."

"There goes your career as a test pilot!" They both laughed.

They continued to sort in silence for a few minutes. Then Jericho asked her, "So, what do you think about all that stuff Dana was saying? Do you think girls ought to be in the Warriors of Distinction?"

"I feel like I'm already distinguished—I don't need a club to tell me I'm all that. But I think this club is pretty distinguished," she added.

"So you don't think I'm dumb to want to do this?"

"No, it's just different—guys need this male-bonding stuff to survive."

"Don't girls ever need to do that?"

"If I feel the need to hang with the girls, I call them up and we go shopping!" Arielle laughed.

"I hate shopping, I hate malls, I hate crowds. Makes me itch," Jericho said, scratching his arm.

"Remind me never to call you to go to a Midnight Madness sale!"

Jericho laughed and watched her reach for another toy. Just watching her move made him happy. "So you think this is the right thing to do—this club stuff?" he asked her again.

"If it makes you happy, then go for it!"

"You make a lot of sense."

"I gotta admit," she said, "I like being around the Warriors and what they do. But that should have nothing to do with your decision to join."

Jericho wasn't sure about that. Being with a girl like Arielle was something he'd never dreamed of. And it seemed like the Warriors were helping to make it happen. But all he said to her was, "I like the way you think."

Arielle continued, "Now, November is different. She wants Josh to get in the club because she's like all into that community stuff. Plus, you know she likes the parties, and the dances, and silk jackets and tuxedos and stuff.

She sees this as a chance to encourage him to be more socially aware, and a chance to do lots of shopping so she can look good at all the Warrior events with him. November always has a dual agenda!"

"What about you?" Jericho asked.

"Me? I just came for the potato chips!" She laughed and stuffed several into her mouth.

To Jericho the time seemed to dance by quickly, and at the end of the four hours, there seemed to be only a small dent in the mountain of work to be done. But Jericho didn't care. Arielle had been laughing and teasing him the whole time, and he would have stayed there till midnight if he could.

As they all got their coats and promised to return on Wednesday, Jericho noticed the Warriors stayed behind and continued working. He liked that—they seemed so dedicated to the project. As he was leaving, he also noticed that Demetrius Stanford whispered a few words to Rick, who scribbled something on his clipboard. Jericho wondered if they were being rated as he hurried to catch up with Arielle, who was heading out the door.

It was dark when they got outside, and snow had started to fall. Jericho trembled a little from the cold, and perhaps because Arielle had grabbed his hand when she started to slip on the snow. "I wonder what they were saying about us," Jericho mused aloud to Arielle and the rest of them.

"Probably wondering how such a messed-up dude like Josh hooked up with a fine-looking thing like me!" November teased. Josh put his arm around her and hugged her.

"Naw, they're probably deciding what size Warriors of

Distinction jacket to order for me!" Kofi joked. Dana, who walked a little behind the group, didn't laugh. No one mentioned her questions at the meeting. She got in her car and drove away without speaking to any of them.

"Hey, here's my dad—right on time," Jericho called to them. "It's colder than a dead dog out here!" Jericho opened the van's huge side door, and they piled in. He made sure he sat next to Arielle on the backseat.

"Thanks, Mr. Prescott," Kofi said as he climbed in the front seat next to Jericho's dad. "Glad you brought the van."

"No problem, son. How's everybody tonight?" Mr. Prescott asked. "And how did your first night go with the Warriors of Distinction?"

"It was fun, Dad," Jericho said. "You wouldn't believe the stuff they've got in there. A whole bunch of kids are gonna have a good holiday because of the Warriors."

"Hey, Uncle Cedric, how's it going down at the precinct?" asked Josh. "What's the latest crime going down in Cincinnati?"

"Josh, it's never very pretty. Frozen homeless people, drug addicts breaking and entering, a couple of bank robberies, a murder by a jealous husband. Not pretty at all."

"So why do you do it?" November asked. "Isn't it depressing?"

"No, November, because sometimes I really get to help. Like the abused wife that I got safely to the shelter last week, or the abandoned newborn baby that I found and saved last summer, or the kids I get to talk to at schools about the dangers of drugs. Sometimes I love my job. Sometimes."

"I understand," November replied quietly. "Believe it or not, I really do."

It took almost half an hour to drop everyone off at their homes, and Jericho knew his dad had worked two full shifts and was very tired.

"Thanks for doing this, Dad," Jericho said gratefully. "Whenever you want to get me a car and let me take over this job for you, let me know!"

His dad laughed. "You know, I used to wonder why they let kids drive at sixteen. Now I know—it's because parents have had just about enough of driving their kids around by that point! But don't worry, I'm not complaining—not yet."

"At least I tried," Jericho whispered to Arielle, who was the last to be dropped off.

"I had so much fun today," she whispered back. "Can I come with you again on Wednesday? The Warriors seem like they've got it together."

"I felt like I was one of Santa's elves," he told her. "I'm really glad you came."

"Pretty big elf!" she teased. Mr. Prescott pulled into her driveway then and she hopped out of the van.

"Thanks, Officer Prescott," she called out. To Jericho she said, "Call me later." Jericho grinned and moved to the front seat next to his dad.

"She seems like a nice girl," his dad commented into the darkness.

"Oh, yeah," was all Jericho said.

"And this Warriors of Distinction project seems like a really good thing," his father continued.

"Oh, yeah," Jericho said again. He reached over, turned on the radio, switched it from his dad's station to the one he liked, scooted down in his seat, and grinned all the way home. His dad just looked over at him and smiled. Sometimes silence is best.

JERICHO FINISHED HIS HOMEWORK AND nervously waited for his father and step-mother to settle down and close their bed-room door. They usually turned in pretty early, and he was often awake long after the rest of the house was silent and asleep. Rory and Todd slept that sweet, deep sleep of children who play hard, but Jericho knew that his dad slept lightly, his police training keeping him aware of everything around him.

Jericho headed down to the kitchen at eleven-thirty, got a piece of Geneva's apple pie from the refrigerator, and listened to see if anyone stirred. All was silent. Geneva's little brown dog, Dimples, woke from her corner in the kitchen to sniff for handouts, but Jericho ignored her. If anyone woke up and caught him going out the door, he'd say he decided to walk the dog.

He pulled on his coat, listened once more for move-ment, and eased silently out of the back door, making sure it didn't slam. The cold night air hit him full force, and he cursed himself for forgetting his hat. He pulled up his collar, hunched down into his coat, and walked briskly down the dark, icy street.

Everything looked different at night. The leftover snow sparkled in the moonlight, and the stars, which Jericho had never bothered to pay much attention to before, seemed like sharp points of light that bounced off the sleeping cars and frozen houses.

The warehouse was about sixteen blocks away, an easy jaunt in the summer, but tonight it seemed unbearably frigid and long. The tips of his ears burned with cold, and his toes had no feeling inside his well-worn Jordans. Jericho tried not to think about the long walk home, or how he would successfully sneak back into the house. For the moment, he just wanted warmth. He wondered why they called this meeting, anyway.

The warehouse loomed ahead, dark and foreboding. Jericho could see no lights. He thought wildly that maybe he was the only one stupid enough to come here tonight. Maybe they're just trying to make fun of him. But he walked on, hopeful and cold.

"Hey, man, you have any trouble sneakin' out?"

Jericho, thrilled to see Josh approaching, said, "Naw, Cuz. I'm just slippery like that."

"I don't see any lights up in there," Josh observed. They got to the door of the warehouse, found it was it unlocked, and opened it tentatively. The door squeaked and groaned. Inside all was dark.

It took a few minutes for Jericho's eyes to adjust to the

darkness. Three candles flickered dimly in the center of the floor. The boxes of toys had been pushed to the walls. Shadowy figures, who Jericho assumed were members of the Warriors, stood silently. No one spoke. Jericho felt stupid. He didn't know whether he should take off his coat, or perhaps say something to the silent boys. But as Josh had not moved, he, too, stood there, waiting.

The door groaned loudly twice more, and several more groups of boys arrived and stood silently in the darkness, waiting for instructions. After one last, loud grinding of the door, when a single figure dressed in a black skull cap and jacket entered the room, the members of the Warriors moved simultaneously to the center of the floor near the candles.

Finally a voice that sounded like Madison's spoke with authority. "Be seated on the floor. Say nothing." They complied.

"What we say here," Madison began, his voice sounding like a drum roll in the darkness, "is to be kept in absolute secrecy." He held in his hands what looked like a large, leather-bound book. He opened it ceremoniously and read from the first page: "'Not one word of what we say or do from this point on is to be shared with another living soul—not your mother, your father, your girlfriend, your priest, not even your shadow on the sidewalk.'"

"Agreed?" Eddie Mahoney spoke fiercely to the awe-struck group in front of him.

"Agreed," the assembled group of boys replied in unison.

"Yes, we do the toy drive. It gives us credibility in the

community and at school," Eddie continued. "But toys are for children, and we don't play."

Jericho wondered what he meant, but was afraid to do anything to call attention to himself.

Madison took over. "If you made it here tonight, you have shown your commitment to the group. We always cooporate with the administration at Douglass. They're proud of us. So you will receive invitations to join the club through proper channels around the first of the new year. But officially, you are pledges now, if you choose to accept our challenge, and we require much more than the pink pledge T-shirt you'll receive."

Madison continued. "We ask for—no, we demand—your dedication, your absolute obedience, your very life, if necessary. In return, we pledge to share with you our secrets, our connections, and our power. Any problems with that? If so, there's the door."

No one moved. Jericho wondered if anyone else felt as uncomfortable as he did. He wondered what Madison meant.

Eddie spoke next. "Since there seems to be full acceptance, we will continue with what we call the 'Bonding of the Brotherhood.'"

"The Bonding of the Brotherhood," Madison explained, "requires not only secrecy and obedience, but also responsibility, loyalty, and honor. Your first responsibility is to your pledge brothers. Look around you. The fifteen young men that you see here will depend on *you* for their success as well as their safety, and you will depend on each of them. You must provide *anything* your brother needs. Each pledge holds the responsibility for the other."

"Agreed?" Eddie Mahoney asked once more to the almost-trembling pledges.

"Agreed," they replied. Jericho shivered in the darkness with them, sitting together on the floor of that warehouse.

"In addition, you must agree to do *anything* you are asked to do," Madison said, an odd smile on his face.

"Agreed?" Eddie Mahoney demanded.

"Agreed," they replied quietly.

"I will lie if I must!" Eddie barked.

"I will lie if I must!"

"I will steal if it is necessary to help my brother!" Eddie continued. He looked almost demonic, it seemed to Jericho, in the dim light of the candles. He seemed to be enjoying himself as he chanted.

"I will steal if it is necessary to help my brother!" Jericho did not like the sound of this, but he wasn't sure how to get out of it. He whispered the words. His stomach was starting to hurt.

Madison turned the page of the book and continued to read. "As a pledge, you must also understand the concept of loyalty. Each of you must think of yourself as one link in a chain that has no beginning and no end. Therefore, all of you must succeed in every pledge activity, or none of you do. The group must work together to help the individual."

"Repeat after me," Eddie demanded. "All of us or none of us!"

"All of us or none of us!" the group of pledges replied.

Then Rick Sharp moved to the center of the circle. "These are the basic guidelines for the Bonding of the

Brotherhood. Please repeat after me," he asked the pledges.

"Number One. A Warrior of Distinction is not afraid to lower himself for his brother."

"A Warrior of Distinction is not afraid to lower himself for his brother," they repeated. Jericho wondered what "lowering himself" actually meant.

"Number Two. A Warrior of Distinction does not show fear," Rick intoned.

"A Warrior of Distinction does not show fear." Jericho said the words with the rest of them, but he was feeling pretty fearful right now. He figured maybe this whole process was designed to intimidate and scare them. It was working.

"Number Three. A Warrior of Distinction is bonded to his brothers."

"A Warrior of Distinction is bonded to his brothers," the pledges repeated.

Jericho glanced over at Josh, who looked intense and serious. He and Josh had been almost as close as brothers since they were born. Their birthdays were only a month apart, and when they were younger, his parents and Josh's parents had apartments in the same building. Josh's dad was working on his law degree while Jericho's dad went through his training at the police academy. The two families shared everything back then—food, trips, baby-sitting. The two cousins had spent hours in the hallway of that apartment building, racing Hot Wheels cars down the long, polished corridor. Jericho wondered how he could ever be "bonded" as close to the boys in this room as he already was to Josh. He turned his attention back to the ceremony.

"Number Four. A Warrior of Distinction *never* breaks the code of silence," Rick continued.

"A Warrior of Distinction never breaks the code of silence." Jericho wanted to think about that one, but the rest of the group repeated it without hesitation, so he joined with the others and said the words as well.

"Number Five. A Warrior of Distinction celebrates obedience," Rick said clearly.

"A Warrior of Distinction celebrates obedience," the pledges replied obediently.

Madison said to them, "Stand, young Warriors. The road ahead will be difficult, but the rewards are great." Jericho, surprised at this sudden, secret confirmation of their membership, stood with the rest of the new pledges and stretched with pride. He hoped they would never be called upon to actually live up to all the words they had just said.

"Are you ready for the challenges ahead?" Eddie shouted.

"Ready!" they roared back at him.

"Are there any questions?" Madison asked.

A single hand went up. It belonged to the last person to arrive at the meeting.

"Yes, young Warrior, what do you need? We are here for you."

Dana took off her skull cap and said clearly, "I'm ready for the challenge. Are you ready for me?"

STUNNED SILENCE GREETED DANA'S SHOCKING
revelation. The anger followed immediately. The Warriors closed in around her.
Dana seemed calm and unconcerned.

"What's up with this? You tryin' to make
some kinda point?" Eddie said in a low, dangerous voice, his face just inches from hers.

"I think I just did," she answered.

"How'd you get in here?" he demanded.

"The door, just like you did," she answered
coolly.

"Don't you know these ceremonies are private and
just for men?" he yelled.

"I don't see any men here—just a few high school
boys."

"You don't belong here!"

"I don't see your name on the door!"

"You playing some kind of espionage game?"

"I never play games."

"Who put you up to this?"

"Your mama."

Dana never lost her composure, in spite of what looked like an angry pack of wolves growling at her.

"You have no right to interrupt what is secret and private!"

"I didn't interrupt. I participated. I took the pledge with everyone else. If they are now pledges," she said, pointing to the astounded Jericho and Josh and the others, "then so am I."

"That's impossible! There has never been a female member of the Warriors of Distinction!" Rick shouted.

"Then it's time, isn't it?" Dana brushed a speck off her black leather jeans.

"You just better get out of here while you still can!" warned Eddie, a fierce sneer on his face.

"Or what?" Dana asked with a calm composure that amazed Jericho.

"Or I can't be responsible for what might happen. You're out in the middle of the night in a warehouse full of men." He paused, then added, "Might get dangerous."

Dana remained impassive. "I just pledged with my brothers that I am bonded to them, and that each of us holds the responsibility for the other. 'All of us or none of us!' Does that have meaning or not?"

The Warriors looked confused now, as well as angry. "It applies to them, but not to you!" Madison finally said.

"Why?"

"Because you were never asked to be a member!" Rick said triumphantly.

"Oh, but I was!" Dana replied. Jericho marveled at her nerve.

"How?" Rick demanded.

"You called me," she replied with a slight smile.

"I know exactly who I called," Rick replied angrily. "And I sure as hell didn't call any stupid girl!" He looked around at the other members of the club as if to make sure they believed him.

"I can't believe you didn't check your attendance before you started pledging," Dana said with a smirk. "Where is Demetrius Stanford?"

No one spoke. Rick frantically checked a sheet of paper. "Demetrius?" he called to the room, which had been stunned into silence.

"I've known Demetrius since third grade," Dana explained. "He got a job a few weeks ago and decided he wasn't going to have enough time to pledge. He knew I wanted to be in the club, so when you had that meeting at Eddie's place, he put my phone number down instead of his. He came to wrap toys this afternoon, but he's not coming back." She grinned in triumph.

"So you knew that call wasn't for you! That's fraud!" screamed Eddie.

"Not so. The message that was left on my phone said, 'Be at the warehouse at midnight on Monday. Tell no one.' So I figured it was for me. I was obedient and said nothing." Kofi glared at her in anger. Jericho wasn't sure what to think.

"You can't be in the club. That's all there is to it." But Madison was starting to sound defeated, Jericho thought.

"Then I'll tell everything I saw and heard here tonight. I'll write it up in the school paper. I'll call the TV news channels and newspaper reporters. I'll call *People* magazine. Then I'll call a lawyer and expose all of you and your discriminatory club, and force you to take me in!" Dana warned.

"You wouldn't dare!" Eddie said between clenched teeth.

"Watch me."

"Why do you want to do this?" Rick asked.

"Because I would be a valuable member of this club," she replied, raising her chin.

"Why do girls like you always want to dip into men's stuff?" Eddie asked angrily.

"Because I can." Dana stood firm.

"Don't be so sure, honey girl. You may live to regret this night," he warned.

"I'm not afraid of you," she told Eddie calmly, looking down at him a bit as she spoke. Eddie's face was twisted with rage.

"Women want to be soldiers and firemen and football players. What's up with all that?" Eddie spoke directly to Madison, as if Dana hadn't spoken.

"Do you really want to be a member, or are you just trying to make trouble?" Madison asked with a sigh.

"I really, really want to do this. When I said the words in the bonding ceremony a few minutes ago, I meant every word of it. I would be loyal—to the death if necessary—for my brothers. Give me a chance. You really have no choice."

The Warriors moved to the other side of the room and conferred together. Jericho could not make out all the words, but he could hear angry voices and pieces of bitter phrases.

"Over my dead body!"

"No way this is gonna go down!"

"She knows too much."

"This sucks!"

"You can't let her . . ."

"How is she gonna . . . ?"

". . . make her sorry . . ."

"This changes everything . . ."

"Kick her out . . ."

". . . lawsuit?"

"Can she . . . ?"

". . . hate this!"

The discussion broke up finally with looks of fierce determination on the faces of the Warriors. Madison and the others returned as a group. Eddie's fists were clenched.

Madison cleared his throat. "We are men of pride and dignity, and we have decided to allow you to honor the commitment you have made as a pledge, even though it was in the role of an infiltrator."

Dana looked him straight in the eye. She was as tall as he was. She said nothing.

"Be warned, however," he continued. "No special consideration will be given to you because you are a female. You will be expected to do everything the men do, and it's difficult for them. You might even be expected to do more.

We will not make your path any easier because of tears or whining. If you survive the activities of the next few weeks, we will welcome you into our organization. If you do not, too bad."

"I can deal with that," Dana replied, showing no emotion at all. "You will not be sorry."

"Yeah, but you might," whispered Eddie. Dana did not indicate that she heard him, but Jericho did.

AFTER A LONG, FRIGID WALK BACK HOME,
Jericho quietly slipped into the house with
no trouble. Even Dimples slept through his
tiptoed walk through the kitchen and
upstairs. When he gratefully got back into his
bed, he thought he'd be awake for hours thinking of the night's unexpected turn of events.
But he nodded off right away.

The next morning at school, Jericho, Josh, and
Kofi said nothing to Dana, who sat with Arielle and
November as usual in the front hall, waiting for
classes to begin. If Dana meant what she had said,
the girls would know nothing yet. They gave no indica-
tion that anything was different. Dana looked up at the
boys, smiled sweetly, and continued her conversation.

"So what you think about Dana?" Jericho asked Josh
as they sat on the other side of the hall.

"Makes me nervous," he replied. "She's in over her
head and tryin' to mess up our stuff."

"It sucks!" Kofi said angrily. "I've been dreamin' about being a Warrior since I first set foot in this school—makin' sure the members noticed me, workin' my plan—here she comes tryin' to prove some women's lib point and messes up everything! It's just not gonna mean the same thing!"

"I don't know, Kofi. Dana's pretty tough. I think I'd be glad to have her back me up in a crunch situation," Jericho said thoughtfully. "More than November, or even Arielle," he added.

"Don't go blastin' on my November," Josh said with a grin. "She couldn't whip a wet noodle, but she'd sure look good while she ran for help!"

The bell rang then with nothing settled and no way for them to judge how Dana's presence in the secret pledge class would make a difference. They had received no word as yet from the senior members of the club. Jericho had a feeling they were evaluating how to proceed.

The next two weeks were extremely busy, but some of the best weeks he'd ever known, Jericho decided. He and Arielle spent hours at the warehouse, sorting and wrapping toys, laughing, sometimes dancing in the middle of the warehouse floor, and slowly getting everything ready for deliveries to be made. November came when she felt like it, and Dana never missed a session. She came early, stayed late, and never once spoke to Eddie, except to ask for an extra pair of scissors or roll of tape. The tension between them was obvious to everyone.

Kofi moped around her, trying to get her to smile at him, but she was all business and ignored him. "This sucks, man," he told Jericho as they were finishing up one night.

"How am I gonna get my wolf girl to get back with me?"

"You still mad at her for trying to get in?"

"She can try out for the Bengals if she wants to," Kofi admitted. "I just want her to talk to me again."

"The way the Bengals have been playin', she might actually help them!" laughed Jericho. "Seriously, though, just watch her back and keep an eye on Eddie. Even a wolf needs protection sometimes."

"You're right about that. Thanks, man," Kofi said, glancing over at Eddie.

Homework was minimal at this time of the school year. Christmas was quickly approaching, and Jericho talked to Arielle late into the night every evening. Even Geneva was in a good mood. She hummed while she decorated the Christmas tree, with Rory and Todd bouncing around like two little wind-up toys. She gave Jericho extra allowance money so he could go Christmas shopping, and even told him to buy a couple of toys to donate to the Warriors' toy drive.

Jericho practiced his trumpet every night, feeling sure that he would be ready for the competition that was now only a month away. For the first time in a long time, Jericho felt good about himself and the rest of the world as well.

"HEY, KOFI," JERICHO SAID AS THEY WERE leaving the toy session on Friday, "I'm going out to Tri-County Mall. Wanna come?"

"Yeah, man, that'd be tight. You're not hangin' with your girl Arielle?"

"Naw, she's going to choir practice or something with her mother. You got bus fare?"

"I'm straight."

Ordinarily Jericho hated shopping, but as they got off the bus in front of the mall, he whistled a couple of Christmas carols to himself as he headed into the frenzy of last-minute shopping.

"You're in a good mood, man," Kofi said.

"I like this time of year. My stepmother ain't sweatin' me so much, my girl acts like she likes me—I can't complain."

"That's good, man. I wish I could say the same. My folks ain't into the holidays. No tree. No lights. Christmas is just another day. I thought I had something goin' with

Dana, but she's fronted on me and everybody else with her stupid plan to be a man."

Jericho sighed. "Well, at least it looks like we're gonna get a chance to be Warriors—with or without Dana."

"I want it bad, Jericho. More than anything I've ever wanted in my life. It would make me feel like I was somebody. You see what I'm sayin'? I ain't never had that."

"I feel ya."

They wandered casually through the mall. Jericho bought video games for Todd and Rory and the perfect little gift for Arielle—a bracelet. Jericho found himself thinking about the smile she would give him when she opened it.

"Hey, young warriors!"

Jericho was surprised to see Mad Madison walking toward them. He was carrying a large shopping bag.

"Whassup?" Jericho answered carefully. He wasn't sure what the rules were. Kofi looked nervous.

"I'm on assignment here," Madison answered, "and now, so are both of you."

"Huh?" As soon as he said it, Jericho could have kicked himself—he hated to sound stupid.

"Your obedience is required—this is your first test," Madison told them cryptically.

"I don't get it," Kofi said.

"I'm collecting donations for the Warriors," Madison began.

"Toys from Toy City?" asked Kofi.

"We have enough toys. These are for our members. Check this out." He showed Kofi and Jericho the items in his shopping bag—a gold ash tray, several cigarette lighters, three pairs of leather gloves, at least a dozen Christmas ornaments, and a pair of Nike basketball shoes.

"People donate stuff for the Warriors?" Jericho asked in amazement.

"Not exactly. They don't know they're givin' it up," Madison explained.

Jericho still didn't understand. "How can they not know?"

"We lift it."

"Steal it? You must be crazy!" Jericho couldn't believe what he was hearing.

"Shut up!" Mad Madison hissed. "You want everybody in this mall to hear you? Insurance pays it all back to the stores. Nobody gets hurt, and we get the goods we need."

Jericho could see that Kofi was looking around uneasily, but nobody seemed to be noticing the three boys looking at a shopping bag in the middle of the mall.

"You *do* want to be Warriors?" Madison asked them, an ominous smirk on his face.

"Yeah, man," Kofi replied quickly.

"Why do you ask?" Jericho wanted to know. He had a feeling he did not want to hear the answer.

"We need some more decorations for the Christmas tree we're donating to the orphanage. Go over there to that store called 'Cozy Christmas.' Bring me back some orna-ments. Two each. Doesn't matter what they look like. Orphans don't care."

"Can't we just buy them?" Jericho asked hopefully.

"Didn't you promise to do *anything* you are asked to

do?" Madison said, looking straight at Kofi rather than Jericho.

"Yeah."

"Then hurry up." Madison sat on one of the mall sofas and looked away. Jericho and Kofi walked slowly over to the Cozy Christmas store.

"What do we do?" Jericho asked Kofi frantically.

"Whatever he says!" Kofi whispered back.

"My dad would *kill* me!" Jericho moaned. He felt nauseous.

"My dad wouldn't care. Look, you cover for me. I'll get all four—enough for you and me. That keeps you clean. Bonded brothers, right?"

"Right," Jericho said weakly.

Kofi looked excited as the two entered the store.

Jericho walked up to the desk. It was decorated with little angels, and snowmen wearing red knitted hats. "Uh, excuse me." He cleared his throat and looked nervously at Kofi, who was browsing in the back of the store.

"Can I help you, sir?" The clerk looked tired.

"Uh, do you carry nutcrackers—like the one in that ballet?"

The clerk smiled. "Yes, let me show you—we have hand-carved models for several hundred dollars, and inexpensive ones for about twenty dollars. They're right over here."

Jericho followed her and let her explain. She showed him several styles: nutcrackers dressed in baseball uniforms and king costumes—even girl nutcrackers. Out of the corner of his eye he could see Kofi leaving the store.

He breathed heavily and asked the clerk, "You got any African-American nutcrackers?"

The clerk looked defeated. "No, sir, I don't think we do."

"I didn't think so. Well, thanks anyway." He left the store in a hurry.

Kofi and Madison waited for him. "That was sweet!" Kofi said with a grin. "It was so easy!"

"You did it that quick?" Jericho's legs felt rubbery.

"Yeah, look what I got!" Kofi removed four ornaments from his coat pocket—a small silver star, a red candy cane, a tiny gold angel, and a candle.

"Good job, young warriors!" Madison thumped Kofi on the back, and tossed the stolen ornaments into his bag. "A Warrior of Distinction never breaks the code of silence," he reminded them as he got up to leave.

Jericho and Kofi said nothing as he disappeared into the crowd. Jericho felt sick.

"It was no big deal, man," Kofi said. "Forget it."

Jericho no longer felt like shopping, and he turned with a sigh to leave the mall. He never even noticed the wheelchair as it approached and he almost bumped into it.

"Hey! Look out, man!" he yelled. "Can't you drive that thing?" Then he realized it was Eric Bell from school. "Oh, whassup Eric? I'm sorry. I didn't mean to yell at you."

"You don't have to apologize. What's up, Kofi?"

Kofi towered over Eric in his chair. "Hey, man," he said awkwardly. And Jericho said again, "I'm really sorry."

"You know, it was my fault. I'd yell at me too," Eric said. "People always act like it's a crime to talk to me like they would to everybody else. My controls wouldn't cooperate. I gotta get this thing checked at the shop next week. Didn't mean to run you over." They had moved over to the soft sofas in the center of the mall near the fountains.

"You have a shop for that thing just like an auto shop?" Kofi asked.

"I gotta get it fixed somewhere," Eric replied. "You'd be surprised what's available for folks in chairs."

"I guess I never thought about it," Jericho said pensively.

"Most people don't, because they don't need to," Eric told him. "I didn't either, until I had my accident."

"I, uh, always wondered—what happened?" Jericho asked hesitantly.

Eric shrugged, "I don't mind talking about it. You know, most kids at school are afraid to even ask me. It's my back that's broken, not my head. I'm the same inside as I always was—I just can't walk."

"You broke your back?" Kofi asked incredulously. "Did it hurt?"

"I never felt a thing." Eric shrugged again. "Like most twelve-year-olds, I was dumb. We were playing Daredevil that night. It was August, almost time for school to start back, and we were bored. Plus it was ridiculously hot—still over ninety degrees after dark."

"Yeah, I know how those nights can be. You're too old to run through the sprinkler like little kids. We used to jump the fence and sneak into Hartwell pool sometimes," Jericho admitted.

Eric let himself laugh. "Believe it or not, that's exactly

what we did. First we played Daredevil by jumping off tree limbs—you know, climbing up, grabbing the highest limb you can, jumping from there to the ground, then daring your friends to do the same."

"Yeah, we've played Daredevil too," Jericho replied, thinking about the garage roofs he had jumped from and lived to tell about it.

"Well, we got tired of tree jumping, so, since we were in that park close to Hartwell pool, somebody made the dare that we would jump the fence and into the water. My friend Andre went first. He looked like one of those Olympic divers. That water looked so cool and refreshing. Then Dashon jumped. The two of them were splashing and laughing in that pool, swimming and diving and yelling at me—calling me all kinds of wimps and punks because I was still on the other side of the fence." He paused.

"So what happened?" Jericho was fascinated.

Eric took a deep breath. "I didn't really want to do it, because it was a long drop to the ground, and to leap far enough to make it into the water seemed to me like something only Superman could do, but Andre and Dashon had done it, so I climbed the fence slowly, really wishing I was home in something safe like my bathtub. When I got to the top of the fence, a police car turned the corner and shined that bright spotlight on my friends in the pool, then directly on me. I got scared, lost my balance, and fell, not into the water, but onto the concrete next to the pool. I heard my back snap when I landed."

Kofi looked away. Jericho was silent for a moment. He

gulped. "What happened next? Can't they fix that kind of stuff in hospitals now?"

"Only in science fiction movies," Eric replied, his voice growing tight. "They took me to the hospital and did all kinds of procedures, but that kind of spinal injury is permanent. My mother was a basket case, and I cried a bucket of tears over the next few months. But I don't want people feeling sorry for me. I've learned to live with it. I am still the same person—I've just had to make adjustments."

Kofi was strangely quiet. Jericho wasn't sure what to say either. He looked at his two strong legs and felt guilty for being healthy. "I've got two younger stepbrothers," he told Eric. "They're dumb enough to pull a stunt like that—do something dangerous on a dare. For that matter, so was I at that age."

"Sometimes the Lord takes care of the stupid; sometimes the stupid gotta think for themselves—that's what my grandma always says," Eric said with a smile. "It's just hard to know when. You finished your Christmas shopping?" he asked, changing the subject.

Jericho felt suddenly clammy and guilty once more. He looked around nervously. "Yeah, just about, now that I found something special for this girl I been talkin' to," Jericho told him.

"Arielle Gresham?"

"You know her?"

"Yeah, I know her. We're in the same history class. But I've seen her with you in the cafeteria. I know most of the girls at school—especially the fine ones. At least, I know who they are. Not that they notice me, except to get out of my way in the hall. Arielle's nice though. She talks to me in class like I'm a real person, instead of just a rolling piece of junk. She takes the time to hold doors for me and she makes kids get their book bags off my ramp."

"You know, the more I know about that girl, the more I like her," Jericho mused.

"Well, I gotta finish my shopping," Eric said. "My mom will be here to pick me up in a few minutes and I still have one more gift to find."

"You need any help?" Kofi finally said.

"Naw, but thanks. I put all the stuff I buy in the bag on the back of my chair, and we have a van with a lift like the bus that picks me up from school." He put his chair in gear to head down the mall.

"It was nice talkin' to you, man," Jericho said honestly. He stood up and noticed how much taller he stood over the seated Eric.

"I'll see you around at school," Kofi called to him.

Eric waved and wheeled away. Jericho stood watching him for a moment or two, thinking not of gifts, but blessings—and guilt.

ALTHOUGH JERICHO KNEW THE ORNAMENTS had been inexpensive, for the next few days he couldn't shake the heavy rocklike feeling sitting on his chest. He had to admit, however, that it *was* a little exciting to be able to get away with it with such ease.

At the next wrapping session at the warehouse, he noticed the Christmas tree in the corner was now almost full of ornaments—some with the price tags still on them. He headed over to it and gazed at it in astonishment. There had to be a hundred ornaments on it! Dana walked up behind him then. She was carrying a small bag of ornaments. She said nothing, but quietly began to place them on the tree.

"All of us or none of us," she whispered to Jericho. She smiled and continued to take ornaments out of her bag. He hurried away.

"Hey, Josh," he whispered as they carried boxes of

wrapped toys out to the truck. "What do you know about the ornaments on that tree?"

"Obedience and silence, my man." Josh would not look at Jericho and made himself very busy lifting boxes. "The orphans will love that tree."

"Yeah, I guess." Jericho sighed deeply in the cold winter air. Some of the brightness seemed to have left the afternoon sky. It looked like snow. It was dark by the time they finished.

When Josh's dad dropped Jericho off at his house, Geneva met him at the door. "Why are you so late?" she asked. "You should have been home hours ago."

"I called, Geneva. I told Rory to tell you I'd be late. We start deliveries tomorrow."

"Well, Rory didn't tell me. Are you sure you want to be involved in this club. It seems like it's taking too much of your time. Your grades are going to slip!"

Jericho sighed. He was too tired for all this tonight. "Geneva, it's Christmas vacation, remember? And all of this will be over in a week. I promise."

"I guess you're right," she said. "You know, it *is* possible that I was worried about you," she added with a small smile.

"Thanks, Geneva," Jericho replied. "That makes me feel good. Can I go to bed now?"

"You're not hungry, are you?" she asked as he trudged up the steps.

"No, thanks. We had pizza at the warehouse. I gotta get up early."

"Well, then, good night, Jericho. Maybe this club is a

good thing. It's certainly making you work harder than I've ever seen you work at anything."

"Good night," he called down to her, but he shook his head. Even her compliments seemed like slight criticisms.

He picked up his trumpet as soon as he closed his door. He needed to work out his feelings. He inserted the mute, partly so Geneva wouldn't bother him, and partly because he loved the way it sounded—almost like it could talk. He played riffs and progressions, improvisations as well as variations on old themes that he knew so well they breathed with him. He felt a little better when he finished an hour later, so he took a quick shower and crawled into bed. Then he picked up the phone and called Arielle. She answered on the first ring.

"Whassup?" he said softly.

"You just getting home?" she answered.

"A little while ago. I'm tired," Jericho said.

"Getting into this Warrior stuff is a real good thing, right?"

"I guess." He paused. "Can I ask you something, Arielle?"

"Sure." Her voice sounded so pleasant and innocent on the other end of the line.

"Can something be both good and bad?"

"I don't get you," she said.

"What I mean is, can something seem like it's good but really be something else?"

"I don't know. I guess it depends on what you're talking about."

He wanted her to understand his confusion. "It's like

roses. They're pretty, you see what I'm sayin', but they've got thorns." He felt frustrated.

"You're not making any sense." She sounded impatient.

"Never mind. It's not important. I'll call you tomorrow. Good night, Arielle."

"Good night, Jericho."

JERICHO DID NOT SLEEP WELL AND WOKE UP before his alarm went off. He was dressed and eating a bowl of cereal when his dad walked in the back door.

"Hey, Dad, rough night?"

"Like you wouldn't believe, Jericho. From petty criminals to real thugs, they all wait till I come on duty to show off!" He yawned, pulled up a chair beside Jericho, and poured himself a bowl of cereal as well. "Why are you up so early?"

"Today is delivery day, Dad. The Warriors will be by to pick me up in a few."

"Oh, that's right. I forgot. You know, I'm proud of you, Jericho. This Warriors of Distinction project seems to be one of the best things you've ever been involved in. You've worked hard, and all for someone else."

"Yeah, I guess." Jericho swirled his spoon in the cereal. The doorbell rang and Jericho bounded over to open the door. Rick, wearing a black leather Warriors of Distinction jacket, stood in the doorway.

"Hey, man, I'm ready."

"See ya, Dad!" Jericho called to his father as he grabbed his jacket.

"Bye, son," his father said, yawning again.

The deliveries that day were unforgettable. They stopped at a huge apartment building downtown and took a stack of wrapped toys into an apartment that had almost no furniture. The mother of the five children living there cried when they arrived. At another house, an older woman who Jericho guessed was the grandmother, her hands bent with arthritis, made them sit down on the old, flowered sofa while she made hot chocolate for them to drink. Seven children sat quietly in the corner while they sipped the chocolate, and watched with wide eyes as piles of gifts were put under their spindly tree. At a trailer park, they left gifts with a young father who wept as he told of his wife's death three months earlier. He had four children.

Jericho was silent most of the day, overwhelmed with the need and the poverty and the thankfulness of those who received the gifts. Many of them needed more than toys—they needed food and a safer place to stay and jobs. By the end of the day Jericho was exhausted, partly from the physical work, but mostly from the emotional impact. The little negatives about the Warriors that he had been harboring in his mind had vanished.

As Jericho and Rick waited in the parking lot of the warehouse, a police car pulled up next to them. Rick looked up with concern. "Don't sweat it, man," Jericho said with a smile. "That's my dad." Officer Prescott waved and got out of the cruiser.

"Hey, son, I figured you might be finishing up here. Want a ride home before I go to work?"

"Yeah, thanks, Dad!" Jericho thanked Rick once again and gratefully climbed into the front seat of the police car. He looked into the side-view mirror and saw Kofi running full speed, trying to catch them before they left. "Hey, Dad! There's a criminal behind you that wants to get arrested! Got your cuffs ready?"

His father laughed, got out, and opened the back door of the cruiser for Kofi, who was breathing hard. "I'm sorry, but you'll have to ride behind the screen," he told Kofi.

"Don't let the neighbors see me like this!" Kofi said, pretending to be a prisoner. Kofi's breathing finally slowed to normal, and the two boys laughed and joked all the way home.

"How'd it go today, Kofi?" Jericho asked.

"It was off the hook, man. At this one house there were about ten kids and five cats. Kids and cats everywhere!" Kofi replied with a laugh. "But they cried when we brought their stuff in," he added soberly.

"Yeah, we got tears too, and hot chocolate and cookies and lots of hugs," Jericho said.

"At one house, a little girl gave me a peppermint stick without the cellophane."

"You eat it?" asked Jericho.

"Naw, man, I saved it for you!" Kofi retorted.

Officer Prescott turned on the siren just as he pulled into Kofi's driveway, and Kofi howled with laughter as two of his neighbors peeked out of their front doors to see what was going on. Neither of Kofi's parents came to the door, however. It occurred to Jericho that he rarely saw Kofi's parents, but the thought passed as Kofi ran up the walkway to his house, waving back at Jericho and his dad. He unlocked his door and went inside.

Jericho and his father rode in silence to their house. "I can't come in, son. I'm on duty in a few minutes, but I hope you had a good day."

"It was the best day of my life, Dad," Jericho said with satisfaction. "The Warriors are straight!"

"Don't get overly excited about getting into this club, son," his father said mildly. "Even though Brock was a Warrior, I made it through Douglass just fine without being a member. Being yourself is more important than being a Warrior of Distinction. Remember that, okay?"

"Sure, Dad," Jericho replied, but he wasn't really listening as he trudged into the house. He went straight to his room, turned on a Wynton Marsalis CD, and played with him until all the pain he had seen, and the guilt and helplessness he felt about it, melted away.

CHRISTMAS DAY WAS, FOR ONCE, LIKE ONE OF those pictures on the Christmas cards that were tacked all over the house. Jericho peeked out of his window and noticed that a fresh snow had fallen; everything was white and glistening. Todd and Rory would be in his room in just a few minutes, jumping on his bed and clamoring for him to come downstairs. He knew it was still the middle of the night in Alaska, but he needed to hear his mother's voice.

He picked up the phone and she answered on the second ring. "Merry Christmas, Jericho!" her cheerful voice rang out.

"Hi, Mom. How did you know it was me?"

"Mother's intuition. I know your ring. Caller ID. All of the above!" She laughed. "Besides, unless you're with us at Christmas, you call me at this time every year."

"Thanks for the package you sent, Mom. I can't believe they sell those new Nikes in Alaska!"

"I knew you wanted them, and yes, they sell everything here you can get back home. I don't live in an igloo, you know." She laughed again and Jericho flopped on his pillow with contentment. Hearing her laughter took him back to when he was a kid.

"I miss you sometimes, Mom. Especially at Christmas. Remember when I was little, how much fun we used to have?"

"Yes, I remember, sweetheart. I keep those memories tucked in a very special place."

Jericho said nothing for a moment, remembering the abundance of those early Christmases, trying to block out the memories of the tension and the problems that his parents had tried to keep hidden from him. "How are the kids?" he asked finally.

"Oh, they're fine. Excited, of course. Will and I have been up half the night putting together stuff for them."

"Yeah, I helped Dad and Geneva put together a couple of things for Rory and Todd."

"It's a little different now that you're older, and not so much on the receiving end like the little ones," his mother said.

"Yeah, but this year, I got to do some real major giving to little kids. Remember I told you I was working with the Warriors of Distinction on their toy project? It was awesome, Mom."

"Yes, I remember that group—your Uncle Brock was a member. They're pretty powerful for a bunch of high school kids. They do some great stuff. You're going to be a member now?"

"Maybe." He decided not to mention his concerns about the club to his mother. After all, it was Christmas.

"They'd be lucky to have you," his mother asserted.

"Of course you'd say that, Mom." Jericho smiled anyway.

"Are you still talking to that girl Arielle?" she asked.

"Yeah, she's really off the hook. I can't believe that a girl like Arielle wants to be with me."

"Well, it's obvious the girl has good taste," his mother teased. "Why wouldn't she want to be seen with a hunk like you? You're good-looking and you play the trumpet like no tomorrow. I bet the other girls are jealous of her."

Jericho grinned. "You're just sayin' that because you're my mom!"

"And you know it's true!" She chuckled. "Tell me more about this girl, son."

"She's smart and she's fine and she makes me feel like, I don't know, I can't put it into words." Jericho hesitated, trying to capture all the feelings that swirled around in him when he thought of Arielle.

"My goodness, this girl must be something else!" his mother said.

"Oh, she is. She's got a great sense of humor and she's caring and she's got more on her mind than makeup and hairstyles. She helped with the Warriors of Distinction project and I'm taking her to the Warriors' celebration party on New Year's Eve." Jericho smiled as he described Arielle to his mother.

"I'm glad you've found someone as special as you are, Jericho," his mother said gently. "I hope I get a chance to meet her one day."

"Yeah, that would be cool," Jericho said. "I guess I better go now, Mom. I hear Todd and Rory in the bathroom. That means I have about three minutes before they pounce on me! Give my best to Will and the kids. I can't wait until summer."

"I love you, Jericho, and have a very Merry Christmas," his mother said fervently.

"I love you too, Mom. Merry Christmas." As he hung up the phone his door flew open, and, just as he knew they would, Todd and Rory jumped on his bed and started screaming.

"Get up! Get up! It's Christmas!" Rory yelled. "Hurry up!" Geneva and his father peeked in his room next, looking sleepy and sorry that the boys had not slept another hour or so.

"I'll make some coffee," Geneva said. "Merry Christmas, Jericho."

"Merry Christmas, son," his dad said.

"Same to both of you. You have to work today, Dad?" Jericho asked as he searched on the floor next to his bed for his bathrobe.

"Yeah, I have to go in at three. Let's go down and do this so I can get another nap. I'm getting too old for this," he chuckled.

Todd and Rory had already skipped down the steps and were bouncing in the living room like hot popcorn when Jericho and his dad got downstairs. The brightly covered boxes and packages, the lights on the huge tree, even the fake fire in the fireplace—the little red streamers waving in the wind from a little blower—reminded Jericho sadly of what others did *not* have, and once again he felt a little guilty for his good fortune.

He sipped the coffee Geneva fixed for him while they watched the boys gleefully rip open their packages. Just as he had predicted, they received everything they had asked for, and more. Then he opened his gifts, and thanked his father and Geneva for the watch and the jeans and the black sweater.

The phone rang. It was Uncle Brock, calling to wish them a Merry Christmas. The two brothers talked a few minutes, then Jericho asked to speak to Josh before they hung up.

"Was Santa good to you, Cuz?" Jericho asked.

"Yeah, he dumped a small load under my tree. But you know what I miss, Jericho?"

"What?"

"Remember when we were little and we got so many toys that the whole living room looked like a toy store? I miss the toys!" he said with a silly laugh.

"I know what you mean. You'd come over here with your new toys, then we'd go over there with my new toys, and we played till we dropped."

"Gettin' older is the pits!" Josh wailed.

"Todd and Rory got laid out with toys, though," Jericho said. "At least I get to play with their stuff!"

"Hey, I gotta go. Mom's got breakfast ready. Maybe I'll come over later and help you play with Rory and Todd's toys!" Josh laughed and hung up.

Jericho was content at that moment, as he gazed at the sparkling lights on the Christmas tree, giving a feeling of safety and comfort to the family scene in front of him. It wasn't perfect, but it was what he had, and it was enough, he thought. Geneva was curled up on the sofa with his father, Todd and Rory ran around the living room like they were on batteries, and Jericho thought about the joy in the homes of the families they had reached, and he hoped their holiday was as happy as his.

"Hey, Jericho," his father said after all the gifts were opened. "Can you go out and get the newspaper?"

"Aw, Dad, it's cold out there," Jericho complained. But he slowly got up and set his coffee down. He put his coat on over his bathrobe, stuffed his bare feet into a pair of his father's tennis shoes, and opened the front door. A blast of cold air rushed inside.

"Close the door, Jericho!" Rory yelled. "You crazy?"

But Jericho didn't hear him. For sitting in the driveway, with a huge red bow tied across it, was a bright red 1994 Pontiac Grand Am! He bounded across the deepest part of the snow, losing the tennis shoes in the process. But he didn't care. Screaming and jumping barefoot in the snow, he shouted, "You got me a car! I don't believe it! You got me a car! You're the best parents in the whole wide world! I love you! I love you! You got me a car!"

"Merry Christmas, Jericho!" his father called from the door. "And get back in here before you wake up the neighborhood and freeze your loud, silly self to death!"

Jericho ran back through the snow and into the house and hugged his dad and Geneva until they almost choked. He was so excited he couldn't breathe. Todd and Rory jumped and screamed in the living room, yelling, "Take us for a ride! Take us for a ride!"

"You never did get the paper," Geneva said mildly.

"Oh, let me go get it! I'll do anything you ask! I'll go naked in the snow and then read it to you—even the ads!" Jericho felt as giddy as the boys.

"With clothes will be fine," Geneva laughed. "And Jericho," she added, "your mother helped with this. She was the real reason we were able to swing it."

Jericho breathed a silent word of thanks to his mother and promised himself to call her back as soon as possible. He went back outside, found his father's shoes in the snow, got the newspaper, and stood there in the icy air, marveling at the wonderful little red car that sat in the driveway.

When he got back into the house, he was shivering with cold and excitement. "You know, Jericho," his father began, "driving a car is a big responsibility. The dangers almost outweigh the freedom it will give you. We'll start off slowly with your driving privileges, and as you show you can handle the responsibilities involved, we'll let you drive more. Agreed?"

"Yeah, sure, Dad. Anything you say. I promise I'll be careful. I promise." Jericho meant every word.

"You get one ticket and we pull the keys. Got it?"

"Got it."

"Your grades go down, we pull the keys. Got it?"

"Got it."

Geneva sipped her coffee, nodding through this exchange. "You know, Jericho," she said finally, "I was against the idea of getting you a car at first, but you seem to have matured a little lately—I like the way you've taken on so much responsibility in working with a strong, positive group like the Warriors. I'm proud of you." Jericho couldn't believe his ears. Could she actually have complimented him?

"Thanks, Geneva. Really. I promise I won't let you down. Ever." He almost felt like hugging her again.

"Can we trust you, Jericho?" his father asked finally.

"I will never make you sorry, Dad. Promise. For real. Can I go and just sit in it for a few minutes?"

"Go ahead," his father chuckled. "But you might want to get dressed first."

Jericho ran upstairs and was pulling some clothes on when the phone rang. It was Arielle.

"Merry Christmas, Jericho," she said pleasantly. "Was Santa good to you?"

"Oh, Merry Christmas to you too, Arielle," he said with excitement. "I don't know about Santa, but guess what my folks had sitting in the driveway this morning? A car!"

"You're kidding! A car? Jericho, that is so awesome!" He could hear the excitement in Arielle's voice. "What does it look like?"

"It's not new—I think it's a '94—but it's a Grand Am, and it's red and it's mine!" he said with glee. "Maybe they'll let me drive it to the New Year's Eve party next week."

"Wouldn't that be awesome?" she said softly. "Wait till I tell November and Dana. Can you drive it over here this afternoon?"

"They've put all kinds of rules and regulations on my driving for now, so I'm not gonna make any waves. I don't want anything to happen to mess this up, so I'll ask later."

"I feel ya," Arielle said. "I'll be here all day. Call me if they let you loose with the keys. I'm really happy for you, Jericho."

"Thanks, Arielle. I'll call you later, and Merry Christmas!"

THREE DAYS AFTER CHRISTMAS THE WEATHER turned unseasonably warm, and most of the snow had melted. Jericho had been allowed to drive his car a bit—to the store for Geneva, to the post office for his dad, and to his friends' houses to show off. Most of the time, Todd and Rory were tucked into seat belts in the back seat, excited to be riding with Jericho no matter where he went.

"Are they gonna let you drive to the party on New Year's Eve?" Todd asked one afternoon as Jericho drove to Arielle's house.

"Yeah, Dad talked to me this morning, spelled out a list of rules and regulations about fifty miles long, and told me that as long as I'm careful, he's gonna let me drive."

"Sweet! Can we come too?" asked Rory.

"Not a chance, Shorty!" Jericho laughed.

Arielle must have been looking out the window, because

as soon as he pulled into the driveway, she, November, and Dana ran out of her house and over to the car.

"Hi, Todd. Hi, Rory. You little cuties," November said to the boys as they rolled down the windows.

"You smell good," Rory said to November.

She laughed with delight. "Your brother is the smartest little dude I ever met. He already knows how to talk to a girl!"

Jericho grinned and got out of the car. He gave Arielle a quick hug and noticed she was wearing the bracelet he had given her for Christmas.

"Nice car," Dana commented as she walked around it. Dana drove her mother's SUV whenever her mother gave her the chance.

"Thanks, Dana. You want to kick the tires or check under the hood?"

"Don't be puttin' me down, Jericho. I know more about car engines than you do!"

"I ain't sweatin' you, Dana," Jericho said with a grin. "I know you could probably take this engine apart and put it back together. I bow down to such power in a woman!"

"Just bow down to the power!" she replied. She laughed as Jericho waved his arms in front of him like he'd seen people do in an old movie about ancient Egypt.

While November chatted with Rory and Todd, and Dana sat in the driver's seat and turned on the engine, Jericho walked with Arielle to the end of her driveway. "They're gonna let me drive," he told her excitedly.

"Sweet!" Her eyes glowed with anticipation. "Me and November went shopping yesterday and I got the sharpest outfit. Tomorrow we're gonna get our hair and nails done."

"You'll look good to me no matter what you wear," he told her.

"That's why I like you, Jericho," Arielle said. "You always know just what to say. Maybe Rory has been taking lessons from you!"

"Is Dana going to the party with Kofi?" Jericho asked.

Arielle glanced over at Dana, who must have decided to look under the hood anyway, for all they could see was the bottom half of her as she leaned into the insides of the car. "She says she'll be there. And Kofi said he'd show up. What happens after that is anybody's guess. It will be worth going just to see what happens." She looked directly at Jericho and smiled. "But I'm going to be with you."

Jericho grinned again. "I'll pick you up at eight Wednesday night. Josh and November are riding with us. What about Dana?"

"She told me that she's driving her mom's car."

"Okay, that's straight. You girls are so tight, like you've known each other forever."

"Not quite forever, but back in seventh grade some boys were teasing November about her name, calling her Turkey and other kinds of foolishness. She was crying, I was scared, and then Dana came out of nowhere and kicked their butts! Sent them running down the hall! She had just transferred here from Hazelwood, and we just clicked. She needed somebody to just be a girl with, and we needed somebody who wasn't scared of middle school! She's really gentle when you get to know her," Arielle added.

Todd and Rory had joined Dana under the hood of the car. "What are we looking for?" Jericho heard Rory ask as he and Arielle walked back to the car.

"Whatever it is, it's dirty," November chuckled.

"Looks good, Jericho," Dana said. "You're a lucky dude."

Jericho watched carefully to make sure that Todd and Rory's fingers were out of the way, then slammed the hood. "I guess I better get these two jokers home." The boys climbed back into the car. "I'll see everybody on New Year's Eve."

November and Dana went back into Arielle's house, but she stood in the driveway until Jericho reached the corner. He looked back in the rear-view mirror and saw her waving. It doesn't get any better than this, he thought.

WEDNESDAY, DECEMBER 31—
NEW YEAR'S EVE

THE WEATHER ON NEW YEAR'S EVE WAS COOL and crisp, with no snow or ice predicted to make Jericho's dad cancel his driving privileges. Dressed in a new black suit with a red shirt and black tie, Jericho picked up Josh and November, then headed to Arielle's house. Arielle's mother took pictures, gave him the same warnings that his parents, Josh's parents, and November's mother had given him about driving safely and not drinking at the party, and finally allowed them to leave. Jericho sighed with relief and pleasure as he glanced over at Arielle, who looked like cotton candy in a pale peach dress.

"Lovely," was all he whispered to her. "Lovely."

She smiled and said nothing. The party was being held in a room at the Westin Hotel downtown. Jericho let the valet park his car, although he winced at the cost and the fact that somebody else was driving his car, even if just around the corner. But he wanted this night to be special, so he, Arielle, Josh, and November walked into the lobby of the huge hotel, blinking a little, trying to act like they did this every day.

Standing in the lobby, dressed in a tuxedo, Rick Sharp greeted them warmly and directed them to take the escalator to the second floor where they'd find the room. As they glided up the escalator, Jericho tried to shake his misgivings about the club. It's got to be worth it, he thought. These dudes are first class. Arielle took his hand as they stepped off the escalator, and he walked proudly to the door of the party room.

Members of the Warriors of Distinction, all dressed in tuxedos, welcomed them and showed them to small tables around the sides of the room, which had been decorated with black and white balloons and gold centerpieces. Mr. Culligan welcomed them as well, then retreated to the shadows. A live band played music in the background and several couples were already dancing on the polished wood floor. Josh and November joined them right away, holding each other closely as they moved to the music.

Dana arrived then, with Kofi, and the two of them came over to their table. "Nice party," Kofi commented. He wore gray slacks and a black leather sports coat. Dana was dressed in a striking black dress with one shoulder bare— the shoulder with her other tattoo.

"I see you two are speaking again," Jericho commented.

"Got to, man. We're bonded, remember?" Kofi looked relieved and reached for her hand, which she didn't pull away.

Jericho noticed Eddie frowning at them. He walked over to their table and right up to Dana.

"Be careful what you wear out in public, little sister," he said in greeting to her.

"What's that supposed to mean?" Kofi asked.

"She's got one shoulder half naked," replied Eddie.

"I'm so glad you like my dress," Dana told Eddie with a smile. Then she took Kofi by the arm and brushed past Eddie, ignoring him. Jericho could tell Eddie was angry, but this was obviously not the time to show it.

While Arielle went to get some punch, Jericho walked over to Dana and whispered, "Do any of the girls know you're a pledge?"

"You expected me to break the code of silence?" she whispered back. "Not until it's official."

"I'm gonna break Eddie's face if he keeps messing with Dana," Kofi said with quiet determination.

"I'll help you," Dana told him with a fierce smile, "when it's time. I'm fine for now, but I have to admit, I'm glad to be with you tonight." Kofi grinned.

"So, do you guys find out tonight if you're members of the Warriors of Distinction?" Arielle asked as she returned with two glasses of punch.

"Why?" Kofi asked her. "You plannin' to dump Jericho if he doesn't get in?" he teased. Arielle just rolled her eyes at him.

"Why you wanna dis me like that, Kofi?" Jericho said with a laugh. He turned to Arielle. "Tonight they give out the official invitations." He tried not to put any special emphasis on the word "official." "I'm not sure what happens after

113

that," he said honestly. "Some kind of pledge activities—
they keep it a big secret."

"Yeah, even Josh's dad won't tell him," Kofi added.

Josh didn't look as if he was worried about anything—he
and November danced wildly in front of the band.

"You want to dance?" Jericho asked Arielle as they
watched Josh and November.

"I can't do that," she said, pointing at them, "but I can
keep *you* busy!"

He and Arielle spent the next couple of hours dancing,
talking with the Warriors, laughing, and sipping punch
from the little goblets with "Warrior" stamped on the side.
She was an excellent dancer, making him look better than
he was on the dance floor.

At ten minutes before midnight, Jericho noticed that all
of the Warriors of Distinction had assembled in the front of
the room near the band. Madison signaled the band and
picked up the microphone. "We just want to welcome everyone here tonight, and we're gonna do the Warrior chant for
you. Hit it, brothers!"

The Warriors huddled very closely together and began to
stomp their feet in a rhythm. Jericho could almost feel the
thunder on the polished floor. Then they began, their deep
bass voices chanting proudly and loudly:

> *You don't know what time it is—*
> *It's time to get live!*
> *It's time to represent!*
> *Warriors rock! Warriors rule!*

You don't know what time it is—
It's time to get live!
It's time to represent!
Warriors rock! Warriors rule!

Jericho had heard the chant many times in school—at football games, in the locker room, in the main hall before school, even on the street corner by the bus stop, but never in such close quarters and never with such balled-up anticipation churning inside him. He found himself whispering the words with them, mesmerized by the rhythm and the young men who chanted them.

Josh stood next to him, dancing by himself to the rhythm of the chant. "You crazy, Cuz," Jericho said, laughing.

Then Rick took the microphone and said, "May I have your attention, please? Very soon our celebration will be over and the new year will begin. We want to thank everyone for your help in making this year's service project the best ever. Just before the stroke of midnight, we will count down to the new year, the lights will go off for thirty seconds, and you may share a private moment with your date. When the lights come back up, the party is over, and the pledge invitations will be available on the table in the hall. If you are invited to pledge, all the necessary instructions will be found inside the envelopes. Once again, we thank you, and hopefully, we welcome you."

Jericho looked at Arielle. She grabbed his hand.

"Would everyone please come to the dance floor for the last dance of the evening?" Rick asked.

Jericho glanced at Kofi and Josh as they all found places on the dance floor. The band played a jazzed-up version of "Auld Lang Syne," and Jericho held Arielle close as they danced. "I don't care about the Warriors of Distinction," he whispered in her ear. "I found you."

She didn't reply, but held him closer as they danced.

The music faded and ended, the lights were dimmed, then Rick yelled into the microphone, "Ten! Nine! Eight!"

"Seven! Six! Five!" Everyone in the room yelled it with him.

"Four! Three! Two!" Jericho and Arielle spoke as one as they looked into each other's eyes.

"One! Happy New Year!" The whole room cheered, then the lights went completely black.

Jericho pulled Arielle very close to him and kissed her gently—once, twice, three times. Those thirty seconds seemed to Jericho like just an instant.

The lights came up slowly. Jericho stared into Arielle's eyes and did not move. He wanted to kiss each eyelash. A full minute passed and other couples had started to file out of the room, but Jericho was content to stay right where he was. He wanted time to stop. But his thoughts were interrupted by November and Dana, who whispered something to Arielle.

"What?" Arielle said, breaking away from Jericho.

Dana repeated, "While the lights were out, someone put his hand on my butt!"

"How do you know it wasn't Kofi?" Arielle asked.

"I had both his hands in mine."

"You think it was Eddie?" Arielle whispered.

"What's up with him?" November asked. "Why is he messin' with you?" Jericho realized she had no idea what was really going on.

"Did you tell Kofi?" Jericho asked.

"No. I don't want to spoil tonight with a fight. Besides, the lights were out. It could have been anybody," Dana replied with a heavy sigh.

"Tell Kofi later, and watch your back—for real!" November warned.

Dana nodded and headed back to Kofi. Jericho, a little annoyed that the romantic mood had been broken, suddenly felt a sense of dread about the weeks to come.

Everyone moved into the hallway quickly, in a hurry to search the table for envelopes with their names on the front. Jericho took his time, not wanting the evening with Arielle to end. They walked slowly out of the room, holding hands, not saying much.

At the table Jericho scanned the names on the envelopes. On the far right-hand side, he saw "Jericho Prescott" handprinted in gold letters on the large black envelope. Next to it was an identical envelope that said "Joshua Prescott." At the end of the table was one labeled "Dana Wolfe." Dana picked hers up slowly, a huge smile spreading across her face.

"What's up with that, girl?" November screamed, clutching Dana's arm. "How'd you pull that off? You're gonna be a pledge?"

Arielle joined her, exclaiming, "How'd you get asked to pledge? This is too deep! Did you know about this?" she asked Jericho. He just shrugged.

Dana grinned slyly. "Sometimes it takes a great group of men to recognize the power of a woman." Madison actually smiled at her with what looked like a bit of admiration, Jericho thought. Then Dana looked directly at Eddie Mahoney, who was standing next to the table. He was *not* smiling.

"You ain't in yet, sweetheart," he said quietly. "I intend to make your life a living hell." Dana turned away from him, took Kofi's hand, and headed for the escalator.

Jericho and Arielle followed them out into the crisp, cold darkness of the new year.

"WOO HOO! IT'S OFFICIAL! WE'RE IN!" JOSH shouted to several middle-aged couples who also waited for the valet to bring their cars. They either smiled or looked annoyed at the teenager who was making so much exuberant noise. Josh suddenly hugged the very surprised, tuxedo-clad elderly man who stood next to him. "I love you, man!" he shouted deliriously. "I love everybody tonight!" The old man chuckled and actually hugged him back.

Jericho and the others cracked up. "You a trip, man," Kofi laughed.

"Wait till I tell Dad!" Josh exclaimed. "He's gonna pop with pride! He'll be proud of you, too, Jericho," he added. After they climbed in the car he opened his envelope and read the invitation to them by the dim glow of the dome light as Jericho drove home. It read:

*You have been selected
By a panel of your peers
And are cordially invited
To become a Warrior of Distinction*

"Awesome!" November exclaimed. "This is like off the hook, Josh! What else does it say?"

"Let's see. We have to turn in a medical form from our doctor, pay a pledge fee—shoulda known that was coming—and there's a bunch of meetings we have to go to."

"Hey, Josh, won't your dad tell you *anything*?" asked Arielle as she turned round to see him better. "What good is it to have a dad who knows all the secrets and then won't help you out?"

"He says the secrecy is what makes it a great organization, and the reason it's lasted so long. Otherwise it would be just like any other club," Josh replied.

"Well, Dana seems to be aiming to make it like no club we've ever seen," Jericho commented.

"For real, though!" Arielle said. "The first woman ever!"

"If she survives," Josh said with a laugh. "I bet they don't make it easy for her."

"I heard Eddie Mahoney threaten her as she picked up her invitation," Jericho told him.

"What can she do?" Josh asked. "She *did* ask for this."

"I don't know, but I bet it was Eddie who had his hands all over her," Arielle replied. "I think there's something wrong with him." She shuddered.

"Dana knows how to kick butt, even Eddie's," November reminded them.

"You guys will look out for her, right?" Arielle asked.

"Yeah, sure. But what could happen? How bad could it be?" Josh reasoned, his usual good mood returning. "If somebody as lame as my dad can get in, it's got to be a piece of cake!"

"When is the next Warrior party?" Arielle asked, changing the subject. "Does it say anything about that?"

"Girl, you're just a party animal!" Josh replied. "No, it doesn't say, but I'm sure there will be a party when all this is over."

"Good," she said.

Then November added, "And find out what other community projects they do the rest of the year. They could do a book drive, or a—" Josh cut her off with a kiss.

"Enough," he said gently. "Let's just enjoy the moment. We can't save the whole world tonight." She giggled and snuggled close to him.

Jericho drove November home, then dropped Josh off at his house. He finally pulled slowly into Arielle's driveway. He didn't want this night to end. "Well, I promised your mom I'd get you home safely and at a decent hour."

"I'm glad you got your invitation," she said quietly.

"Me too. I talk big, but I woulda been hurt if I hadn't gotten it."

"Especially if Josh and Kofi got invited and you didn't."

"I didn't want to say anything, but we kinda knew ahead of time," Jericho admitted.

"Did you know about Dana?" she asked.

"Sorta. I think they were forced to do it. I heard she threatened them with lawsuits and exposure and stuff."

"I gotta call her as soon as I get home!" She scooted over and looked directly at him. In the chilly moonlight Jericho could barely see her eyes. "I'm proud of you, Jericho," she said softly.

"I'm no big deal."

"Don't be hatin'—especially yourself."

"Josh is a good athlete and his father was a Warrior. Kofi is super smart and knows all that computer stuff. Me, I'm just Jericho—large Jericho." He bowed his head. He couldn't believe he was saying this to her!

"First of all, you got your invitation, so they must think you're all that," she reasoned.

"Yeah, I guess you're right," he admitted.

"Besides, you've got something that Kofi and Josh *don't* have," Arielle whispered.

"What's that?" he asked. But he knew what she was going to say.

"You got me!" she replied quietly, moving even closer to him.

He touched her chin with the tips of his fingers, then kissed her gently. "And that," he whispered, "makes my life magic."

"This has been the best night of my life," she said softly.

He kissed her once more in the darkness of the car, then got out and walked her to the door, where he kissed her again.

"Good night," he whispered.

"I'll talk to you later," she said, "and Happy New Year!"

"Happy New Year, Arielle." Jericho walked back to his car, glancing happily at the moon and breathing in the cold night air.

TWO DAYS AFTER THE NEW YEAR'S EVE PARTY, as far as Jericho was concerned, it could have been the middle of summer, even though the weather had turned bitterly cold. Nothing could erase his good mood, even though Geneva had tried her best to do so. He had pulled his hat down over his ears and headed out the door to his car.

"Maybe you shouldn't go, Jericho," Geneva had said as he was walking out the door.

"I'm just going to hang with Josh for a little— maybe go get something to eat."

"You know you get careless when you two get together," she said, although Jericho could not figure out how she came to that conclusion. He tried to stay calm.

"It's not even snowing," he said reasonably.

"Yes, but it's cold. You be careful, you hear me?"

"I will, I promise," he mumbled, determined not to argue with her.

"You know you're still a new driver, and I really don't trust you in this weather."

"I'll be careful."

"You know you have a tendency to drive too fast."

Jericho wasn't sure how she would know that—she had never ridden in the car with him. "I've never had a speeding ticket," he reminded her.

"You just haven't been caught yet."

He took three deep breaths. "I don't speed, Geneva," he said softly.

"The roads are pretty icy," she said as she peered through the curtains out the window.

"I promise I'll drive very slowly and carefully," Jericho had said through clenched teeth.

But she went on and on. "Don't play your radio and be sure to wear your seat belt."

Jericho sighed. "Okay, Okay! Can I go now?"

"Okay, I guess."

Jericho left before she had a chance to think of something else. He scraped the windows while the car warmed up, then he climbed in and savored the smell of the inside of it. It reminded him of auto shows and crayons for some reason—maybe because when he was little all he ever drew pictures of were cars. He carefully put it in reverse, popped in a CD, turned it up as loud as it would go, and headed down the icy streets to Josh's house. He stopped in front and honked twice. It was too cold to get out.

"What's up, Cuz!" Josh said as he opened the passenger door.

"Where's your hat, man? It's two degrees out here!" Jericho said as Josh climbed in.

"You sound like my mama! What do you care if I freeze my ears off?" Josh asked jokingly.

"I don't care if you freeze your buns off, man, but that glow-in-the-dark hair you got might stop traffic!" Both of them laughed.

"Where you want to go?" Josh asked.

"I dunno. I'm hungry, I guess. What about you?"

"Man, I'm always hungry! Mom's on this health food kick, so I gotta get junk food any way I can. Last night she fixed carrot salad and asparagus to go with some kinda fish. It was pretty disgusting."

"Geneva's got her faults, but at least she can cook."

"I got a taste for chicken wings. There's a new place that just opened up down the street from the mall."

"Gotcha." Jericho drove carefully down Montgomery Road and turned into the parking lot. "Looks like it's crowded."

"Good. I love a crowd!"

They headed into the restaurant, which had two huge television screens playing the University of Cincinnati basketball game, as well as the latest rock music blaring in the background. They ordered a huge basket of hot wings, cheese fried potatoes, and a pitcher of Coke, and headed for a table.

"This is tight!" Josh said with pleasure. "And talk about tight—look at that girl over there!"

"You better not let November hear you talk like that!" Jericho teased.

"A man can still look, can't he?" Josh said with a grin. "Hey, what's the score?" he asked the girl as she walked past their table.

"They're up by twelve," she replied, smiling.

"Thanks, sweetness," Josh said, winking at her. She ignored him and returned to her table.

"You and November as tight as ever?" Jericho asked Josh as he occasionally glanced at the game.

"Yeah, man. I look at the other girls, but November got me wrapped around her finger and the rest of her body too!" He seemed a little embarrassed.

"I'm still a little scared of Arielle," Jericho admitted.

"Scared? Of what?" Josh scoffed.

Jericho shrugged. "I don't know. She's just, you know, all that!"

"I can tell by the way she looks at you, man, you got nothing to worry about," Josh declared. He was sprinkling salt into the sugar bowl at their table.

"You think she'd be with me if I wasn't pledging the Warriors?" Jericho asked quietly. He was afraid of the answer.

"Be for real, man. Give yourself some credit. You got it together—the girl ought to be glad to be with you, no matter what," Josh told him sincerely.

Jericho was thoughtful for a moment. "You've been with November a long time, man. Don't you get tired of her?"

"November is really heavy, my man. You just see her from the outside. I know the real person inside. She's been through some real mess."

"Like what?" Jericho asked. By this time he was helping Josh to salt the sugar bowl.

"Did you know she had a twin sister who died when she was nine? Complications from chicken pox. I think that's why she spends so much time with the kids at Children's Hospital."

"For real? I didn't know that."

Josh continued. "She's got a mentally disabled brother who lives in a group home on the other side of town. So every summer she works with the disabled kids at Camp Stepping Stones."

"Deep," Jericho replied.

"Then when she was ten her father was murdered. I think her mother has spoiled her because she's all she's got left. Nothing is ever as it looks from the outside, my man. There's a lot of pain floating under there."

"It's funny what you don't know about people," Jericho said thoughtfully. "I guess everybody's got a secret side."

The waitress brought their food to the table then, and Josh jumped up and kissed her on the cheek. She laughed and pushed him back into his seat.

"Well, we go back to school Monday and all the official Warrior stuff begins," Jericho said, grabbing a cheese potato.

"Yeah, and the unofficial stuff, too. Wonder what's up with that?"

"I don't know. You worried about it?"

"Naw, not really. How bad could it get?" Josh looked thoughtful.

"What do you think about Dana?" Jericho asked.

"I don't know, man. Girl power and all that stuff, I guess. I wish she woulda chosen some other time and place to make a point," Josh said as he balanced a cheese potato on his nose.

"Me too," Jericho admitted. "Dana in the pledge class changes everything. She might mess everything up for us." Then he changed the subject. "Hey, what do you know about the ornaments on that Christmas tree for the orphans?"

Josh was quiet for a minute, watching the game as Cincinnati scored again. "I know Dana brought in a bag full of ornaments," he said quietly.

"What about you?" Jericho wanted to know.

"I was in the drugstore a couple of weeks ago and I ran into Rick Sharp. He told me about, uh, how the orphan tree was decorated, and what I had to do."

"Did you do it?"

"It was one stupid ornament—worth about a dollar. Was that a major crime?" Josh asked defensively. "What about you?"

"I was with Kofi in the mall and Madison told us we had to get two each. I talked to the clerk while Kofi got the ornaments," Jericho explained.

"You feel bad?" Josh asked.

"Yeah, a little."

"I did, but I got over it." Josh turned his attention back to the game. "Hey, three points! Look at that!"

Jericho said nothing else, but concentrated on the wings in front of him.

"Hey, Cuz, you ate all the food, man!" Josh exclaimed.

"I told you I was hungry," Jericho grinned as he licked his fingers.

"I got an idea!" Josh jumped up and ran back to the counter where the orders were placed and came back with two fresh baskets of wings.

"What you gonna do with all that food?" Jericho asked in amazement. "Even I can't eat that much!"

Josh walked over to a table near theirs, and climbed up on a chair. The two middle-aged women who sat nearby tried at first to ignore him, but Josh was not to be ignored. "I got free wings for two lucky tables!" he yelled at the top of his lungs. "Free!"

The two women looked interested, but Jericho thought they looked too stuck up to take Josh's silly offer. "Get down, man. You're crazy!" Jericho said, glancing around uneasily for a management-type who might throw them out.

"Ah, my good man," Josh said to a bald-headed, sweatsuit-wearing fat man who walked over to the chair where Josh stood, "your dinner is on me tonight."

"How come?" the man asked.

"I did a terrible wrong a couple of weeks ago, and this is my penance."

The man looked at Josh like he was crazy, but took the food anyway. "Whatever," the man said as he walked away.

"Now I feel better," Josh told Jericho as he sat back down.

"You think that makes everything straight?" Jericho asked. They got their coats and headed out the door.

"Absolutely!" Josh replied. "Hey, let me drive! I haven't

had a chance to get behind the wheel of the Red Queen yet."

Jericho hadn't let anyone except the valet parking guy drive the car. He fingered the keys hesitantly, then took a deep breath and tossed them over to his cousin. "Just be careful, man. I don't feel like Geneva sweatin' me. When she gets on my case, her voice sounds like fingernails on a chalkboard."

"I'm straight, Cuz. Hop in and put on your seat belt."

Jericho climbed in, turned the radio up loud, and relaxed. Josh was taking the long way home, he noticed. He pulled onto I-71, which was freshly salted, and surprisingly free of cars for a Saturday afternoon. They zipped along, laughing and singing with the music, the car going faster and faster. Jericho noticed they were doing sixty, then sixty-five, then seventy. The car sped along smoothly, effortlessly.

"I love this car!" Josh shouted over the music. He rolled the windows down so that the cold, two-degree air blew into their faces as they sped down the expressway.

"Roll up the windows, Josh! It's freezin'!" Jericho gasped.

"Maximum stimulation! It's good for you!" he said, laughing. But he rolled the windows back up. "Can't hear the music with the windows down!" He continued to do about seventy.

"Slow down, man," Jericho warned. Jericho glanced over at Josh and noticed the car in the next lane. It was Eddie Mahoney's beat-up black Toyota. "Look, man, there's Eddie!"

Josh rolled the window back down and waved. Eddie nodded to them, rolled down his window, gunned his motor, and made it clear that he wanted to race.

"Let's see what this baby can do! You got it, my Warrior brother!" Josh yelled out the window.

"No, man! You crazy! Don't do it!" Jericho cried.

"Relax! I got it under control. You're not gonna let this dude punk us out, are you? If I had a Warrior car, I'd take care of it—he's got that thing lookin' like a piece of junk!" He gunned the motor of Jericho's car and pressed down on the accelerator. Seventy. Seventy-five. Eighty.

At eighty-five Jericho looked around, almost hoping for a police car so they could slow down. The road was inexplicably deserted. Josh drove faster. Eddie sped up. Josh kept up with him. The car was beginning to shake.

"Josh!" Jericho finally yelled. "Slow down! You've made your point!"

"I got ya. We're at the exit anyway." Josh gradually slowed the car, and carefully clicked the right blinker to indicate he was about to move over to the exit ramp. Eddie's car slowed and moved to the exit lane as well. Josh sped up again, hurrying to beat Eddie's car to the ramp.

Jericho wasn't sure what happened next, but suddenly the world was spinning out of control. He saw a dark tree, a patch of unmelted snow, a telephone pole, and Eddie's car, then the same tree, patch of snow, pole, and car, then the same scene again, only at a dizzying speed as the car spun out, doing complete three-sixties on the exit ramp.

Jericho screamed. He felt like he was going to throw up all those wings he'd eaten. "Take your foot off the brake!"

131

he said finally. "Turn the wheel gently in the direction of the spin," he said, although he felt far from gentle at that moment.

Josh said nothing, but he nodded. His face was as pale as the winter sky outside. Gradually the car slowed and stopped just a little off the road, amazingly still facing the right direction. Eddie's car had disappeared, and other cars rushed past them, obviously unaware of what had just happened. No one stopped.

"You okay?" Jericho asked in a whisper.

Josh nodded. His hands were shaking.

"I didn't see that patch of ice, did you?"

Josh shook his head.

"We didn't hit anything, did we?

Again Josh shook his head. He turned the music off. They sat without speaking for a very long time. When he was able to breathe normally again, Josh said quietly, "Why don't you drive the rest of the way?"

Jericho, his feet still wobbly, slid out of his seat and moved around to the driver's side. "We'll laugh about this one day, won't we?"

Josh looked serious. "Yeah, but not today. I'm sorry, man." They drove the rest of the way home in silence.

When Jericho got home, he said nothing about the near-catastrophe. He needed his car privileges for the Warrior pledge activities. His father had just come in from work and was sitting in the kitchen while Geneva fixed dinner. Jericho wasn't hungry, but he got a cold glass of water from the refrigerator. He needed to clear his head a little.

"What happens next with the Warriors, son?" his father asked.

"I've got to get a physical, we have a bunch of meetings, and by the end of the month, it'll all be over!"

"Sounds almost too easy," Geneva commented.

"Oh, and we have to pay a pledge fee," Jericho added.

"How much?" asked his dad. "I think it was fifteen dollars when Brock pledged."

"That was back when gas cost fifteen cents a gallon!" Jericho laughed. "It's a hundred dollars now," Jericho added quietly.

"Good grief!" Geneva exclaimed. "Do you want to join this club or buy it?"

"Aw, you know you love me, Dad. I'm worth it! Didn't I come home safely and on time today?" Jericho thought briefly how easily the day could have been a disaster.

"Okay, okay. Don't get started. When you go to bed tonight, I want you to dream about ways you can make your poor old dad a bunch of cash this summer." Mr. Prescott shook his head and chuckled as Jericho headed up the steps to his room. Jericho got out his trumpet and tried to play, but the world kept spinning in his mind. He gave up after a few minutes and went to bed, burying his head under his pillow. The dizziness didn't stop until he fell into a restless sleep.

THE FIRST WEEK OF JANUARY

THE FIRST WEEK OF JANUARY SEEMED TO be just about perfect. Everything was falling into place for Jericho. He went to his doctor, got his physical, and was told he was healthy, but a little overweight.

"Hey, man," he told Dr. Irvin. "I promise to eat carrot sticks for lunch every day."

"Carrot sticks dipped in ranch dressing or followed by two bags of potato chips won't make it, Jericho," Dr. Irvin replied. "You've got to think before you eat."

"But I'm always hungry!" Jericho said as he put his shirt back on. "And when they have the five burgers for five dollars special, I gotta help 'em out!"

"Five cheeseburgers is too much food for one meal. You can live on two."

"Maybe *you* can live on two. I'm a growing boy!" Jericho grinned. "But I promise to eat better and exercise more, okay?"

"Anything strenuous in these pledge activities?" Dr. Irvin asked as he signed the Warriors of Distinction medical form.

"No, just fun stuff—you know—acting silly," Jericho told him.

"My cousin was a Warrior of Distinction years ago," the doctor said, looking as if he were thinking back. "But I can't remember what he did as a pledge."

"It's supposed to be a big secret," Jericho replied. "Well, thanks, Dr. Irvin. I'll see you in a couple of years for my college physical."

"Take care, Jericho, and cut back on the hamburgers!"

"You got it!" Jericho grabbed the medical form and rushed out of the door.

Occasionally his father let Jericho drive the new car to school, which made him feel good, because very few kids had cars. "You lucky, man," Kofi told him one day after school as he was driving him home. "Half the time my folks forget to leave me bus money. The other half they leave me too much." Then he smiled quickly, as though it didn't matter.

"You get your physical yet?" Jericho asked Kofi quietly.

"Yeah, last week. Doctor called me back and said I gotta come in Wednesday for some more tests. No big deal."

Jericho wasn't sure how to reply. "You need a ride tomorrow?" he asked.

"Yeah, thanks, man." Kofi got out of the car and headed to his house. Jericho drove home thoughtfully.

In school, Jericho was pleased to find, his grades were soaring. He'd always received good grades in music, but

Mr. Tambori took extra time with him after school to help prepare him for the competition. Jericho wondered why all of his classes couldn't be like music—as easy as drinking a glass of water.

His math teacher, Mr. Boston, smiled at Jericho as he passed back the exam taken before the holiday.

Yes! Jericho said to himself. "I can't believe this— an A!"

"You ace it, man?" Kofi whispered across the aisle.

"Yeah, what about you?"

"I'm straight. No reason to call the troops out, but I'm straight."

"I'm gonna kiss Mr. Boston on the lips!" Josh whispered from the next aisle. "I got a B!"

"Don't do that, man," Jericho whispered back. "I bet even Mrs. Boston don't kiss that ugly dude."

"You got that right!" Josh kissed his paper instead, and Kofi and Jericho cracked up.

"Gentlemen? Am I boring you?" Mr. Boston's voice interrupted.

Jericho wanted to say, "Actually, you're the most boring thing I've seen today except for that telephone pole outside the window!" but he just sat up in his seat and said, "Sorry," and cleared his throat as he glanced at Kofi and Josh, who tried not to explode with laughter.

ON THE TUESDAY BEFORE THE MARTIN LUTHER
King holiday, the Warriors of Distinction
held a meeting, once again in the shabby
recreation room of Eddie's apartment building. Jericho was sure that this time Eddie's
father would not be interrupting. Fourteen
young men and Dana Wolfe waited nervously for
instructions.

Michael Madison walked to the door and made
sure it locked when he closed it firmly. Next to
him stood Rick Sharp and Eddie Mahoney. Mr.
Culligan was nowhere to be seen. Jericho glanced
at Kofi and Josh, who looked deadly serious. Dana
looked intent.

"We will begin with a recitation of the vows," Madison said quietly. "It is imperative that you remember
and obey every word." He nodded at Rick Sharp, who
repeated the vows and made the pledges stand at attention and chant them once more.

"Thank you, pledges. You may be seated," Madison told them. "The paper that is being given to you now is a copy of the pledge you just recited. If you agree to everything, please sign your name on the bottom and pass it to the front of the room. These forms will be kept on file, but will not be circulated. As we have said, secrecy is our greatest strength."

Jericho read the form and hesitated just for a moment, but he signed it and passed it to Kofi, who was sitting in front of him.

Rick cleared his throat and announced, "I want to tell you a little about Pledge Week. It lasts from Monday until Friday of the last week of January. Get your homework done early, because every night you will be involved in pledge activities that are designed to strengthen you, teach you to depend upon each other, and test your honor, loyalty, and courage. The very last night, Friday night, lasts well past midnight, because included in that night is a celebration party—just for us, the former pledges and the current members. Saturday evening is a formal dinner-dance to which you bring a date. At that time you will be officially welcomed into the group."

Jericho thought about Arielle and how proud she would be of him that night. Then he gasped. The last Thursday of January was the trumpet competition! There's no way he could miss that! What was he going to do? Jericho's mind swirled as he forced himself to pay attention to what Rick was saying.

"The form that is being distributed now is one for your parents to sign," Rick continued, "indicating their permission for you to be involved in Pledge Week activities.

Please return that to Mr. Culligan's box at school first thing tomorrow morning. This is our school connection—don't screw it up."

Eddie took over then. "Between now and the last week of this month, anything that a pledge master asks you to do—anything," he repeated, looking directly at Dana, "you are required to do. That's at school or any place off campus. Understood?"

"Understood," the pledges repeated.

"Let's see if you really do understand," Eddie smirked. "Luis, come here!" Luis jumped from his chair and ran to where Eddie stood. "Stand on one foot!" Eddie ordered.

Luis, an accomplished track star, lifted one foot and balanced with ease. A minute turned into two and Luis began to hop to maintain his balance. Three minutes, four. Finally Eddie commanded, "Enough! Good job, Morales." Luis went back to his seat, a frown on his face.

"Who wants to be next?" Eddie barked, staring right at Dana.

"I'm game," Kofi said with a loud cough. Jericho wondered if he had volunteered because of the way he had seen Eddie looking at Dana.

Eddie picked up two folding chairs, one in each hand. "Hold these two chairs, arms straight, elbows unbent. He placed one chair in Kofi's right hand, and another in his left. Kofi looked at Eddie strangely, but he obeyed. The room was silent as everyone watched. At first it was easy, then his arms began to tremble a little.

"Kofi's skinny as a pencil and probably just as strong," Josh whispered to Jericho.

After six minutes Kofi's face was red and his breath was coming in harsh bursts. "Enough!" Eddie commanded. He seemed to enjoy wielding such power. Kofi dropped the chairs with a sigh, and rubbed his arms.

"Next?" Eddie offered. He looked again at Dana, who did not move.

Josh said loudly, "Try me!"

Eddie looked at him coolly. "Okay, Mr. Prescott. Sing us a song!" Eddie commanded. Josh grinned and burst into "Ninety-nine Bottles of Beer on the Wall" at the top of his voice. It broke the tension as everyone in the room laughed. Even Eddie managed a slight smile.

"That's all we have time for now, Eddie," Rick said. "I'm sure they get the idea about obedience." Eddie looked disappointed, and Dana looked relieved. "Are there any questions before we dismiss?" asked Rick.

"Is the pledging process going to be difficult?" Kofi asked.

"You will never forget it," Eddie Mahoney replied without smiling. Again he looked directly at Dana as he answered.

"When do we get the Warrior jackets?" Josh asked cheerfully.

"The very last Friday night, assuming you've paid your pledge fee by then," Eddie replied. "And Josh," he added, "you better learn how to drive."

Josh and Jericho looked at each other in amazement. They hadn't spoken of the driving incident since that day. Jericho stared at Eddie, who look self-satisfied and victorious.

A sense of uneasiness crept quietly into Jericho's mind. He raised his hand slowly. Rick nodded to him. "Uh, suppose a pledge had something really, really important to do on the fourth night of the final week of pledging?"

"I'd suppose that pledge wouldn't need to bother to come back on the last night," Rick replied clearly. "Any pledge who does not complete the entire week is automatically eliminated."

Jericho's heart fell to his shoes as he thought about the trumpet competition. How could he choose one over the other?

JERICHO SAT IN THE MAIN HALL WAITING for Arielle, who had to stay after school to make up a biology test. He felt only slightly guilty as he munched on a large bag of potato chips and slurped a soda. After all, the soda was diet.

Eric rolled over to where Jericho was sitting. "Whassup, man?"

"Not much. Want some chips?" Jericho offered.

"Yeah, sounds good. Thanks." Jericho handed Eric the bag. Eric took a handful, handed it back to Jericho, and said, "So the Warrior stuff kicks off next week, I hear."

Jericho felt uncomfortable. "Yeah, that's what they tell us." Jericho hoped Arielle would hurry up so he could leave.

Eric was quiet for a moment. "You know, I woulda loved to be a part of that."

Jericho wasn't sure what to say. "It's no big deal, really."

"Yes, it is. It would put me on the inside of everything instead of the outside."

"I wish there was something I could do," Jericho said lamely.

Eric sighed. "I don't mean to lay this on you. It's just been one of those days. You know what? All my life I dreamed of going to the prom. I can't even get a girl to talk to me for more than five minutes. How am I gonna get a date? And if I did, what would I do there—wheelies to the music?"

Jericho wasn't sure how to answer. "You know, Eric," Jericho said quietly. "Sometimes I feel like I'm outside lookin' in on the rest of the world too."

"Yeah, but you do your lookin' standing up, while I have to do mine sitting down—all the time."

"Don't you just want to scream sometimes, Eric?"

Eric smiled. "I'm sorry. I'm just feeling a little down today. And yes, sometimes I want to scream so bad, I think I'll explode!"

"So do it!" Jericho challenged him.

"Explode?" Eric looked at him, astonished.

"No. Scream!"

"Here? Now?"

"Yep. Right here. Right now. Scream your head off." Jericho was grinning now.

"There's still people in the building," Eric said hesitantly.

"So?"

"So what if I get in trouble?"

"What are they gonna do? Break your legs?" Jericho looked at Eric to see if he had gone too far. But Eric was laughing hysterically. "Scream, Eric, scream!"

"Ahhhhhhhhheeeeeeee!" Eric screamed at the top his voice. The empty halls echoed.

"Do it again!" Jericho said with exultation.

"Ahhhhhhhhheeeeeeee!" This time it was even louder. They looked at each other and cracked up.

A door opened down the hall. "What's going on out there? Is somebody hurt?" It was Mr. Boston and he was headed in their direction. "Was that you two making all that noise?" he asked angrily.

"Yes, sir," Eric replied between giggles. "I told myself if I have to sit in this chair one more second, I'm just gonna scream. So I did."

"Do you feel better?" Mr. Boston asked. Jericho noticed that he seemed to rein in his anger a bit. Even teachers tiptoed around disabled kids, he realized.

"Yes, sir, I do," Eric replied. "Here's my bus. I'll be going now." With that, he gave Jericho a high five, rolled out of the door, down the ramp, and to his bus. Jericho waved as Eric sat on the electric lift, slowly being raised up. Eric was still smiling when the bus drove away, but Jericho couldn't stop thinking what Eric's life must be like. Mr. Boston, shaking his head, returned to his classroom.

Jericho checked his watch and wished once more that Arielle would hurry up. He was hungry and he had a lot of homework to get done tonight. He looked up and saw Kofi coming down the hall.

"Hey, Jericho. Did you hear all that screaming a little while ago?" asked Kofi.

"That was me and Eric Bell."

"The kid in the wheelchair?"

"Yeah, he needed to let off some steam, so he did. It was too tight!" Jericho told him.

"That's good. I'd hate to be stuck in a chair like that." Kofi glanced outside at the handicap ramp. "Why you still here, man?" he asked. "Everybody's gone home but the janitors and Mr. Boston. I think he must sleep here."

"Waiting for Arielle. Slowest female in the world!" Jericho joked. "What are you doing here?"

"Mrs. Walton asked me to fix something on her computer. I swear, if I drop dead, all the computers in this school will just fizzle up and die too. Half the teachers, 'cause they were born back in the Dark Ages, are scared of the computers, and the rest either don't know what to do with them or don't know how to deal with the details of running the programs."

Jericho laughed. "You ought to see my little stepbrothers on the computer. They'd probably make *you* feel like a dinosaur! How'd you learn so much about computers, anyway?"

"My grandmother won a complete computer setup—printer, modem, scanner, the whole bit—in a contest at the grocery store a couple of years ago. She told me, 'Kofi, come get this thing outta my house 'fore it tries to get all in my mind and my business!' I tried to tell her it was just a machine, but that's exactly why she didn't like it! She wouldn't even open the box. So I took it home, set it up, and taught myself. I'm as good on a computer as you are on a trumpet," Kofi teased.

"Maybe," Jericho admitted. He frowned in thought a moment. "Let me ask you something, Kofi. I got a trumpet competition comin' up real soon. If I do well, and since my lips got magic, I know I will . . ." He paused and smiled a moment. Then he finished seriously. "It could mean a scholarship to Juilliard."

"So what's your problem? You scared your lips will fall off from kissin' Arielle before you have a chance to play at the competition?"

"Naw, man, it's just the contest is the last Thursday of the month—the fourth night of pledge week," Jericho told him glumly.

"Man, that sucks! Can you reschedule the contest?"

"No."

"What are you gonna do?"

Jericho sighed. "What choice do I have. I gotta pledge, man. I can't quit now."

Kofi looked at him quietly. "Hey, Jericho, remember when I told you the doctor told me to come back and see him for some tests?

"Yeah, what happened?"

"Well, he ran the tests and he said I had a slight heart murmur or something."

Jericho looked up in surprise. "For real? What does that mean?"

Kofi shrugged. "Well, there goes my chances with the NBA!"

"You couldn't shoot a hoop straight to save your life

anyway! You're lucky the NBA lets you buy tickets to their games!"

"Yeah, I know. I never did like sports much. I just played ball with you all 'cause that's what dudes are s'posed to do, I guess. I'm more into computers and video stuff anyway."

"Did your doctor sign your Warrior medical form?" asked Jericho.

"Yeah, he signed it, with a note about my 'heart condition,' as he called it. He said as long as I don't decide to run a marathon or something, I'll be okay." Kofi chuckled. "No danger of that! He said takin' toys to little kids was cool and wasn't stressful, and he wished me good luck in the club."

"Well, that's good to know. What did your parents say?"

"Nothing. I don't think they got the message on their machine yet. It usually erases itself before they bother to check it."

"You gonna tell them?"

"Maybe. They won't think it's a big deal."

"Why you say that?" Jericho asked.

"To them, nothing is a big deal, except hangin' out. They party with their friends all night long, then sleep it off the next day wherever they end up. Life is just one big high for them." He drummed his fingers on the wooden bench.

"That's some deep stuff. I know they're hardly ever home when I stop by there," Jericho replied.

Kofi grunted. "I live there, and I never see them either. Sometimes I feel like I'm the grown-up in the house. It's been like that since I was little. I grew up on words like 'maybe later' and 'I don't care.'"

"I know they're glad you're around, Kofi. Maybe they'll change," Jericho suggested. "Ever think about that?"

"All the time. But for now, I just hope they remember to leave a couple of dollars for lunch and bus fare," Kofi admitted. He picked up his book bag.

"You need a ride?" Jericho offered.

"No, but thanks. I'm taking the bus downtown. I have to do a report for English and I have to use a real book, not something I downloaded." Kofi slung his backpack onto his shoulder. "Old-fashioned teachers," he muttered as he headed out into the cold January air.

"You take it easy, now," Jericho called as Kofi left. He noticed Mr. Boston, with his coat and briefcase, walking purposefully toward where Jericho sat. "I'm sorry about all the noise, Mr. Boston," Jericho began.

"Oh, that's okay, Jericho. Actually, I understand. I feel sorry for Eric. If screaming is all he needs to do to vent his frustrations, then let him scream once in awhile."

Mr. Boston sat down and Jericho tried not to groan. Why couldn't this dude just go home? Why did he feel like he had to talk to him? Out loud he said, "Why do you always stay at school so late, Mr. Boston?"

"Grading papers. Preparing for tomorrow. I like the silence and the solitude of an empty classroom."

"Hey, we can make that happen for you. Just say the word and you can have a solitary classroom every day! We'll just disappear."

"Thank you for your kind offer, but nothing that drastic

will be necessary," Mr. Boston replied, rolling his eyes. "I also like the noisy activity of a busy classroom. I just like school."

"Is there a pill you can take to cure that?" Jericho asked.

"Retirement, I guess," he replied with a laugh. Then he cleared his throat and said, "I hear you're on the list of pledges for the Warriors of Distinction."

Jericho nodded. "Even teachers know?"

"Everybody knows."

"That's cool," Jericho said with a shrug.

"We've heard about Dana Wolfe as well—the first girl to try it."

Jericho sighed. "Well, she's gonna make it interesting at least. Nobody's sure how it's gonna turn out."

"You look out for her, Jericho," Mr. Boston said sharply.

"Me? How come?"

"A young man of true distinction would do that."

Jericho said nothing for a moment. Then he asked, "Were you a Warrior when you were in high school, Mr. Boston?"

"I didn't go to Douglass. I'm from Oklahoma. Believe it or not, I was on the football team in high school."

"For real? You don't look big enough," Jericho said in amazement.

Mr. Boston laughed. "I wasn't the best kid on the team, and I only played for a year. I quit in my sophomore year."

"Too much competition?" Jericho asked.

Mr. Boston inhaled and replied, "No, I quit because of the initiation activities the team practiced every year."

"What kind of initiation? Don't you just make the team because you're good enough?"

"Yes and no. After you make the team, the returning players put the new kids through hazing rituals."

"How can that happen? Wouldn't the coach stop anything bad?"

Mr. Boston looked at the ceiling. "The coach turned his head and pretended it didn't happen—he'd been doing that for years."

"Then it couldn't have been that bad," Jericho reasoned.

"I remember the coach saying that the initiation activities built team spirit and such. But it was horrible."

"So what did they do?" Jericho was fascinated.

"After our first practice, while we freshmen were in the shower, the upperclassmen took our clothes, so we were left there, nude, in the locker room."

"No big deal. We're naked in the locker room all the time," Jericho countered.

"Yes, but then we were blindfolded and marched, without our clothes, onto the football field, where the cheerleaders, the marching band, and the drill team were practicing. We had to stand there, naked and blindfolded, while kids took pictures and called us names. It was only seconds, but it seemed like hours. Everybody laughed and thought it was great fun, but I was embarrassed and humiliated." Mr. Boston picked at the latch of his briefcase.

"So you quit?"

"No, I was also too embarrassed to complain to anybody, so I played that one year. The next year, when I heard them making the same plans for the new kids, I just quit. I didn't want to be a part of the hazing, but I didn't have guts enough to stop it."

"Are they still doing it at that high school?" Jericho asked.

"No, someone with more guts than I had finally told the authorities. The coach was fired, and the practice was stopped."

"Why are you telling me this?" Jericho asked, amazed.

"Because I've heard rumors about the pledge activities of the Warriors of Distinction, and I don't want you to get hurt. I'm also a little worried about Dana."

"What kind of rumors? I haven't heard anything like that," Jericho replied, agitated.

"As you know, they keep it pretty secretive. But bits and pieces of information escape."

"The Warriors of Distinction is the best club in the city!" Jericho said defensively. "Look at all the good stuff it does!"

"I don't deny that, Jericho. Just be careful, all right?"

"Yeah, I'll be careful. But if it was dangerous, my Uncle Brock, Josh's father, wouldn't let us pledge. He's been through it and he said it was a piece of cake!"

"Were those his exact words?" asked Mr. Boston.

"Well, he said it would be an 'unforgettable experience.'"

"That's not exactly the same thing, is it?" Mr. Boston got up to leave. "You're a good student, Jericho. I enjoy having you in class. I just wanted to share my concerns with you."

"Thanks, Mr. Boston. I appreciate you worrying about me, but everything will be cool."

Mr. Boston opened the main door, letting the cold winter air into the front hall. Just then Arielle came around the corner.

"Thanks for waiting for me," she said. "That test was really hard. Were you bored while you waited?"

"Surprisingly not. I'll tell you about it in the car. Let's get out of here!"

THEY STOOD IN THE WAREHOUSE THAT HAD been used for the toy drive. Jericho was nervous but not frightened. He looked at the other members of his pledge class—Josh, Kofi, a big football player named Cleveland, the track star Luis he knew from math class, two basketball players named Rudy and Deshawn, a wrestler who was simply known as Ram, three honor society members named Arnold, Simon, and Jesse, a swimmer the kids called Fish, a boy named Kenyon who liked to write poetry, a drummer named Jack, and Dana, who stood a bit off by herself. There were fifteen pledges, all waiting to see what would happen. No one spoke. Jericho felt a tickle in his stomach when he thought about what the first night's activities might be. He had thought about it all weekend, and he couldn't imagine what they might ask him to do. The room, completely empty of boxes and toys now, echoed strangely in the darkness.

The Warriors entered the room together. They all wore black Warrior T-shirts and stood in a line before the pledges. Eddie Mahoney seemed to be in charge tonight. He lifted weights every day after school, and his upper body was tight and hard with muscles. Jericho figured he forced himself to be tough to make up for his lack of height.

Eddie spoke with authority. "We will ask very little of you during the school day. After all, academics are important. But we will ask you each day to complete a school service activity."

Rick spoke next. "You will address the seniors, who for the duration of this process are your pledge masters, by their proper title. For example, I will be known as 'Master Senior Sharp,' and you must address me as 'sir.' Mr. Madison here will be 'Master Senior Madison, sir.' And we will call each of you by your proper title, which is 'Pledge Slime.' Any requests we make of you at any time must be fulfilled—immediately. Understood, Pledge Slime?"

"Understood, Master Senior Sharp, sir!" the pledges repeated.

"When this is over, if you survive," he paused and looked directly at Dana, "we will no longer be your masters, but your brothers, and we will welcome you into the Warriors of Distinction. But until then, you must undergo the Bonding of the Brotherhood. Understood?"

"Understood!" the pledges repeated loudly. Their voices echoed strangely in the now empty warehouse. It sounded different from how it had in the daytime, Jericho thought, when sunlight streamed through the wire-covered windows. Tonight the warehouse was slightly darkened, full of shadows and echoes.

"Tonight it begins," Eddie said suddenly. "The sweetness is over. We did a good job with the toy drive. No one will bother us now while we get down to the business of making sure you are worthy of us."

A feeling of dread began to creep up Jericho's spine.

"Our first activity," Eddie Mahoney continued, "is designed to test your loyalty and obedience. Sit on the floor in a circle, hands behind your back." He held a medium-size plastic bowl in his hands. Rick held an identical bowl. In each bowl was a spoon. Jericho couldn't see what was in either bowl. "Pledge masters, the blindfolds please."

Rick and Madison and the others swiftly tied black scarves around the heads of the pledges. Jericho could feel the scarf being wrapped around his head and it felt uncomfortably tight. He could see nothing. Then he felt his hands being tied behind his back. He suppressed a wild notion to pull off the blindfold and run out of there.

"Warriors and Masters," Eddie said. "It's time to make our very own pledge slime. Let's spit in the bowl for the Pledge Slime at our feet." Jericho wasn't sure he heard correctly, then he could distinctly hear the disgusting, wet sounds of deep gobs of mucus being spit, dropping thickly into the container.

"Enough!" Eddie commanded. "Now, Pledge Slime, one spoonful of spit will prove your loyalty and obedience. Who will be first?"

The room was silent.

"We don't have any potential Warriors here, men," Eddie said. "We have a room full of wimps! Again I ask you—who will be the first to swallow a spoonful of spit?"

Then Jericho heard Dana's voice. "I'll go first, sir."

"I gotta admit, the girl's got guts," Jericho heard Madison say. Jericho silently agreed.

"Open your mouth," Eddie said. "One large tablespoon of spit for the girl with the guts!"

Jericho heard Dana gagging a little, but she must have swallowed it, because she said clearly, "That was delicious!"

The pledge masters laughed at that, and Eddie said, "Who's next?"

Kofi, probably not wanting Dana to show him up too badly, volunteered next, then Luis, then Cleveland, who almost vomited. Josh volunteered then, and the rest of them. It took a very long time, but finally it was Jericho's turn.

"Jericho, you get what's left in the bowl. Can you handle it?" Eddie asked him.

"Yes, sir," Jericho replied weakly. He heard the spoon scraping the bottom of the bowl, then felt the spoon at his lips. He felt sick to his stomach.

"Swallow it, Pledge Slime!" Eddie said, a maniacal tone to his voice.

Jericho took a deep breath, opened his mouth, and the contents of the spoon were poured into his mouth. It was warm and thick. He swallowed quickly before he could gag. He felt like he might faint.

"Take off the blindfolds and hand restraints," Eddie

commanded. Jericho gazed at the pledges sitting on the floor. They all looked ill.

Madison took over then. "You did well, Pledge Slime. You know, of course, that we wouldn't really make you drink spit. Let us show you what you swallowed." He removed a Styrofoam egg container from his book bag. "Rick, show them your bowl."

"Egg whites. Just egg whites—room temperature. Not exactly pleasant, but not dangerous, at least. That's what you swallowed." Rick smiled maliciously, but none of the pledges smiled back.

Jericho sat on the floor, unable to move for a few minutes. He was trying to figure out how his mind had made it all seem real. "And this is just the first day," he whispered to Josh, who was also unusually quiet.

Before they had a chance to recover completely, Eddie stepped forward again. He handed each pledge a photograph of the black silk Warriors of Distinction jacket. "I want you to look at what you're striving for. The jacket you see in the picture can be yours if this week is successful. But it is much more than a jacket—it is a representation of obedience and loyalty and dignity. It is symbolic of the pride we feel in knowing that we are Warriors of Distinction." He spoke with fierce passion and frowned at Dana.

"Now you run!" he barked. "I want you to hold this photograph in front of you as you run so you can see what you are striving for. Let it be your strength and your inspiration. Hold it high and run! Run until I tell you to stop. If you slow down, you get beat down."

Jericho held the picture of the jacket in front of him and

joined the others as they thundered around the sides of the warehouse. He looked around and saw that all of the pledges were doing as they had been told—holding the picture high and looking at it as they ran. He wasn't sure if they felt inspired by the picture or not. He just knew that he had to do as he was told in order to make it into the Warriors of Distinction. So he ran.

Eddie was true to his word. When Cleveland stumbled over a shoelace, Eddie hit him on his back with what looked like the handle of a snow shovel. Cleveland looked at him angrily, but said nothing. He got up and continued to run. Luis got a cramp and sat down in pain. Eddie hit him with the shovel handle and told him to get up. Luis got up, but he walked instead of ran. Rudy ran smoothly, but he bumped Eddie on one of his rounds. Jericho thought it looked like he had done it on purpose.

Two laps. Five laps. Ten. Jericho was breathing hard and hoping that Eddie would let them stop. Twelve laps. Fourteen. Sixteen. Dana ran smoothly, seemingly without much effort. She didn't frown or slow her stride, even when some of the boys started to falter. *Go, girl, go,* Jericho thought. Then he glanced back at Kofi, who was running far behind the others. He let Kofi catch up and noticed his breathing was raspy and rapid.

"You okay, Kofi?" Jericho asked as they ran together, much more slowly than the others.

"Yeah. . . . Fine." But his words seemed to be stretched wide.

"You need to stop, man?" Jericho asked.

"Don't . . . sweat . . . it. . . . I . . . can . . . beat . . .

you!" Kofi breathed as he managed to push past Jericho.

They ran longer and harder than in any gym class or basketball practice that Jericho had ever been in. Fifteen minutes, twenty, twenty-five. None of the pledge masters seemed to notice that Kofi was having difficulty. Thirty minutes of nonstop running. "One more lap," called Eddie. He had stopped using the stick.

Jericho and Kofi finished the last lap together. Jericho was definitely winded. But Kofi took deep gulping breaths.

"I'm going to go tell Mahoney to take it easy on you," Jericho declared as they finished.

"Don't you dare say anything to anybody!" Kofi exclaimed. He grabbed Jericho's arm and whispered, "This is the only thing I have ever done in my life that makes me feel proud. So just shut up!" Kofi stuffed the picture of the Warrior jacket into his pocket.

Jericho looked at Kofi and said grudgingly, "Okay for now, but if it gets crazy, I'm not gonna shovel you off some floor. You got that?"

"Thanks, man. I'll be fine. I can't let my girl Dana beat me, can I?"

Dripping with sweat in spite of the chilliness of the room, Jericho glanced around at the group. The heavier boys like Ram and Cleveland heaved loudly and sweated profusely. Josh looked energized instead of being tired, Kofi looked almost ashen, and even Dana looked drained and exhausted. She wasn't breathing nearly as hard as Kofi was, however.

Madison passed out small bottles of water, and for a moment Jericho thought the worst was over. "I have a question," Madison said to the group of pledges sitting on the floor. "Are you willing to do anything to be a Warrior of Distinction?"

"Yes, sir! Yes, Master Senior Madison, sir!" they all chanted. Jericho didn't know whether he was excited or frightened.

"Don't ever forget that," Madison commented dryly.

"You're hot and sweaty," Eddie said then. "Take off your shirts."

Jericho started to obey immediately, but stopped when he remembered Dana. A bunch of dudes taking off their shirts was one thing, but a girl in the room made it different. The other pledges hesitated as well, looking at each other and not sure what to do.

"I said take off your shirts—all of you!" Eddie yelled.

Kofi removed his shirt first. His thin, wiry body was still heaving from the run. He was sweating heavily. Cleveland was next. He wore a heavy sweatshirt and removed it slowly. Rolls of fat hung over his waistline. Josh and Jericho removed their shirts at the same time. Josh was fit and slim; Jericho looked down at his large belly and wished he had eaten more carrot sticks. Luis had the best build of all the boys, with deeply rippled muscles. Jericho wondered how Luis managed to be blessed with such a physique. Rudy, the tallest of them, towered silently over the rest. Ram, thick and solid, flexed his biceps. Fourteen shirts lay next to fourteen boys. The room was silent. They waited for Dana.

DANA LOOKED AROUND HER, SHRUGGED,
and swiftly removed her T-shirt. She wore
no bra. She looked straight ahead. Eddie
grinned as he stared at her. At first, no one
moved, then Kofi walked over to where she
sat on the floor. He stood, arms folded across
his chest, directly in front of her, facing forward, like a human shield. Jericho realized what
he was doing and joined him, his back to Dana,
his arms folded across his chest as well. Josh ran
to join them, then the rest of the pledges did so as
well. When they were finished, fourteen boys surrounded the half-naked girl on the floor, each facing
outward.

"Well done," Madison said, nodding his head. He
said nothing else to them.

The pledge captains then handed out bright pink
T-shirts to the pledges.

"Toss one over your barrier to that pledge who wants to

be just like a man," Eddie sneered. Unlike Madison, he did not seem to be very pleased that they had shielded Dana. "You will wear this shirt every day at school to every class and every school function. You will wash and dry it every night and iron it every morning. Failure to wear this shirt will mean you have failed as a pledge, which means that the entire class of pledges will have failed. Why?"

"All of us or none of us!" Jericho and the rest of the pledges said in unison.

Rick spoke to them next. "You will be living two lives for the rest of this week. During the day you will participate in school-sanctioned pledge activities. At night you belong to the real world of the Warriors. You will say nothing about these two worlds. You will tell no one of our evening activities. Understood?"

"Understood," the pledges repeated obediently, but Jericho continued to feel uneasy about the "other world" Rick spoke of.

"Go home. You are dismissed for tonight. Be in Mr. Culligan's room tomorrow morning at seven thirty." With that, he and the other members of the club left the room.

Dana stood up then, wearing her pink shirt. "I want to thank you guys," she said shakily. "Especially you, Kofi, for starting it. But I'm gonna do my best to hold my own. I would have sat right there in just my jeans—all night, if I had to—just to prove it."

"You would have?" Josh asked in amazement.

"Yeah, but I'm glad I didn't have to," she admitted. "I promise never to let any of you down. I'm determined that I'm going to do whatever they make me do."

"We got your back, Dana," Kofi said quietly. "I didn't like what you did and how you did it to get in here, but you got guts, girl. I gotta give you your props for that."

For the first time all night, Dana smiled.

"Hey, Dana," Kofi asked her, "how did you know the spit was fake?"

"I didn't. I just figured they had to be faking us out somehow, and I had to prove myself. I don't want them to have an excuse to kick me out of this group."

"Why do you want this so bad?" Josh asked.

"I've never had a chance to make a real difference," she said. "I talk big, but talk changes nothing. This is my chance to prove what I believe in."

"You're doin' great so far," Cleveland added. "If it hadn't been for you, I woulda just sat there and vomited my dinner all over their fancy shoes."

The fifteen pledges collapsed in laughter then. Jericho felt really close to them at that moment, and wondered if this was what was meant by bonding. "We're bonded, right?" Jericho asked the group.

"I guess so," Kofi said.

"All of us or none of us," Luis reminded them.

"Yeah, yeah. Enough of that. What's up with the shirt?" Josh asked. "Pink? November is gonna trip when she sees this!"

"They used the same ones last year," Jericho reminded him.

"Yeah, but not on me," Josh complained.

"Well, I'm gonna have to listen to Arielle all week about this slogan on the back," Jericho said with a sigh. "'I am not distinguished yet.'"

"Yeah, that's pretty cold," Josh admitted. "But it's only for a week. I figure I can put up with anything for five days."

"Even being called 'Pledge Slime'?" asked Rudy.

"I guess. All this is worth it, right?" Jericho asked.

"Yeah, you got that straight! I'd do anything to be a Warrior," Cleveland said as he looked at the ugly pink shirt.

"Anything?" Jericho asked.

"Yeah, man, just about anything."

Jericho took Kofi and Josh home, then eased into his house quietly. Everyone had already gone to bed. He took a long, hot shower and called Arielle when he had slipped under the covers.

"How was it?" she asked.

"Pretty disgusting, but not bad. Nothing scary—yet."

"That's all you can tell me?"

"Aw, you know, the code of silence thing. It's dumb, but I'm following their rules for now."

"How did Dana do?"

Jericho thought back to the intensity of the evening. "Better than most of us, actually. She's tough."

"That's for sure. Well, I'm just glad you're okay."

"Sleepy. Tired. And better now that I've talked to you."

"You always know what to say, Jericho," she said softly. "Good night, and I'll see you tomorrow."

"Good night, Arielle."

Even though he was tired and still slightly nauseous, Jericho practiced his trumpet for a half hour after he hung up. He winced as he thought about the competition, however, and he put the trumpet away.

THE FIFTEEN PLEDGES, DRESSED IN THEIR flourescent pink T-shirts, waited quietly for instructions. No one mentioned how Dana had answered the challenge the night before, but Jericho was sure they were all thinking of it.

Madison moved to the front of Mr. Culligan's room. "I have a question," he began. "Are you willing to do anything to be a Warrior of Distinction?" he demanded.

"Yes, sir!" they all replied.

"We will see," Madison commented dryly. "Today we begin the school service assignments. We meet for the serious stuff again tonight. Eight o'clock. Don't dare be late!"

"Yes, sir!"

"For your first assignment this morning," Madison continued in his gravelly voice, "we ask that all of you stand in the main hall by the front door and greet each and every incoming student. You will say, 'Good morning. We are the undistinguished pledges who strive to be Warriors of Distinction. We hope you have a pleasant day.' Understood?"

"Understood, Master Senior Madison, sir!" the pledges said in unison.

"When the bell rings for first-period class, you are to go to your classes as usual. For now, you are dismissed. Have a great day."

With that, he and the other Warriors of Distinction left the room. Jericho and the other pledges looked at each other excitedly.

"So what do you think is gonna happen tonight?" asked Kofi.

Jericho shrugged, "I don't know, but I'm not worried."

"You ready for this, Dana?" Kofi asked her.

"I'll be fine," she said with a smile, "as long as I can keep my clothes on!"

"Well, we better get this over with," Josh reminded them. "Let's go meet and greet the world!"

The first person all fifteen pink-shirted pledges met in the hall was November. Rick Sharp was standing nearby, watching them. The pledges looked at November and said in unison, "Good morning. We are the undistinguished pledges who strive to be Warriors of Distinction. We hope you have a pleasant day." Jericho felt pretty stupid saying it, but he reminded himself that he was just one of the group, and his voice blended in with the others.

November looked at the group, gasped, then sat down in the middle of the floor and howled with laughter. She laughed until tears were streaming down her face. She couldn't stop laughing.

"I don't think it's so funny," Kofi said saltily. "Quit laughing, November!"

"But you all look so *funny!*" she howled. "Dana, girl, you better watch out! These dudes look like they're tryin' to be fashion statements!"

"The shirt is supposed to show who we are and that we're proud to be pledges," Jericho tried to explain.

"A pledge is a promise, not a person," November said to them. That kinda made sense, Jericho thought, but then November started laughing at them again. "Well, you sure can't miss any of you coming down the hall! Where's my shades?" She dug in her purse and pulled out a pair of sunglasses.

Other students had started to arrive by then. They either joined November's laughter or simply shook their heads in bemusement at pledges who greeted each and every one of them with, "Good morning. We are the undistinguished pledges who strive to be Warriors of Distinction. We hope you have a pleasant day." Jericho had thought he would enjoy this, but even though he didn't mind November laughing at them, because he knew where she was coming from, it made him uncomfortable to see kids he didn't even know join her. A few kids had cameras in their book bags and they snapped pictures of the group that even Jericho had to admit looked pretty silly.

Mr. Boston arrived as the pictures were being snapped, and Jericho thought about what he had told him about hazing. But this wasn't hazing, was it? They weren't naked. True, the pink shirts were a little over the top, but this was all in fun, right? Jericho wasn't sure. The group recited loudly, "Good morning, Mr. Boston. We are the undistinguished pledges who strive to be Warriors of Distinction. We hope you have a pleasant day." Mr. Boston said nothing, but made eye contact with Jericho, who looked away.

The principal, Mr. Zucker, walked through the hall, carrying a clipboard and a cup of coffee. He was wearing a three-piece blue suit and a red tie. Jericho admired how well the man dressed. Mr. Zucker smiled and nodded at the pledges and continued on to his office.

Soon the whole ordeal became monotonous and Jericho just wanted to go to class. When Arielle walked in the front door, she joined November, who had moved from the floor to a bench near the door. Arielle didn't laugh, but she did take a picture.

When Eric Bell arrived, struggling to push his way through the heavy front door, the group said the speech once more. "Good morning. We are the undistinguished pledges who strive to be Warriors of Distinction. We hope you have a pleasant day." Jericho couldn't bear to look at Eric. Eric wheeled his chair right through the middle of the group, purposely running over a few of the pledges' toes, before he headed down the hall to his first class.

By the time the bell rang, Jericho figured he and the other pledges had said the speech about two hundred times. His mouth was dry and he stopped to get a bottle of water from the machine in the side hall just before class.

Eddie Mahoney appeared out of nowhere. "Thank you, Pledge Slime. I'm really thirsty. So nice of you to buy me this sweet cold bottle of water." He held out his hand.

"But I don't have any more money, and I'm—"

Eddie interrupted him and roared, "Are you questioning me, Pledge Slime?"

"Uh, no, sir, Master Senior Mahoney, sir!" Jericho almost trembled at the rage in Eddie's voice. "I bought this water for you, sir!"

Eddie snatched the bottle of water and continued down the hall. Jericho went on to class, thirsty.

Just after lunch, where he finally got enough to drink, Jericho saw Eric rolling toward him and he knew he couldn't avoid him this time. "Hey, Eric," he said slowly.

"You look awful in pink," Eric answered. His face showed both envy and derision.

"Yeah, well, you know," Jericho stammered.

"What's the secret pledge stuff like?"

"No big deal. Lots of running and shouting and promising and stuff," Jericho replied evasively. He looked around uncomfortably, searching for an excuse to get away.

"You don't have to feel bad about me, Jericho. I know I lost my chances in a club like that when I broke my back. I can still dream, though. Catch you later." With that he directed his chair down the hall, the wheels whistling on the smooth, polished floor.

JERICHO AND THE PLEDGES WAITED QUIETLY in the chilly warehouse for the night's events to begin. He worried a little about Dana, but she looked calm and unruffled. Eddie and the fourteen other Warriors walked into the warehouse at precisely eight P.M. Eddie seemed to be in charge again.

"Good evening, Pledge Slime," he greeted them.

"Good evening, Master Senior Mahoney, sir!" the pledges repeated loudly. Their voices echoed and bounced off the bare walls.

"First of all this evening, we want to make sure you understand your position as pledges. Gentlemen? The collars please." Eddie motioned to Rick and Madison, who pulled from a brown paper bag fifteen dog collars with attached leashes.

"You gotta be kiddin' me," Josh whispered to Jericho.

"Line up and kneel!" Eddie commanded. The pledges

knelt obediently on the dirty warehouse floor. The seniors then proceeded to attach the dog collars to their necks. Jericho felt the leather being pulled around his neck and latched snugly. He felt choked, as if he couldn't breathe, even though the collar wasn't really fastened that tightly.

"Let's pretend we're at one of those dog shows," Eddie said. "Warriors, make sure your doggie knows how to run and sit up and do tricks. Let's get started!"

The Warriors gleefully began dragging the pledges across the filthy floor, making them bark or jump or roll over. They seemed to be having great fun. "I couldn't wait until this year so I could do this to another group of pledges!" Madison boasted as he made Kofi crawl on his stomach.

"Yeah, man," agreed Deon, a six-foot senior. "They did it to us, and it sure feels good to do it to them now!" He yanked Josh by his neck and made him pretend to wag his tail.

The Warriors hooted with laughter. Jericho felt like dirt. He looked up at Rick Sharp, who held his leash.

"Next year you get to do it to another group. That's the beauty of the system!" Rick explained. "Now bark!"

Jericho barked.

Rick led him all the way across the room with the leash; Jericho had to crawl quickly to avoid being choked. He glanced at Dana, who, to no one's surprise, was being yanked around the room by Eddie. Jericho tried to keep an eye on Dana as he did his own set of stupid dog tricks for Rick.

"Roll over!" Eddie yelled at her. She obeyed, but the

look in her eyes was not of a loving puppy, but rather a caged beast.

"Sit up!"

She sat on her knees and glared at him.

"Now down!" he commanded. "All the way to the ground—flat on your stomach." Dana obeyed slowly. He yanked the collar around her neck. "Now back on your hands and knees. Let me see you wag your tail."

Dana shook her backside almost imperceptibly.

"I said wag that tail!" Eddie ordered. "Let me see it shake!" Dana obeyed, but Jericho could see her eyes were squeezed shut. He then watched in disbelief as Eddie put his hand on her behind and patted it as if she were really a dog. "Good doggie," he whispered to her. Dana, amazingly, said nothing.

"Let's race our dogs," Eddie called suddenly to Rick. He pulled Dana by her neck, lined up with Rick, who led Jericho into place, and the four of them sped across the warehouse floor. Rick and Eddie shouted with glee as they dragged Jericho and Dana as fast as they could by their collars. Trying to run on his hands and knees was difficult, and Jericho feared he would stumble, get caught up in the leash, and choke to death. He sighed with relief when Rick and Eddie stopped.

Eddie wasn't finished with Dana, however. "Jump!" he commanded. "Let me see how high my doggie can jump. Jump, dog, jump!"

Dana hesitated, then from her crouching position on the floor, jumped up as smoothly as a leopard attacking its prey, her arms outstretched toward Eddie. As she was landing, she reached out with her hand as though to catch her balance and managed to scratch Eddie's face with her fingernails. But Jericho could tell it was no accident.

Eddie jerked his hand to his cheek, his face contorted in surprise and rage, but he said nothing. Jericho caught Dana's eye and smiled.

Eddie walked back to the center of the room, holding his cheek, pulling Dana sharply by the collar on her neck. "Gentlemen," he announced. "Bring your dogs to the center of the room and line them up in front of these chairs." Jericho allowed himself to be pulled with the others back to the center. "Remove the collars," he told the Warriors. Jericho rubbed his neck with relief as the collar fell from his neck. He wasn't sure if he'd be glad to do this next year to a new pledge or not.

"Next," Eddie announced to the pledges, "we test your strength and endurance. We don't want you if you're not tough."

"Pledge masters, the chairs please." The fifteen pledge captains each pulled an old brown folding chair from where they had been stacked against the wall, and lined them up in a row. Now what? Jericho wondered.

"Now, Pledge Slime, face the chairs, and get ready for the blessing! We have done this every year for fifty years, and the blessings just get better!" His odd laughter echoed in the darkened warehouse. The pledges shuffled to the line of chairs hesitantly. Kofi stood to the left of Jericho, Dana stood to his right. "Bend over," Eddie commanded, "and hold the seat of the chair firmly with both hands."

As the pledges obeyed, Jericho could see what was about to happen. *Oh, no,* he moaned silently.

"If you move from the position, if you make a sound, you get blessed twice—maybe three or four times," Eddie explained. "It's up to you."

Madison and Rick appeared in front of them holding huge wooden paddles. The pledge captains then walked quietly behind the chairs to where the backsides of the pledges waited. The room was silent.

Whack! Intense pain exploded on Jericho's butt, spreading down his legs and up his spine. Involuntarily he stood up from the chair. He did not scream, however. For once he was glad of his extra padding of fat.

"You like the blessing so much, I see you want it again," Rick told him. "Bend over, Pledge Slime, and take it like a man!"

Everything in Jericho's being screamed inside him—not so much from pain, but from anger. *How dare somebody hit him like that! He didn't have to take this!* But he clenched his teeth, grabbed the seat of the chair, and leaned over so that Rick Sharp could strike him again. *Whack!* This time Rick hit him even harder. Jericho seethed, but held on.

Kofi was next. Jericho glanced over at him and tried to give him a smile of encouragement, but Kofi had his eyes squeezed shut. *Thwack!* Kofi let a small involuntary noise escape. *Thunk!* He was hit again.

Ram, Cleveland, and Jack were heavyweights who took their swats with relative ease. Rudy and Arnold screamed, so they both got three fierce beatings with the paddle.

Josh stood up twice, so he got hit three times as well. Luis escaped with only one swat. All of the pledges except for Dana had endured the beatings. She waited in silence, head down, arms taut as she held on to the chair.

Eddie took the paddle from Rick and said quietly, "This one is mine." Jericho bent forward so he could see Dana. She looked determined and tense. He wanted to say something to stop her from getting hit, but he couldn't think what. He didn't want to mess up her chances of getting in the club, or his own chances for that matter, but he knew somehow that Eddie was going to go way over the line. He was right.

He heard Eddie take a deep breath, heard him say "Umph!" as he struck Dana with so much force that he knocked her forward into the chair. She collapsed into the chair which broke as she fell into it. Amazingly she did not scream.

"Get her another chair," Eddie said calmly. "She needs another blessing."

"That's enough, man," Rick said, grabbing Eddie's arm.

"Didn't we agree we were gonna make her understand what she was getting into, to show her she has no place here?" Eddie hissed.

"Yeah, man, but—"

"I know what I'm doing! Get her another chair!" Rick said nothing more, but brought Eddie a chair.

"Get up, Pledge Slime!" he commanded Dana.

Kofi moved from his chair to help her. "Stay where you are!" Madison snarled.

Jericho looked at Dana. She had a long scratch on one

arm, and her nose was bleeding a little. Her face was a mask of anger and determination. She assumed the position once again. *Thwack! Whack! Smack!* Three times Eddie beat her with the paddle. Three times she held on to the chair and made no sound at all, not even a whimper.

Jericho thought that if he hit her one more time, he was going to punch that punk in his face. He didn't care if he didn't get in. This was crazy! But just then Eddie stopped and tossed the paddle to the floor.

"Stand up now," Eddie told the pledges. He said nothing to Dana and refused to look at her. She stood with difficulty, but managed to smile at Jericho and Kofi.

"You all right, Dana?" Kofi asked. Jericho couldn't say anything; he was disgusted with himself for not having the courage to stop the whole thing.

"I'm okay," she said shakily. "Let's just get this night over with. If you guys can do it, I can too."

"Now we test your courage and obedience," Eddie told the pledges. "Sit down in the chairs." They all sat, some of them very carefully. Jericho could see that Dana winced in pain as she sat. But she said nothing.

Eddie, Rick, and several of the other seniors walked toward the seated pledges. Rick carried two glass jars with lids, one in each hand. They looked like used mayonnaise jars, Jericho thought. He couldn't see what was inside the jars, but it was reddish-orange in color.

"Pledge masters, tie their hands, please," Eddie continued. Jericho felt rough rope pull his wrists tightly as it was expertly tied to the back of the chair. He tried to pull it loose and found he could not. He felt trapped and nervous.

Suppose there's a fire! he thought irrationally. He looked at Dana, who had her eyes closed, and Kofi, who also looked scared. Josh, in the seat next to Kofi, tapped his feet nervously.

"Now their feet," Eddie commanded, "and place the blindfolds over their eyes." Jericho felt even more confined as he felt his feet being lashed to the legs of the chair and the scarf being pulled around his eyes. He wanted to run kicking and screaming out of there, feel his arms moving freely as they beat several of the Warriors in their faces. But the point was to be tested for courage, wasn't it? So he tried to take short easy breaths and stay calm for whatever was to come next.

Madison's voice broke the silence. "Are you willing to do anything to become a Warrior of Distinction?"

"Yes, sir," the pledges replied obediently. But their voices lacked the power they had carried earlier.

"Good!" Madison's voice replied. "Then you'll enjoy the meal we've prepared for you!"

"Do you like spaghetti?" Eddie asked sweetly.

Jericho hadn't been expecting that question. "Yes, sir," he answered cautiously with the others.

"You will have a choice in our next activity," Eddie explained. "One jar holds soft candy gummy worms dipped in tomato sauce. The other jar holds real earthworms, also dipped in spaghetti sauce." Jericho knew what was coming next. "You will say one word—'left' or 'right.' If you guess in which hand Master Senior Sharp holds the candy, you will have a mildly pleasant treat. If you choose the hand that holds the worms, that is your meal for the evening."

"We will begin with Josh!" Madison announced.

"Hey, pick somebody else," Josh said. "I admit I'm not brave—I'm scared of puppy dogs!" Jericho smiled at Josh's never-ending good humor. He was sitting there terrified, and Josh was making jokes about it. It helped Jericho relax a little.

"Silence!" Madison roared. Josh said nothing else. "Now choose!" Madison commanded.

"Right," Josh announced clearly. Jericho heard the sound of the jar being opened. He could smell the rich, deep aroma of spaghetti sauce.

"Chew!" Eddie's voice demanded.

"Delicious!" Josh's voice yelled victoriously. "I don't often dip my candy in my spaghetti sauce, man, but I like your recipe!"

The pledges giggled, and some of Jericho's tension eased.

Jericho was chosen to go next, and with great relief, he, too, chose the candy. So did Luis and Ram and Rudy. Every single pledge, whether he said "right" or "left," ended up with the candy. Only two pledges remained. Jericho was beginning to think maybe there were no real worms when they called Dana's name.

"Do you like worms, little girl?" he heard Eddie whisper in her ear.

"You *are* a worm!" Dana replied fiercely. Jericho knew that if her feet were free, she would have kicked him.

"I am your master, whether you like it or not, sister," Eddie continued to whisper. "If you're gonna be in this group, we'd better learn to get along with each other."

"Bite me!" she retorted.

"Not tonight," Eddie replied deliberately and quietly. "I think I'll take a wet, sloppy kiss from you instead."

"Leave me alone! Don't you touch me!" Jericho could hear Dana's chair scrape along the wooden floor as she wiggled, trying to get away from Eddie. "Don't you da—" Her voice was muffled then as Eddie carried out his threat. Jericho could hear Dana struggle. The other pledge masters laughed uproariously.

"Quit, man!" Kofi shouted from his chair. "Leave her alone!"

"Are you speaking to me, Pledge Slime?" Eddie asked harshly. "How dare you raise your voice to a pledge master!"

Kofi didn't respond, but Jericho could hear his breathing, heavy with frustration. Eddie's footsteps moved to where Kofi was sitting. "Choose!" he commanded.

"Left," Kofi replied immediately. Jericho heard the jar being opened, smelled the sharp tomato odor.

"Open your mouth!" Eddie's voice commanded.

"Arrgh! Real worms! You did that on purpose!" Kofi screamed angrily.

"Eat!" Madison's voice commanded. "Suck it, chew it, enjoy it! And to the rest of you, we will tolerate no insubordination!"

Kofi said nothing else, though he gagged a little. Then he said in a whisper, "Spaghetti, spaghetti, spaghetti!"

"I have not forgotten you, Miss Dana," Eddie said next. "Choose!"

"Right," Dana replied. Jericho knew that Eddie would make sure she got the worms. He figured Dana knew that

SHARON M. DRAPER

as well. He heard her gag, chew slowly, then swallow with a loud gulp.

"You could have had the candy," Eddie told her quietly.

"The worms were delicious, thank you," she replied.

"All of you could have had the candy," Eddie told them. "We knew the swats were pretty hard to take, so we decided to lighten things up a bit by letting you think you were getting worms, but making sure all of you got the candy. But your slimy brother Kofi screwed things up!"

Madison continued, "We know the pledge process is intense, but you must trust that we have your best interests at heart. These pledging activities are designed to aid with your bonding to us and us to you. We chose you because we want you to become part of our group. We have never seriously harmed a pledge in fifty years. But we will *not* tolerate any talking back to the pledge masters. Ever! Obedience is essential! Is that understood?"

"Yes, sir," the pledges replied meekly.

"May I have permission to speak, sir?" Jericho heard Kofi ask.

"You may not!" Eddie answered harshly. "The female pledge in the group is bound by the vow of obedience as well. She asked for everything she has received. She must undergo the Bonding of the Brotherhood as we see fit. There will be no more discussion!"

"That's enough for tonight," Rick Sharp announced then. "Untie them. Pledges, you are dismissed until seven tomorrow morning—room one-oh-four. Good night, Pledge Slime."

"Good night, Master Senior Sharp, sir!" the pledges replied quietly as their hands and feet were released.

180

Jericho breathed deeply as the blindfold was removed as well. He glanced over at Dana, who sat trembling in her chair.

"You okay, Dana?" he whispered.

"He's gonna pay," she vowed between clenched teeth. She walked over to Kofi then and buried herself in his arms. Jericho watched quietly, impressed that through the entire evening, she had not cried.

WITH A LITTLE LESS ENTHUSIASM THAN THE DAY
before, the pledges trooped into Mr. Culligan's room to await the day's instructions. A few of them walked uncomfortably, the bruises from the previous night's beating painfully evident. Their pink T-shirts, some of them still damp, were clean and fresh.

"What'd you do to your shirt?" Jericho asked with a laugh as Josh took off his winter jacket. "It looks like it's got chicken pox!"

"I used my mom's soap powder. Box said it had 'bleach crystals' in it. How was I supposed to know what that was?"

"Are you trying to make a fashion statement, Pledge Slime?" Madison asked as the Warriors entered the room. "Or are you incapable of washing your own clothes?"

"I'm sorry, Master Senior Madison, sir. The detergent sorta had a mind of its own last night . . . sir," Josh added.

"Well, at least it's clean, and it certainly makes it very clear that you are 'not yet distinguished'," Madison replied with a cold smile.

"Yes, sir," Josh answered.

Rick moved to the front of the room and cleared his throat. The pledges looked to him immediately. "This morning's activities," he began, "will focus on the teachers. Each of you will go to the main office and as the teachers come in, you will greet them, walk them to their classes, carry their books, get them a cup of coffee—anything they need to begin their day."

"Do we get to pick which teacher, sir?" asked Kofi.

"No, each of you has been assigned to two teachers—that will include about a third of the teachers on the staff. Here is the list. As you know, many teachers arrive early and are already in the building. Get busy, because you must complete this task before the bell rings for first period."

"Suppose they don't want any help, sir?" Jericho asked.

"They must sign your sheet to indicate that at least you offered your help," Rick replied.

Eddie Mahoney spoke next. "Tonight we meet once again at eight P.M. sharp at the warehouse." He said nothing else. Jericho looked at Kofi and Josh. They looked a little worried. Dana, the only one of them who looked good in the pink T-shirt, stared at Eddie, her chin held high. She did not seem to be overly concerned.

Rick gave them their assignments and sent them off to find their teachers. Jericho looked at his sheet and groaned. He had been given Miss Hathaway, the English teacher, and Mr. Boston, his math teacher.

Jericho hurried to Miss Hathaway's room. She was tall and skinny and talked in a loud, squeaky voice. She asked Jericho to run up to the library and find a book for her. He did so gladly so he wouldn't have to listen to her squeaky conversation about her new car. He found the book, rushed back downstairs to give it to her, got his sheet signed, then headed slowly to Mr. Boston's room and knocked on the door.

"Come in," Mr. Boston answered.

"Hey, Mr. Boston. I, uh, want to know if there's anything you want me to do this morning to help you."

"Would you be offering this help if you were not pledging the Warriors of Distinction?" Mr. Boston asked. Jericho hated when teachers answered a question with another question. Why couldn't he just say yes or no?

"I'd help you anytime you needed it, Mr. Boston," Jericho replied honestly, "but yes, today it's because of a pledge activity." He hoped Mr. Boston would just sign the form so he could get out of there and be done with it. "Can I go get you a cup of coffee or something?"

"Did you know hazing is illegal in forty-one states?" Mr. Boston asked.

There he went again—answering a question with another question! "Uh, no, I didn't know that," Jericho answered. "But the Warriors have been pledging kids from this school for years. If it was illegal, it wouldn't be allowed, would it?"

"Is everything going all right, Jericho? Is Dana okay?" Mr. Boston asked.

He'd done it *again!* "I promise, there's no problem at

all. Actually, it's fun!" Jericho said with what he hoped sounded like conviction. "And Dana is probably tougher than I am!" he added honestly.

"You asked if there was a task you could complete for me. Yes, there is. If anything happens this week that makes you uncomfortable or you feel is not quite right, I want you to come to me."

"Oh, I couldn't do that, Mr. Boston!" Jericho said in alarm. "They've got really strict rules about secrecy and silence and stuff. I'd get in really big trouble if I told anybody anything."

"I'm not asking you to break any confidences. All I'm asking is that you come to me if you need help. Do you understand?"

Jericho nodded, but Mr. Boston just didn't understand. There was no way he'd ever breathe a word to him. The rest of the pledges would suffer if he broke the rules and there was no way he was going to rat on anybody.

Mr. Boston signed the teacher participation sheet. "I'll see you in class, Jericho." He returned to grading math papers. Jericho dashed off to his first-period class.

The rest of the day went by quickly. When Jericho got to math class, Mr. Boston, even though he had three pink-shirted students in the class, conducted it as usual—strict discipline and no nonsense. He made no comments or references to Jericho about their earlier conversations.

At lunch Jericho sat with Kofi, Dana, and Josh. "What you gonna do about Eddie?" Josh asked Dana.

"Nothing yet. Try to stay out of his way as much as possible."

"That's hard to do," Jericho commented. "He makes sure he's assigned to you every night."

She nodded slowly. "I did ask for this, you know. I knew it wouldn't be easy, and I knew they'd make it really hard for me. As long as I know I've got you guys behind me, I'll be fine." She nibbled on a carrot from her salad.

"Uh, how's your . . . uh, the place where he beat you with that paddle?" Jericho asked her delicately.

"Bruised," she replied. "Extremely bruised."

"When this is over, Eddie is due for some one-on-one rehabilitation!" Kofi declared, slamming his fist on the table. "Nothing would give me more pleasure than bringin' him down!"

"Let's change the subject," Dana said suddenly. "What's that you're eating, my pink-shirted brother?" she asked Jericho.

"Salad," he answered. "I don't know how you do it. May as well be eatin' air!" Jericho was glad they were now talking about something easy like food. Thoughts about the Warriors were making him feel confused and angry. He got up then, went to the quick lunch line, and bought two hamburgers and an ice cream sandwich. "Now that's more like it!" he said cheerfully as he gobbled the first burger.

"I hear ya, man! Bein' a vegetarian is for the birds!" laughed Josh, who was eating spaghetti and meatballs.

"Don't get me started on you, Mr. Polka Dot Man," Dana said to Josh. "Looks like a bird found your shirt and pooped all over it!"

Jericho and Kofi choked with laughter. It felt good to

laugh and act silly once again. "She blasted you, man!" Kofi gasped.

"Do you guys have any idea what's in the meat they serve here in the cafeteria, or what animal it came from?" Dana asked with mild disgust.

"I don't really care. It died well, and I appreciate the sacrifice!" Jericho grinned as he finished off his second hamburger. He burped loudly.

Dana grabbed her book bag and got up, a look of disgust on her face, but she was laughing as well. "I've got a test to study for. I'll see you guys tonight."

Kofi laughed. "Why you chase away my girl, man?"

"Your girl got too many opinions!" Jericho replied. "You want half this ice-cream sandwich, Josh?" Josh started to say yes when Jericho stuffed the whole thing in his mouth. "Too late!"

"So what do you think of the Warrior stuff so far?" Josh asked them.

Jericho swallowed the last of his ice-cream sandwich and said, "I'm not sure. It's not so bad, I guess." He wanted to tell them he was having serious doubts about the Warriors and the pledging and how the whole process made him feel. But he simply said, "It's got to be worth it, man. The Warriors are so tight!"

"That's true," Kofi began, "and runnin' never killed anybody." Jericho looked at him sharply, but said nothing. "The swats were rough, but I hear they do that in all clubs. But I don't like how they're treatin' Dana—especially Eddie. I was ready to choke him when he kissed her!" He brought his fist down on the table with such force that it shook.

Josh nodded. "You knew that was gonna happen, man. She set herself up for it, but why do you think she's puttin' herself through all this?"

"She told me once that her father, the big time military man, wanted a son and was really disappointed when Dana was born that she was a girl. So he decided to teach her everything he would have taught his son. She played baseball and basketball as a kid, took flying lessons, and boxing, too."

"She's not the only girl to do that stuff," Jericho reasoned.

"Yeah, but she's the only kid her daddy had, and I think Dana always felt like she was never quite good enough for him. So she keeps pushin' the limits."

"I think she'll do fine," Jericho said with a confidence he didn't feel, even about himself. "We just gotta make sure we look out for her."

"I've seen Dana in action!" Josh laughed. "Maybe we ought to get her to look out for us!"

"What do you think they're up to tonight?" Kofi whispered.

"I don't know." Jericho licked his fingers and the wrapper of the ice-cream sandwich. "Hey, Josh, has Uncle Brock said *anything* to give us a hint about what's coming up?"

"No, he just keeps smilin' and struttin' around like some kind of rooster. He's so proud he's about to explode."

"Too bad. It would help to know," Kofi said with a sigh.

"I kinda like the idea of surprise. Every night is a new adventure," Josh said as he cleared his tray.

"Do you think they do the same pledge activities now that they did when he pledged?" Jericho wondered.

"Probably not. I bet ours are a lot more intense," Kofi said thoughtfully.

"Yeah, I guess, but I don't know how I'm gonna make the rest of this week. I am *so* tired!" Jericho said as he walked out of the lunchroom with them.

By the end of the school day, Jericho felt like he was dragging. He was anxious to get home and get a quick nap before the night's activities. But then he noticed Arielle coming down the hall, talking to Eric Bell. She was smiling at Eric and laughing, touching his hand lightly as she talked, and looking at him with the same sparkling eyes that Jericho loved to look at. Eric looked deliriously happy as he rolled along beside her.

Arielle didn't notice Jericho at first. He watched her as she sat with Eric in the main hall near the door. She was looking directly in Eric's face, her face very close to his. They seemed to be whispering and giggling. Jericho felt ill.

Arielle finally saw Jericho and waved. "Hi, Jericho. I was just telling Eric about my silly little sister. He has a sister about Kiki's age." Jericho didn't even know that Eric had a sister. He'd never bothered to ask. He said nothing for a moment.

"What's wrong, Jericho?" Eric asked. "You look tired."

"I guess I am," he said deliberately. "And this is just day three of the Warrior pledge week." *Where does he get off talkin' to my girl with his crippled self?* Jericho frowned. *I hope he gets his feelings hurt!*

Eric looked at Jericho with a pained expression. "My

bus is coming early today," he said. "I think I'll wait for it outside." He moved to the front door. Before he left he turned his chair back to face Jericho and Arielle. "I'll see you tomorrow, Arielle," he said pointedly before going out the door to wait for his bus.

"What was that all about?" Jericho asked Arielle.

"All what?" she asked. "What's wrong with you?"

"What's up with you and Eric? I see you walking down the hall with him, and sitting here where anybody can see you, laughing and giggling like he's some kind of movie star." Jericho could not explain why he felt so angry.

"What do you mean 'where anybody can see me'—like I'm supposed to hide when I talk to him?" Arielle replied, her dark eyes flashing.

"That's not what I meant," Jericho said, feeling even more confused and upset. "It just doesn't seem right."

"So what are you tryin' to say?" she asked. She was really getting angry.

"I'm sayin' that it's not fair to give him hope or make him think about something that's not possible." The words weren't coming out right, but Jericho was unable to express himself clearly.

"Give him hope about what? You think he hasn't got a chance with me just because he's in a wheelchair? If you think that, you're a narrow-minded punk! I like Eric because of who he is, not for how he gets around."

"So now you *like* him?" Jericho sneered. He knew he was twisting her words unfairly.

"So what if I do like him? You don't own me!"

"I didn't mean that. It's just that I saw you with him

and . . ." Jericho couldn't finish. He wished he were in a hole at the bottom of the ocean. The whole situation was getting out of hand.

"He's smart, he's good-looking, and he makes me laugh," Arielle said as she angrily tossed her book bag onto her shoulder. "He's my friend, and I *do* like him," she added defiantly.

"Maybe he's the wrong kind of friend to have," Jericho muttered. He was saying it all wrong, but he knew what he had seen in Eric's eyes.

"I can't have friends?" she asked as she headed for the door.

"Not friends that look at you like he did. You didn't see how he was lookin' at you, Arielle—like you were a piece of soft chocolate candy."

"So what if he did? You can't tell me who to talk to or who to laugh with or who to like!" She stormed out of the front door and purposely went over to talk to Eric.

Jericho couldn't understand why he was so furious, but he knew he had to get out of there. He left by the back door and drove home alone.

JERICHO ARRIVED AT THE WAREHOUSE A LITTLE before eight, still upset about his fight with Arielle. He had tried to call her, but she wouldn't come to the phone. He knew he'd been wrong, and he wanted to apologize, but she wasn't ready to talk. He sat in his car in the dark parking lot, taking deep breaths, trying to focus on whatever the Warriors had in store for him tonight.

Josh and Kofi got dropped off by Josh's dad, Dana arrived a few minutes later, and soon the other pledges arrived. Jericho got out of his car and joined them on the front steps. It had started to rain and the temperature had dropped close to freezing.

The Warriors arrived at eight. "It's cold out, so I think you need a good run tonight to warm up," Eddie Mahoney said.

Jericho groaned and glanced over at Kofi, who looked away.

"Around the warehouse until I say stop," Eddie said. "And get those jackets off! They'll just slow you down." Jericho looked at the other pledges, who reluctantly had begun to peel off their winter coats.

"Are we runnin' inside or outside, sir?" Cleveland asked.

"Outside. Fresh air is good for you. And if you're fast enough, you won't get cold. Begin."

The fifteen pledges began a slow, miserable jog around the building. After five times around, Jericho's chest ached from inhaling the cold air into his lungs. His nose was running, and even though he was sweating, the cold and rain penetrated his clothes and skin. Why was he doing this? he thought miserably. Kofi ran slowly, taking huge, gasping gulps of breath as Jericho passed him. "Don't you dare," he whispered to Jericho between gasps. Dana ran with Kofi, matching her stride with his.

The front of the warehouse had a sidewalk, and a dimly lighted parking lot was located on one side. On the other side of the building was a narrow driveway that led to a house that had long been boarded up. Along the far side of that driveway a tall, concrete wall had been built to separate the warehouse property from the buildings next to it. It extended all the way back to the deserted house. But the ground in back of the warehouse was unpaved. It might once have been a yard, but it was now just a cold, muddy area filled with trash and rocks. It was not lighted, so Jericho and the others weren't sure what they were running over as they made their laps around the building. In the very back of this yard was a huge Dumpster, which even in the cold air reeked of garbage and decay.

Eddie and some of the pledge masters sat in Eddie's car, watching the pledges run. Finally, after fifteen times around the building, Eddie got out and told them to stop. Jericho glanced over at Kofi, whose face, instead of his usual tan color, looked almost blue. He was heaving and leaned against Eddie's car. Dana stood near Kofi and as far from Eddie as she could. Jericho had never felt so cold and so hot at the same time. He just wanted to take a steaming shower and go to bed. But Eddie wasn't finished with them. Jericho noticed with irritation that the Warriors all had put on long, heavy rain jackets with hoods.

"Okay, Pledge Slime. Now we search for treasure." He and the other pledge masters, who carried flashlights, led them to the backyard.

"Remember doing scavenger hunts when you were a kid?" Rick asked. "We have hidden several objects in this Dumpster that you must find. I know you're cold and wet, so the sooner you find them the quicker you can go home."

"We should tell you," Eddie added with a cruel smirk, "Madison's dad works at the slaughterhouse downtown. He gave us a load of manure to add to the fun."

"What's manure?" Cleveland whispered.

Josh answered, "Cow dung. Doo-doo. Feces. Sh—"

Cleveland groaned and interrupted, "I get it."

"What do we have to find?" asked Jericho. "Sir," he threw in quickly.

"Here's the list," Eddie replied. "One ripe unpeeled banana, one whole peeled grapefruit, one used baby diaper, one whole pizza—uncut but not in its box—a shoe, a large rock, a wig, and a gun."

A gun? *A gun?* Jericho looked in alarm at the others, who were clearly thinking the same thing. Yet not one of them spoke up.

Eddie barked at them before they had a chance to think about it any longer. "Get in that Dumpster, all of you, and find that stuff!" He left one flashlight on the ground next to the stunned pledges, then he and the rest of the Warriors retreated and watched. The back of the warehouse was suddenly dark and ominous once more.

This was not what Jericho had in mind when he dreamed about getting into the Warriors of Distinction. But he still didn't say anything. No one else did, and he couldn't let the others down.

"What's up with that—a gun!" Josh exclaimed.

"Where'd they get a gun?" Luis asked.

"And what they gonna do with it?" Cleveland mused.

Kofi, whose breathing seemed to be back to normal, said quietly to Dana, "The rest of the stuff they make us do is what I'd expect—just stupid stuff—but I don't like this gun business."

"I don't either," she said, "but all they asked us to do was to find it—they didn't ask us to shoot anybody."

"Yet," Rudy added ominously.

They were divided as to what to do. Some wanted to get in the Dumpster right away. A few wanted to go home. Josh finally said, "I'm cold, I'm wet, and I'm tired. The motto is 'All of us or none of us.' Let's just do it and get it over with."

The Dumpster stood about eight feet high and ten feet wide. About two feet from the bottom was a door in the front with a large steel latch, large enough to accommodate huge garbage bags and boxes. It was certainly large enough for a person to climb through.

Jericho opened the door. The stench greeted them made them jump back in disgust.

"I'm not gettin' in there!" Kofi exclaimed.

Jericho held his nose and looked inside with the flashlight. "Looks pretty gross in here. This stuff is ripe! Hey, I see the shoe already!" He reached in and pulled out an old tennis shoe. It was covered in brown muck and smelled like manure. Jericho gagged a little and removed his head from the Dumpster to get some fresh air.

"This is just gross, man!" Luis declared.

"Let's get this over with," Dana urged them.

"What about rats?" asked Cleveland. "I can't deal with no rats, man."

Josh turned to the group of pledges. "This is a test. They want to know if we're working together as a group. They want to see if we really believe in this 'All of us or none of us' idea. So do we do it? It's gotta be all of us. Raise your hand if you're not going to get in the Dumpster."

Jericho really did *not* want to get in that Dumpster. He figured none of the rest of them did either. They looked at each other uncomfortably, but no one raised a hand.

"Okay, let's do it," Josh said decisively. He climbed in first, followed by Kofi and Dana. Jericho climbed in next, the others giving him a hand as he hoisted himself into the bin. His feet sunk several inches into the soft, smelly muck. Jericho helped the next few boys climb in, then others followed. Soon fourteen pledges stood huddled together—all of them in the Dumpster except for Cleveland Wilson.

"I ain't sharing no space with no rats," he said defiantly.

"There's no rats, man," a couple of the pledges said, trying to reassure him. "Just stink and garbage."

"Where there's garbage, there's rats. I hate rats." Cleveland was immovable.

"Hey, Cleveland," Josh called from the back of the Dumpster. "All of us or none of us, man. Come on! We need you!"

Cleveland hesitated. "If I feel something moving, I'm jettin' outta here. Got that?" He climbed in slowly and stood very close to the door. "Now what?" he asked.

Jericho was wondering the same thing. He was finding it hard to breathe in that stinking enclosure. He wasn't sure what he was standing on, but it was soft and felt squishy under his shoes. "Oh gross! I found the peeled grapefruit! I hate to tell you what this feels like," he called out to the others.

"Toss it out there!" Luis said.

"Here's the banana!" Josh called out next. "Yuk!"

Dana found the wet and dripping wig, Kofi announced he'd stumbled over the rock, and Luis exclaimed with disgust that he'd picked up the very dirty baby diaper. All of the objects they tossed out of the door of the Dumpster. Josh reached down and pulled up the pizza.

"I don't think I'll ever eat pizza again," he murmured.

"Hey, the pledge masters are standing out there, watching and waiting! Let's hurry up!" whispered Jericho.

"Let 'em freeze," Cleveland replied sullenly.

"Rats don't freeze," Josh said, teasing him.

"Aw, man, why'd you have to remind me. Let's get this done and get out of here!"

"We just have to find the gun," Dana reminded them. "A gun is hard, and has a recognizable shape. The sooner we find it, the sooner we can get out."

"She's right," Josh agreed.

It was difficult for them all to move around in the Dumpster, each of them trying desperately to feel for the hard, cold shape of a gun. The flashlight was very little help, its dim rays barely piercing the darkness. The smell of the sweat from their bodies, the load of manure, and the rotten garbage was almost unbearable. It was all Jericho could do not to explode out of there.

"Will somebody tell me what digging in garbage for a gun in the middle of winter has to do with delivering toys to kids at Christmas?" a voice asked from the darkness.

No one had an answer.

As they rooted around for the gun in the stinking trash, Jericho thought about Mr. Boston and his warnings. Was this hazing? He wasn't sure. Nobody was getting hurt, he reasoned. It's just a harmless prank, right? But he wasn't sure of anything anymore.

Jericho moved so he could be closer to the door of the Dumpster, ready to be the first out once the gun was found, when his foot stumbled over something. He leaned down, reached under his left foot and his hand touched the icy barrel of a small handgun. It had been carefully wrapped in plastic.

"I found it!" he shouted. "Let's get out of here!"

"I'm outta here!" shouted Cleveland, who was the first to climb out. Jericho was right behind him. When they all were out, they stretched and breathed deeply of the clean night air. Jericho tossed the gun to Eddie.

"Why a gun?" Jericho asked coldly.

"You don't need to know that now," Eddie replied.

"Even you ought to know better than to play with guns. Sir," he added. Eddie ignored him.

"Good job, pledges," Madison said quickly. "Don't get too close, though!" He handed out wet paper towels to the pledges, but nothing could quite remove the smell on their hands and clothing. No one mentioned the gun.

"WE HAVE ONE FINAL ACTIVITY FOR THIS evening," Eddie announced. "Follow me." Jericho wondered dimly if they would be allowed to get their jackets, but the thought disappeared as the pledge masters marched the fifteen pledges to the middle of the soggy yard. The ground was muddy and squished as they walked, and the frigid air whipped across their wet T-shirts. Sharp needles of rain stung them as they stood there silently waiting for instructions. A pledge master stood directly in front of each pledge.

"Kneel!" Rick Sharp shouted to Jericho.

Jericho wanted to disobey, but instead he knelt immediately. Cold mud soaked through his jeans in seconds.

"Take off my boot, Pledge Slime!" the six-foot, broad-shouldered senior shouted to Jericho over the noise of the pouring rain. He glanced down at Jericho, who huddled at his feet.

Jericho shivered as the rain came down harder and made him sink deeper into the mud of the desolate warehouse yard. His fingers were wet and stiff, but he reached for Sharp's big, black army boot and slowly began to untie the laces.

"Hurry up, Pledge Slime!" Sharp shouted. Jericho dejectedly struggled to untie the wet laces of the pledge master's boot, his fingers aching. He wasn't sure what to do when he finished. He had no idea how to get the boot off of Rick's foot.

He glanced over to see, if he could, the line of the other pledges, also kneeling in the mud at the feet of their pledge masters. But the rain and the darkness made it difficult to see very much. Jericho could barely even see Josh, who was closest to him in the line, but he could hear Mad Madison shouting at him in the darkness. Jericho couldn't see Kofi or Dana at all.

"All of us have been where you are tonight," Sharp told Jericho. "A Warrior of Distinction is not afraid to lower himself for his brother. A Warrior of Distinction does not show fear. Are you afraid, Pledge Slime?"

"No, sir," Jericho replied. "I'm not afraid."

"Then get busy! The rest of your pledge class, slimy and disgusting as they are, seem to be doing fine. Do you want to let them down?"

Jericho inhaled slowly. It was all of them or none of them. "Can you lift your foot, Master Senior Sharp, sir?" Jericho asked timidly. As he raised his face to look at Sharp, he gasped as the icy rain stung his eyes.

"Did I give you permission to speak, Pledge Slime?"

Sharp snarled. Jericho said nothing, but Rick lifted his right foot, using Jericho's head to balance himself.

Jericho pulled the boot off with difficulty. He was afraid that he would fall or would make Rick fall as he tugged at the boot. Either would have been disastrous, but he managed to get the boot off smoothly. The stench of Rick Sharp's foot was enough to make Jericho choke.

"Now take off the sock," Rick barked.

Jericho hesitated and hoped they would be able to go home soon. He slowly peeled off Rick's sock. Rick's foot reeked of sweat.

"Place the sock on the ground, then set my foot down on it. Make sure not a speck of mud touches my foot," he commanded.

Jericho did as he was told and Rick Sharp removed his hand from Jericho's head as he lowered his foot to the ground.

Master Senior Sharp bent down and whispered into Jericho's ear, "You havin' fun yet?"

Jericho didn't dare tell the truth—that he had stopped having fun long ago.

"You really want to be a Warrior of Distinction?" Rick asked.

Jericho nodded. He thought of the prestige of having one of those black silk jackets, the admiring glances in the halls at school, but mostly he thought of Arielle. He tried not to think of the rain and the mud and the stink of Rick's feet.

"Are you willing to do anything to be a Warrior of Distinction?" Rick demanded. "You have permission to answer."

"Yes, sir! Yes, Master Senior Sharp, sir! I am willing to do anything to be a Warrior of Distinction, sir!" Jericho repeated the words that he and the other pledges had been chanting automatically since the whole process began. But he wasn't sure if he meant them anymore.

"Are you willing to do anything to help the others become Warriors of Distinction?" Rick demanded.

"Anything, sir." Jericho just wanted it to be over.

"Then suck my big toe."

"Sir?" Jericho wasn't sure if he had heard correctly.

"If you want to be a Warrior of Distinction, you must suck my big toe. Now!"

Jericho looked around desperately; he had no idea what the others were being forced to do. As he lowered his head close to the mud and closer to Rick Sharp's foot, Jericho wondered miserably how he could have sunk so low.

STILL, JERICHO HESITATED. BUT IT WAS DARK, and no one could really see what he was doing, he reasoned. So he lowered his head, and felt his lips touch the top of Rick's toe. He held his breath and moved his mind to another place—any place other than where he was—and then he took the whole toe into his mouth and sucked it.

"Enough!" Rick shouted. "Stand up now."

Jericho stood stiffly. He was soaking wet, filthy dirty, cold, and angry. All he wanted to do was walk away from that yard. But what would everybody think of him if he quit?

The rest of the pledges, none of whom would make eye contact with the other, waited silently in the rain while the Warriors put their shoes back on. Jericho shivered uncontrollably. He wasn't sure if it was from the freezing rain, his humiliation, or his fearful anticipation of what was still to come.

Eddie walked away from the group and over to his car. He carried one shoe in his hand and he walked with a noticeable limp.

"What's up with Eddie?" Jericho whispered to Dana, who was covered in mud.

She replied with bitter satisfaction, "I bit his toe—crunched it like an almond! I bet he won't be wearing shoes for a couple of days!"

Jericho chuckled. "Serves him right!"

As soon as they were dismissed, the pledges left quickly. Jericho took a long, hot shower when he got home, trying to warm his chilled and aching body. He felt he'd never be completely warm or completely clean ever again. As the hot needles of water relaxed him, he thought of the last three days. Somehow he couldn't quite remember why he'd wanted so badly to be a member of the Warriors of Distinction. The pledge activities weren't really what he'd expected, but then they were all designed for a good purpose, weren't they? Jericho figured he could last two more days.

And tomorrow was the competition. He groaned as the water splashed over him. He tried to wash away the sick, helpless feeling, but it remained like a stone in his gut.

He thought about what Mr. Boston had told him and sighed as he dried off. Even if the pledging was hazing, it didn't make any difference. He couldn't tell anybody, and he couldn't quit.

He rinsed out his pink shirt and almost gagged at the sight of it. Picking up the phone, he hoped that this time Arielle would let him talk to her. He dialed. "Arielle?"

"I don't want to talk to you, Jericho." She hung up the phone.

Jericho felt like the dog the Warriors made him pretend to be. He listened to the click, then the dial tone, and dialed her number once more. "Please, Arielle," he began. She hung up once more. He decided to try one last time. *Ring. Ring. Ring.*

On the fourth ring she picked up the phone, but said nothing.

"Please don't hang up on me," he begged. "I'm sorry. I'm so sorry. I was way out of line yelling at you like that."

"Well, you got that much straight." She said nothing else, but at least she hadn't hung up on him again.

He sighed. "Look, I've been stressed with all this Warrior stuff and I'm tired, and I just let loose on you. I hated myself even while I was talkin' to you, but I just couldn't shut up," he said lamely.

"Maybe you ought to practice," Arielle replied tersely.

"I deserve that. I promise it will never happen again. I can't stand it when you won't talk to me," Jericho told her miserably.

She was silent for a moment. Then he heard her sigh. "Look, Jericho, I'm not going to have you or anybody tell me who my friends are or who I can talk to! You got that straight?"

"I got it."

"And I will *not* be with a dude who treats me like a piece of property."

"I understand—I really do."

"I like you, Jericho, and I'm excited about the fact that in two days you're going to be a Warrior of Distinction, but you were scaring me today. I don't like being under-estimated, and I won't be put down by you or anybody!"

Jericho knew not to argue with her. So he said, "I'm so sorry, Arielle. It's just that I love your smile and the way you laugh, and it seemed like Eric was enjoying your laughter and your smile just a little bit too much."

"My smile belongs to me and I can share it with who-ever I want!" she said clearly.

"Will you still share it with me?" he asked meekly.

"Yeah," she said finally. "I guess. How can I resist a dude who wears pink every single day? Besides," she added, "being in that club will be good for both of us."

"Thanks, Arielle." Jericho breathed a sigh of relief. "You know you're my boo."

"Don't be tryin' to sweet-talk me," she replied, but he could tell by her voice she was not as angry. "I'll see you at school tomorrow."

Jericho figured he could make it through anything the Warriors gave him to do as long as he had Arielle to show off for when it was over. He hung up the phone with new determination to endure—and maybe even enjoy—the last two days of pledging.

He picked up his trumpet then, trying not to agonize over the competition that he knew he would miss. He care-fully shined its gleaming bell and played a song of his own creation to Arielle. He wasn't sure where the notes were going, didn't really care, but Zora took him to a place of green trees and romance, a place where he and Arielle danced in the moonlight, she dressed in dazzling white, and he in his black silk Warrior jacket.

THE ALARM STARTLED JERICHO AT SIX THE NEXT morning. He got up quickly, ironed the pink shirt, grabbed a doughnut, and headed off to school before Todd and Rory even got up.

In Mr. Culligan's room, the pledges looked a little tired of the whole process, and a little embarrassed as well, Jericho thought, but they waited patiently for instructions for the day. Rick reminded them, as he did every morning, about the code of silence.

Then Madison announced, "Your service activity this morning will be to work with the janitorial staff. Any dusting, cleaning, or sweeping that you can assist with is always greatly appreciated. Remember that we are a service organization and we want to be helpful to every aspect of the school community."

Jericho wondered how a gun figured into this helpful service picture that the club showed at school.

"Here are your assignments," Madison continued.

Jericho looked at the sheet and found he had been assigned to put salt on the icy patches on the front and back steps and walkways of the school. He thought briefly of his spinout with Josh in the car.

"Tonight," Eddie reminded them, "we will once again meet in the warehouse, eight P.M. Wear jeans and tennis shoes." Eddie was walking with a slight limp this morning. Dana was trying to hide a smile.

As the pledges left to do their morning assignments, Jericho went downstairs to the office of Mr. Redstone, the head custodian. Kids said he had worked at the school for forty years. Jericho thought he looked like a tree trunk—tall, brown, strong, and wrinkled. "I've come to help, Mr. Redstone," Jericho offered. "I'll be glad to help you put salt on the walkways this morning."

"Oh, yeah, is it time for the Warrior service projects already?"

"Yes, sir."

"Seem like they come quicker every year. They still doin' that dumb Dumpster trick and the Leap of Faith?"

Jericho wasn't sure what to say. Maybe Mr. Redstone had been a Warrior. So he just said, "I don't know what you mean, sir." He'd honestly never heard of the Leap of Faith.

"Oh, I know I'm not supposed to know about their stupid little pledge activities, but not much slips past me. I know what they do every year—and I'm not sure if I approve of all of it."

"The principal knows what we're doing, and he seems to think it's okay," Jericho said, a little defensively.

"Zucker is an idiot," Mr. Redstone declared. "Culligan, too."

"I'll, uh, just get busy on this salt now, okay?" Jericho said. Maybe this was a trap to see if he'd keep the code of silence. He had no intention of getting in trouble by talking to Mr. Redstone or anybody.

"Doesn't it bother you—some of the stuff they make you do?" Mr. Redstone asked. "You look like an intelligent young man. Doesn't some of this stuff make you feel like less than yourself sometimes?"

Less than myself. Jericho didn't respond, but the phrase kept repeating in his head. He wasn't sure if he felt less than himself last night in the Dumpster. He just wasn't sure. He looked at Mr. Redstone quizzically.

"Okay, son, don't get all nervous and upset. I know about your code of silence. I won't spoil your little games. Grab a bag of that salt and hit the back walk. I already did the front, but I sure appreciate your help."

Jericho took the salt and hurried to leave Mr. Redstone's office.

"You be careful now, you hear?" Mr. Redstone called to him.

Jericho mumbled, "Yes, sir."

"And, son?" Mr. Redstone added. Jericho looked back as he was leaving. "Watch out for that girl you got doin' that foolishness with you."

"I will. But she's pretty tough."

It only took him a few minutes to finish salting the walks and the steps, and he looked up with pleasure to see Arielle walking toward him.

"Hi," he said softly. "Still mad?"

"A little." She looked at him pensively. "How much longer before you're finally a Warrior?"

"It's all over tomorrow night and there's that big party to celebrate on Saturday." He hesitated. "Will you come to the party with me?"

"I'll think about it," she answered with a slight smile. Jericho breathed a sigh of relief. "My mom is picking me up today, but call me later," she said as she went through the door. "Maybe I won't hang up on you!" Jericho just shook his head as he smiled and waved at her. Girls were so hard to figure out.

Just as he reached the front door of the school, he heard the deep bass voice of Mr. Tambori calling him. Jericho cursed silently and turned around. "Hey, Mr. T. Uh, I guess you got my note, huh?" Jericho couldn't look at him.

"You weren't man enough to tell me this to my face?" Mr. Tambori was livid. "You left a scrap of notebook paper on my desk with this paltry, scribbled excuse?"

"I knew you'd be angry," Jericho replied quietly.

"I am more than angry—I am deeply disappointed," Mr. Tambori replied sadly. "You are giving up a possible scholarship, a potential career, for a high school club? How can you be so foolish?" His voice trembled with emotion.

Jericho was afraid Mr. Tambori was about to cry. "You gotta understand, Mr. T. This is the most important thing that's ever happened to me. It's my chance to be on the inside instead of always looking from the outside, wishing

I had the magic. You couldn't possibly understand."

"I understand so much more than you know, Jericho. And I know that one day you will regret this decision."

Jericho couldn't take any more. "I gotta go, Mr. T. I'm sorry." He ran to his first class in a hurry.

When Jericho got home from school, his father was in the kitchen. "Hey, Dad," Jericho said with surprise. "What are you doing home?"

"I live here!" joked his father. "Actually, since I had the evening off, I figured I'd go with you to the trumpet competition tonight. Listening to you toot that horn makes me so proud."

Jericho sat down with his dad and nervously began shredding a paper napkin on the table. "Uh, Dad," Jericho began, "I decided not to go to the competition tonight." He closed his eyes and waited for what he knew was coming.

"What do you mean, you 'decided not to go'? You can't just drop out on the night of the contest! What about all that practice? Where is that determination you said you had?"

Jericho hung his head. "I can't go, Dad."

"What could possibly stop you from doing what you love?"

Jericho hesitated. "The Warriors of Distinction," he finally admitted.

"What! You mean they won't give you one night off for something that can possibly affect your entire future?"

"If I miss one night, I'm out for good," Jericho explained miserably.

"I don't care what kind of club this is—they can't control your life like that! Who can I call to get you out of this? Mr. Culligan?"

"Nobody, Dad. It was my choice. I can't quit. I can't let the other pledges down. If one of us quits, we all fail. And Dad, even if that wasn't true, I just gotta be in this club. I'll be a nobody at school if I fail the pledging process— less than nobody. I'd never be able to show my face there again," Jericho pleaded. "Besides, I'd lose Arielle."

"Is the club the only reason she's with you?" his father asked, looking surprised.

"No, Dad, I think she really likes me. But she'd be embarrassed just like I would if I didn't make the Warriors. You don't understand."

"I understand that a girl should care about who you are, and not what club you're in."

"That's so ancient, Dad. You don't have the faintest idea about how it is for kids today."

"Let's forget the girl for now. What about your chance for Juilliard? You have the possibility of a scholarship, Jericho. A chance to live your dreams!" His father touched Jericho's arm gently; his eyes were soft with the same look of disappointment Mr. Tambori had shown.

Jericho thought back to what Mr. Tambori had once told him: "Don't be afraid to dream beyond where you can see." But Jericho knew his dreams were with the Warriors right now. He couldn't see much further than that. "There'll be other competitions, Dad," he told his father. He now had a huge pile of shredded paper napkin in front of him.

"Sometimes opportunities come once in a lifetime,

Jericho. This club is high school, which is temporary. Your music is yours for life."

"This *is* once in a lifetime," Jericho argued. "I will never get another chance to be part of the best group in the school—even in the city. You saw the good stuff they do, Dad. And look at Uncle Brock—he's still proud and still feels good about himself. I *need* that, Dad! And I need Arielle. No girl like her has ever wanted to be with me."

"I thought your music made you feel good, Jericho," his father replied quietly.

"I keep tellin' you, Dad—you don't understand!" Jericho answered angrily. He knew why he was so angry—because his dad was probably right. But he knew he had no choice.

"Is it all you imagined it would be, Jericho? Is it worth it?" his father asked with resignation.

Jericho hesitated. "I'm not sure what I imagined, Dad—I really didn't know what to expect—but so far, it's been okay, I guess. Not too hard. Not too stupid. They call the stuff we do 'bonding activities.'"

"I think you're making the wrong decision, Jericho, but I can't force you to quit. You wouldn't play well anyway if you didn't want to be there. But I'm afraid you'll be sorry about this decision. Very sorry."

Jericho tried to ignore the look of disappointment on his father's face. "I have to do this, Dad. I just have to."

"How will you feel when this is over?" his father asked.

"Tired. Relieved. Very proud," Jericho answered.

His father got up to go upstairs. "I hope you won't feel sorry, Jericho. You and Josh be careful. Take care."

Jericho sat in the empty kitchen for a few minutes, trying to do his homework, but he couldn't stop thinking about what his father and Mr. Tambori had said. Suddenly he ripped up his homework paper, balled it up fiercely, and threw it as hard as he could against the refrigerator.

AT SEVEN THIRTY THE PHONE RANG. IT WAS
Kofi. "Can you give me a ride tonight?"

"Sure. I was just gettin' ready to leave.
You feelin' okay?"

"Yeah, man. Leave it alone. I'm fine." Kofi
sounded annoyed. "Hey, Jericho, what did
your folks say about missin' the competition?"

"My dad is really upset," Jericho told him.
"But he let it be my decision—I appreciate that.
I'll be there in a few." He got his coat, yelled a
quick good-bye to his father and Geneva before
either of them could say anything more about the
competition, and hurried out to his car.

When he and Kofi got to the warehouse, they joined
the other pledges and waited for instructions. The Warriors opened the warehouse door and let them in.

"At least we don't have to stand around in the cold
tonight," Jericho whispered to Kofi.

"And no rats!" Cleveland said with relief.

"You sure about that, man?" Josh teased.

"Don't play like that, Josh," Cleveland warned.

"You think they're gonna make us run again?" Kofi asked.

"Probably," Dana replied. "They seem to like to watch us run."

"What do you think happened to the gun?" Jericho wondered out loud. No one even made a guess.

"Hey, somebody brought a CD player," Dana noticed. "Maybe we'll get to dance tonight."

"Not likely," Luis whispered.

As usual Eddie was in charge. "We'll begin with a quick run to get you ready for the evening," he began.

The pledges looked at each other and rolled their eyes.

"Let's start with fifteen laps—one for each of you. Watch those corners. Begin!"

The pledges began their noisy romp around the warehouse, Jericho moving purposely slower, trying to keep an eye on Kofi, who seemed to have no problem tonight. When they finished, Kofi glanced at Jericho and gave him a thumbs up.

Eddie walked to the center of the room. "I have a question," he began. "Are you willing to lower yourself for each other?"

"Yes, sir!"

"Are you willing to lower yourself for the senior Warriors?"

Jericho wondered how much lower they could make them go after last night. And he could not figure out why

217

he was shouting in agreement with the others. But he didn't stop. "Yes, sir!"

"Are you willing to do anything to become one of us?" Eddie asked in a loud voice.

"Yes, sir! Yes, Master Senior Mahoney, sir!"

"Anything?"

"Yes, sir!"

"Good. I thought so." He paused. "Each of you must now be cleansed of all impurities and joined with us, body and soul. Tonight we take care of the body. The soul we save for tomorrow night."

Jericho didn't like the sound of that. He shifted his feet nervously.

"Bring out the branding irons," Eddie said loudly. The pledges looked up in alarm.

Rick disappeared into a back room and returned with a large, covered metal bucket, which was steaming and smoking in the dim light. Jericho could smell the heated coals in the bucket. It was a dangerous smell.

Sticking out of the bucket were numerous long-handled barbecue forks. Jericho knew without counting there would be fifteen. Madison carried a smaller bucket, also covered, but at least it wasn't smoking.

Madison walked over to the corner and pushed the button for the CD to play, and ominous-sounding music with deep drum beats filled the warehouse. "Soon, if you survive, you will become a Warrior of Distinction," Eddie began. "Tonight you will receive the mark. All of us carry the Warrior mark in the center of our backs. It is very small, hardly noticed by others, but it is our sign of unity and bonding."

A mark? Jericho thought fearfully. He wondered if Josh had ever noticed such a mark on his father.

"Are you ready and willing?" Eddie asked the nervous pledges in front of him.

"Ready and willing, sir," they answered dutifully, but not much enthusiasm could be heard in their voices. The Warriors did not notice, but Jericho never said a word. He could not bring himself to agree to be marked or branded, but he didn't complain or do anything to stop them either.

"Sit on your knees, with your backs to me. Lift up just the back of your T-shirts!" Rick now commanded, glancing at Dana. The pledges obeyed slowly. Jericho shivered uncontrollably, from the cold of the dirty wooden floor, and from fear.

Eddie used a pair of tongs to remove one of the red, glowing coals and made sure they all saw it and felt its heat. Then he removed one of the barbecue forks from the coal-filled bucket. The end of the fork was glowing red. He walked around the group slowly, passing the fork close to their faces, making sure that each of them could see how hot and how sharp the end of it really was. When Eddie passed by Dana's face, he held it for a long time, very close to her cheek, trying to make her wince in fear. Jericho was glad to see she didn't.

"This will hurt for just one second," he said finally to the group. "But all of you must receive the mark. Are you ready?"

"Yes, sir," the pledges replied quietly.

Each of the fifteen Warriors pulled a glowing fork from the bucket and each stood in front of a trembling pledge.

Then they walked around the group and stood behind them.

"Bow your heads and prepare to receive the mark!" Eddie commanded. They bowed. The music continued to beat, heavy and foreboding.

The pledges knelt on the floor with their heads down and the backs of their shirts pulled up.

"Apply the mark!" Eddie called out.

Jericho squeezed his eyes shut and tensed with fearful anticipation. The smell of the hot coals reminded him of summer picnics, but this, he thought with a shudder, was no picnic.

Then he felt a sudden, sharp sting burned into the center of his back. It was like cold fire. He screamed in spite of himself. He heard a couple of the other pledges cry out in pain as well. And he knew he heard Dana scream.

"Turn around and face us!" Eddie commanded once more. "And face your fear!" Jericho had to blink to see clearly. In Eddie's hand, and in the hands of each of the Warriors in front of them, was not a burning fork, but an ice cube.

"I don't get it," Cleveland said.

"We never burned you," Madison explained. "That would be criminal. We just let you *think* that you were being burned. The mind is very powerful, you know. Ice, when it is applied to bare skin, can feel just like fire."

"Tell me about it," Josh muttered as he rubbed the place on his back where he thought he had been burned. The pledges grumbled among themselves, relieved and a little embarrassed at their outbursts.

"I heard you scream, Dana," Kofi said softly.

"I'd feel bad, but I heard you scream too!" She frowned and tried to rub the place on her back. "Kofi, my back still hurts!"

"It's your imagination, Dana. It was just a piece of ice."

"Yeah, but it still hurts." She kept rubbing her back.

Jericho wondered again why he was doing this. He remembered a family trip they had taken when he and Josh were six. The whole time Josh had kept asking, "Are we having fun yet?" That's exactly what Jericho was thinking now.

Eddie was not finished with them. "Your final activity for the evening," he said without smiling, "is the final act of the purification ceremony. Are you learning to trust us?"

"Yes, sir," the pledges said grudgingly.

"Are you still willing to do anything to become a Warrior?"

"Yes, sir," they all replied.

"I couldn't hear that! I couldn't feel that!" Eddie yelled at them. "Are you still willing to do anything to become a Warrior?"

"Yes, sir!" they yelled back with more enthusiasm.

"Good. Let me remind you—you must be cleansed of all impurities and joined with us, body and soul."

Jericho felt like he was trapped in a cave from which he couldn't escape. He didn't like being there, yet he liked what the cave had to offer. He did not know how to get out.

Eddie continued, "One at a time, you will be taken into the bathroom with a senior Warrior and there you will be purified. Who will be first tonight?"

Dana whispered to Kofi and Josh, "I'm tired of going first—it's you guys' turn for a change."

Kofi squeezed her hand and told her, "You're right. I'll do it."

But before Kofi had a chance, Josh said loudly to Madison as he walked to the center of the room, "I'm not afraid. I'll go first."

Josh disappeared into the bathroom with Rick Sharp and the door was slammed. The CD continued to play loudly, but no one moved to the music. The pledges could not take their eyes from the door. They could hear nothing. A few minutes later the door opened slowly and Josh emerged, looking embarrassed, but not really upset. His hair, face, and neck, were soaking wet.

"What happened, man?" Jericho asked.

Josh did a little dance, turning around like a ballerina. "Toilet swirlies. Hold your breath—it's not so bad."

"Oh, man, this sucks," Cleveland said. "I hate puttin' my face where somebody's butt used to be!"

"Now that you put it like that, man, it seems pretty gross!" Josh agreed.

"Next!" Eddie yelled.

Kofi volunteered next. He was in the bathroom a lot longer than Josh. He emerged frowning, wet, and breathing hard. "Toilet stinks!" he told them.

"I warned you to hold your breath!" laughed Josh.

When Kofi sat down with a towel, he whispered to Jericho, "He held my head down and made me hold my breath till I thought I was gonna explode!" Kofi put his hand to his chest and took slow, deep breaths.

"You okay, man?" Jericho whispered back.

"I'm fine now. The worst is over," Kofi said firmly. "Look, hundreds of dudes have survived this before me, and now even a girl. Don't sweat it."

Rudy emerged quickly. When he got back to the group of pledges, he whispered, "At least the water's fairly clean—the toilet is flushed before they start."

Jericho volunteered to go next, just to get it over with. He walked in with Madison, who told him, "Close your eyes, hold your breath, and get your head as wet as you can. If it's not wet enough, I'll have to push it down. Got it?"

Jericho nodded. He kneeled in front of the toilet, which was quite old and very dirty. Crusted yellow and brown stains encircled the inside of the bowl. The water, even though it had just been flushed, was slightly cloudy. It smelled like the remnants of the hundreds of uses it had received since it had last been cleaned.

"Are you ready?" Madison asked. Jericho thought he looked oddly excited.

Jericho nodded again and slowly lowered his head into the toilet bowl. The water was icy cold and felt like a wet, slimy beast as his chin touched it, then his lips. He thought about where he should be at that moment: on stage, dressed in a tuxedo, lips not kissing the water from an old toilet, but pressed against his beloved trumpet, and basking in the glory of stage lights and applause from the audience. He also thought briefly of the professor from Juilliard who would see many talented players tonight, but not him.

Then he tossed those thoughts aside, held his breath,

squeezed his eyes shut, and lowered his head all the way down into the water. It crept into his hair, his ears, and up his nose. In spite of the fact that he had clenched his lips together tightly, a couple of small air bubbles escaped from his mouth. Afraid to open his eyes, he almost panicked, sure he would drown in a toilet bowl. He felt his head being pushed down then, and he almost gasped in fear and surprise.

Jericho tried to lift his head up—he wasn't sure how much longer he could hold his breath. But Madison's hand, heavy like a stone, held Jericho's head firmly under the water. He flailed his arms, trying to signal he needed to get up, needed to breathe. He knew he couldn't hold on one second longer. Suddenly he felt his head being pulled up, almost sucked out of the jaws of that toilet. He gulped in air, inhaling droplets of water that remained in his nose. He coughed and choked and angrily refused Madison's extended hand of congratulations. When he stood up as Madison flushed the toilet, cold fingers of water trickled down his back.

"Good job!" Madison said. "Proud of you, man! Wait till you get to do this next year. It's so much fun!"

Jericho didn't smile. He stomped out of the bathroom in a hurry, his head dripping wet. He returned to the rest of pledges, got his towel, and dried off without speaking to them.

Deshawn, Ram, and the others submitted to the procedure without complaint, although none of them looked pleased. Dana was the last pledge to enter the bathroom. Jericho saw her tense when it became apparent that Eddie

Mahoney was the Warrior who was to accompany her into the bathroom. She walked slowly, not looking at him. They all watched quietly as the door closed. Then they heard it lock.

"They didn't lock it for anybody else, did they?" Kofi asked, concern in his voice.

"I don't think so," Jericho replied.

"Mahoney's got it in for Dana," Cleveland whispered. "He's harder on her than the rest of us."

"She's been holding her own in all this," Josh said. "I'm kinda proud of her!"

"Yeah, if we had to have a girl in the group, I'm glad it was Dana," Luis admitted.

Three minutes passed, then five, then seven. The pledges looked around in concern. Even the Warriors checked their watches. Kofi stood up to go and check on her, but Rick Sharp finally went to the door of the bathroom and knocked. "How long does it take, Eddie?"

The door opened then, and Dana ran from the bathroom, dripping wet and crying. She smelled awful. She ran past the pledges and out of the door. Jericho and Kofi followed her into the parking lot and caught up with her at her car.

"Dana, what happened?" Kofi asked.

"Eddie peed in the toilet before he pushed my head into it!" she screamed. She sped off into the darkness.

AS JERICHO LEFT FOR SCHOOL ON FRIDAY morning, a cold, harsh rain was falling. It had rained all night, and he felt damp and chilled by the time he ran from the parking lot into the school. He and the rest of the pledges got to Mr. Culligan's room early—before the senior Warriors got there. Dana was the last of them to arrive. She walked with a dignity that Jericho didn't think he could have managed.

The pledges instantly gathered around her.

"They can't do you like that, Dana," Kofi began.

"It wasn't all of them—it was just Eddie," Jericho reasoned.

"They had to know what he was gonna do," Cleveland said angrily.

"Maybe not. Eddie's just plain mean," Luis added. "I think he hates you, Dana."

"I don't think he hates you—I think he wants you," Rudy

observed. "And since you're obviously more of a woman that he is a man, he treats you like dirt!"

"I think they ought to punish Eddie—kick him out or something," Kofi suggested.

"Why don't you ask me what I think," Dana said softly. They were suddenly quiet and attentive. "I was ready to quit last night," she told them. "I swore I could handle anything they asked me to do, and I swore I would not let them see me cry. But what Eddie did was too much." She stopped and bowed her head.

"If you quit, Dana, I'm quitting too," Kofi stated.

"So will I," Luis added.

"Me too," Cleveland offered.

Jericho listened to the others. He knew this might be his only chance to get out. Finally he took a deep breath and spoke. "If Dana quits, we all quit. We're bonded, right?"

They looked at him carefully, then one by one they nodded their heads. "Right," most of them agreed. Josh was uncharacteristically quiet.

"Think about this, Dana," Josh said finally. "I think you should stay and show them that not even a lowlife like Eddie can chase you out. They'd be glad if you quit, glad to tell everybody you failed. Eddie would win."

"I see what you're saying, Josh, but there's more," Dana said quietly. "All of you got ice on your back last night instead of the hot fork. Eddie didn't use the ice. There is a legitimate burn mark on my back. It's small, but it is very real."

Jericho was shocked. "What are you going to do?"

227

Dana looked thoughtful. "I told you that last night I was ready to quit, but I decided, after taking about fifteen showers, that I would not let Eddie Mahoney stop me from doing what I really want to do." She stopped and gazed at all of them intently. "But understand, this is not about making a mark for girls—this is about me and who I am. I am better than Eddie Mahoney, and I intend to prove it!" Kofi gave her a hug.

"So Eddie just gets away with what he did?" Rudy asked finally.

"Not exactly. I intend to make sure he's punished, but not now. I am going to finish what I started."

"Are you really sure about this, Dana?" Jericho asked. "Is this what you really want?" He wasn't sure if he was asking Dana or himself.

"Yes, I'm very sure," she answered clearly. "You guys have backed me up through this mess, even though I *know* you didn't really want me at first," she added with a smile. "And I am *not* going to be the one who spoils your chances to be Warriors! All of us or none of us!"

The pledges cheered in agreement. Jericho knew that his path had been chosen.

The senior Warriors walked into the room then. Eddie was not among them. Madison, his head freshly shaved bald, spoke first. "Good morning, pledges."

"Good morning," the pledges replied quietly. They did not include the usual "Master Senior Madison, sir," and Madison did not remind them.

"We have much to discuss this morning," Madison began, "but we must remember the rules. Rick?"

Rick Sharp spoke with quiet intensity. "It is my duty to remind you, pledges, about rule number four: A Warrior of Distinction never breaks the code of silence. Repeat after me, please."

"A Warrior of Distinction never breaks the code of silence," the pledges all said dutifully.

"Nothing of last night's events, or any of our activities, is to be shared with anyone. Never. Understood?"

"Understood," they repeated.

"Now," Madison continued, "we must deal with what happened. What we call the cleansing ceremony has been done dozens of times—hundreds if you count each individual member—and what happened to Dana was a first. It was not planned, we did not know, and we truly apologize."

"It's not you who owes me an apology," Dana replied sharply.

"Eddie Mahoney has been officially reprimanded by the senior council of the Warriors," Madison explained. "He understands what he did was totally inappropriate."

"He didn't get kicked out?" Jericho asked, astonished.

The pledges crowded close to Rick, who held up his hands. "We stand by each other, even if we make mistakes."

"So who will stand by me?" Dana asked.

"The Warriors of Distinction are very proud of your efforts as a pledge, Dana, and we will stand by you, no matter what you decide," Rick continued. "But we fully understand if you choose to drop out of the procedure at this point."

Dana looked at them in amazement. "So you're gonna *let* me quit?" she asked angrily. "How noble of you!"

"Sounds to me like you're tryin' to get rid of her!" Kofi yelled.

"Not at all," Rick replied calmly. "She simply might decide the effort and embarrassment are too much for her."

"You just finish what you have to do!" Dana shot back at Rick. "But you're going to have to deal with me while you do it! *I will not quit!*"

Jericho glanced at the other pledges, who had gathered around Dana in encouragement. Josh looked relieved. Kofi looked proud. Jericho wasn't sure how he felt, but he knew he was glad to be a part of the group that stood there together as one powerful team.

Rick and Madison glanced at each other. Then they smiled at the pledges, and Rick said, "We have eliminated this morning's service activity. However, normal pledge activities will resume this evening at eight at the warehouse. Tonight is the final night, and it will be an experience you will never forget."

Madison added, "Be aware that nothing will change tonight, and no activities will be made easier or less intense because of last night's incident. Got that?"

The pledges nodded without comment. At that point, Eddie Mahoney walked into the room. All was silent.

"I want to apologize," he said without hesitation, "to my brothers who are Warriors, to the pledges, and especially to you, Dana." He looked directly at her. Jericho thought his eyes looked cold and distant; he didn't look very sorry at all. "What I did was not worthy of a Warrior of Distinction," Eddie continued. "Please forgive me."

Everyone looked at Dana. She stared at Eddie for a full minute. He finally had to turn away from her gaze. At that point she said, "Of course, Master Senior Mahoney, *sir*." Her voice dripped with sarcasm. "But sometimes forgiveness comes with a price."

The bell rang then and she walked proudly out the door. Jericho and the rest of the pledges followed.

"She's some kinda woman!" Kofi said as they walked down the hall.

"Probably more than you can handle, dude!" Josh teased.

"Wonder Woman!" Jericho chuckled.

"Super Girl," added Kofi.

"Do I hear you talkin' about me?" Dana asked as they walked into the classroom.

"Yeah, I was tellin' Jericho about how sweet and feminine you are," Kofi told her.

"Feminine is powerful, and don't you forget it!" she told him as she pretended to punch him on his arm.

"You're not likely to let us forget that!" Josh said with a laugh.

Then, by the pencil sharpener, Kofi asked her seriously, "You okay, Dana?"

"Yeah, I'm fine—ready for tonight," she answered with quiet determination. She headed to her seat as the bell rang. "You know, Josh," she teased, "if I looked as bad as you do in that shirt, I'd never say a word about anybody else. I didn't think it was possible for you to make that shirt look any worse, but how did you manage to get black splotches all over it, along with the white spots from the other day?"

"Skills!" he said simply. "Skills!"

AFTER LUNCH JERICHO SAW ERIC BELL IN
the distance, and he knew he should say
something, but he was embarrassed. Still,
he hurried over to him when he saw Eric
struggling with a door that would not stay
open long enough for him to get his wheelchair
through.

"Let me help you with that, man," Jericho
offered. He couldn't look Eric directly in the face.

"I can do it myself," Eric said sullenly.

"I know. Hey, Eric, I was a butt the other day."

"You got that right," Eric agreed.

"I didn't mean to hurt your feelings," Jericho told
him.

"My feelings get hurt all the time. I ought to be used
to it, but it never gets any easier."

"I'm sorry, man," Jericho said sincerely.

Eric sighed. "You know what bothered me the most?"

"What?"

"You figured Arielle wouldn't like me because I'm in a wheelchair."

Jericho was silent for a moment. "Actually, that wasn't it—honestly. The wheelchair had nothing to do with it. I was just afraid she wanted to be with you and not with me. I got scared."

It was Eric's turn to be quiet. "So what did Arielle say when you talked to her?"

Jericho laughed. "She told me where I could stuff my opinions about who she talked to or who she associated with. She got me told real good!"

Eric laughed with him this time. "Serves you right! I better get through this hallway before the bell rings. I'll talk to you later, Jericho."

"Take it slow, Eric."

"Hey, Jericho," Eric called as he rolled away.

"Yeah?"

"Good luck tonight with the Warriors of Distinction."

"Thanks, man," he replied quietly. "Thanks." He watched Eric roll down the hall and around the corner.

"Why you got that funny expression on your face?" Arielle asked, walking up to Jericho.

"Nothing," Jericho said as he took a deep breath. "What's up, Arielle? You look good today."

"Thanks. Aren't you supposed to be running around the school doing good deeds for the Warriors?" she asked Jericho.

"Not today. Tonight is the big whatever, so they're letting us take it easy."

"You nervous?"

"Of what? How bad can it be? Naw, I just want it to be over so on Monday we can come to school in our new silk jackets. You still goin' to the celebration party with me tomorrow night?"

"Me and Dana and November are going shopping after school to get outfits for the party. Does that give you a hint?"

Jericho grinned. "There's the bell—I gotta get to class. I won't call you tonight because it will be too late, but I'll call you first thing in the morning."

"And tell me all about it?" she teased.

"All that I can," he answered.

"Whatever! Good luck, Jericho." She hurried off in one direction to her class, and Jericho in the other direction to his.

Jericho was tense with anticipation, but the day seemed to crawl by. The cold rain and dreary clouds and the muddy puddles on the brown and sodden grass didn't help. Finally the last bell rang. Jericho saw Josh coming from his last class.

"What's up, my almost-Warrior cousin?" Josh called.

"I wonder if they give a prize tonight for the ugliest pledge shirt," Jericho told him as he gazed on Josh's blotched, spotted, and now shrunken T-shirt.

"Well, I wonder if they give a prize for the ugliest pledge!" Josh shot back at him. "You'd win face first!"

"Don't let me start talkin' about your cookie-dough head!" Jericho laughed.

"Aw, man, well at least I'm not mistaken for Godzilla when I walk down the street!"

The two of them headed out into the rainy afternoon,

laughing and punching each other. Jericho shivered. "We're gonna freeze our butts off tonight."

"I got my love to keep me warm," Josh boasted.

"November won't be anywhere near there—I heard they're all going shopping together."

Josh pointed to his heart. "I got my girl here where it counts." For a second he looked pensive and serious. Then, running around the parking lot and oblivious to the rain, he shouted to the sky, "Hey, world! This is Josh! Tonight I get my black jacket, and I'm gonna look goooood!"

"Man, you losin' it!" Jericho laughed as he watched Josh splash through all the puddles in the parking lot. Maybe he just needed to relax like Josh and get this week over with.

Josh's father pulled up in front of the school then. Josh, soaking wet and out of breath, opened the car door and greeted his dad. "Tonight's the night, Dad, and I'm charged up!"

"What you are is messed up, boy! You out here playing in the rain like a ten-year-old? Get a towel out of the trunk." Uncle Brock wasn't really angry, Jericho realized as he watched them tease each other. "Do you need a ride, Jericho?" Uncle Brock asked as Josh, still laughing, got in the car.

"Thanks, Uncle Brock. I'm driving today." Josh had rolled down the window and Jericho leaned inside to talk.

"Be careful, Jericho. The roads are wet and slick from all this rain," his uncle said.

"I will."

"Are you two ready for tonight?" he asked.

"Josh sure is!" Jericho replied.

"It will be the most memorable night of your lives," Mr. Prescott replied with a pleasant smile, as if he were thinking of fond memories. "It will make a man of you."

Josh rolled his eyes. "Sure, Dad. Does this mean I get a car like Jericho?"

"It may make you a man, but it's not going to make me a blockhead!"

"He shut you up, man! Nice goin', Uncle Brock," Jericho teased as he punched Josh once more through the open car window.

"See you tonight!" Josh called cheerfully as they left the parking lot.

Jericho waved as they drove away.

WHEN JERICHO GOT TO THE WAREHOUSE, A
little early, Dana was already waiting at the
door. The night was cold but clear—filled
with stars and promise.

"You scared?" he asked her.

"I can't imagine anything worse than last
night," she whispered, shuddering a little.

He nodded. *This girl is, like, too tough,* he
thought. He didn't think he could have accomplished what Dana had. They shivered nervously in
the darkness, waiting for they knew not what. The
rest of the pledges arrived a few minutes later, and
at exactly eight P.M. Rick opened the door to the
warehouse. "Good evening, Pledge Slime. Please
come in."

The room was dark and shadowy. Fifteen chairs had
been placed in a circle in the center of the room. A single
candle flickered on a table in the middle of the circle. The
silence was thick.

"Remove your coats and be seated," Rick said quietly. The pledges stacked their winter jackets on a table in the back of the room. There sat fifteen neat white boxes, unopened, the coveted black silk jackets waiting to be caressed and admired by the new members of the club. Jericho smiled with anticipation, then walked quickly back to the circle, ready for whatever might happen that night.

The pledges found seats within the circle. They looked at each other hesitantly. Rick stood in the center by the table. The other pledge masters stood behind the pledges at various points around the circle.

Jericho noticed, once his eyes had become accustomed to the dim light, that sitting on the table next to the candle was a mirror, a rusty brown brick, what appeared to be a whiskey bottle, and the gun they had found in the Dumpster. All of Jericho's feelings of dread and foreboding flooded back.

"Tonight," Rick began, "is the final night of pledge activities. Soon you will join us as Warriors of Distinction. Tonight's activities will be intense, perhaps overwhelming. So we will begin with a quiet reflection."

Rick's quiet, serious tone made Jericho even more nervous about the final activities than ever. Rick picked up the brick from the table and passed it to Jericho.

"This brick," Rick said, "is a symbol of our brotherhood. Slowly pass it around the circle. Look at it. Feel its weight and its rough edges. Notice it is not perfect. All of us have rough edges and imperfections." Jericho noticed that Rick stopped then and glanced at Eddie.

Jericho felt the roughness in his hands. He'd never

bothered to look at a brick up close before. It had little holes and ridges in it, but it was surprisingly heavy.

"Jericho, pass the brick to the person sitting next to you. Hold it at eye level as you do. This is to remind you that you may not always see things eye to eye, but you should be man enough to confront each other and solve your problems face-to-face."

Jericho passed the brick to Josh.

"Bricks can be found anywhere," Rick continued. "They are strong and powerful, but are rarely noticed individually. Only when a brick is missing does a building look unusual. Together we have power."

Josh passed the brick to Luis, who passed it to Kofi, who passed it to Dana. It traveled slowly to all the pledges in the circle.

"This brick is also a symbol of our unity," Rick said. "It's made of cement, rocks, sand, and water. Just like this brick that is made up of a combination of materials, the Warriors of Distinction are also a group with diverse cultural and social backgrounds, values, and experiences. Like the composition of the brick, that's what makes us strong."

As Rick spoke, Jericho began to relax. The Warriors are off the hook, he kept telling himself. He was so lucky to be part of this. He thought about the faces of the people they'd helped through the toy drive, and the pride on Arielle's face the night of the New Year's Eve party.

The brick had made it completely around the circle. Rick placed it back on the table, then picked up the small mirror and handed it to Jericho. "Next I want you to pass this mirror around the circle. What do you see?"

Jericho saw a round brown face with slightly crooked teeth, fuzzy hair, and ears that stuck out too far. He didn't like looking at himself in the mirror. He passed it quickly to Josh.

"Your face is just one of many, but it is unique. No other face in the world is exactly like it, yet all human faces are basically the same. Remember that each of you is an individual, yet each of you is responsible for the other tonight. Very soon we will be proud to include your face with ours as a Warrior of Distinction."

Just as Jericho was ready to agree with him, Rick then picked up the gun. The room instantly grew so quiet and tense Jericho imagined he could hear the sound of the flame from the candle as it flickered in the darkness.

"The gun," Rick began, "symbolizes our power. It is cold and silent as you see it now, but it can become hot and deadly in an instant."

Jericho's heart pounded as he considered what the presence of a gun could mean. For the first time since the pledging began, he was genuinely scared.

Rick took the end of his shirt and carefully wiped a tiny speck from the barrel of the gun. "The gun also represents our strength and our silence. A gun never speaks unless it has to," he said ominously. "As I pass it around, I want you to feel its power, its strength, as well as its silence. Touch it, explore it, learn its mysteries." He gave it first to Jericho. "Don't be afraid," Rick told him. "Be brave enough to discover a new and powerful reality!"

Jericho took the gun. His hands shook. He turned it over and gazed at it in the dim light with fear and foreboding. It was heavy and cold. He passed it quickly to Josh.

Josh, his usual cheerful lightheartedness missing for once, took the gun carefully. He made no jokes as he held it for a few moments, then passed it on to Luis. The rest of the pledges all explored the gun silently and fearfully and it was quickly returned to Rick.

"I want to reassure you," Rick told the solemn group of pledges, "we have never used the gun." He paused. "It has never been necessary," he added without explanation.

Eddie then took over the ceremony. The candle burned lower, the flame a wild and confused point of light as Eddie brushed close to it. Eddie picked up the bottle. In his other hand he held fifteen very small plastic cups—the type that comes on the top of a cough medicine bottle. "We began with reflection," he said. "The next part of our ceremony is for relaxation." He gave Jericho the plastic cups and told him to take one and pass the rest to the others.

Eddie then opened the bottle. The strong smell that escaped the bottle instantly let them know that this was no whiskey bottle filled with tea to fool them. This was hard liquor. Eddie walked around the group of pledges and filled their cups.

Jericho looked at the brownish liquid in his cup. He'd had beer before, but he didn't like the taste of it, so he rarely drank, even when his friends decided to party more than he cared to. He had never even tasted whiskey or any other hard liquor before. And he had no desire to taste any tonight.

"The purpose of this part of the ceremony," Eddie explained, his voice syrupy and sinister, "is to release your inner strength, and to show your willingness to become one of us. It will also relax you for activities to come later tonight."

Jericho felt trapped. He knew he should leave, but there was no way he had the nerve to walk out now. After all, it was almost over. In just a few hours he'd be a Warrior! So he sat where he was.

"Drink!" Eddie commanded.

The pledges hesitated.

"Drink!" Eddie yelled again. "If you want to be a part of this group, do it now and do it quickly!"

Cleveland was the first to empty his cup. "Ahhhh!" he blurted loudly. Then he burped. The pledges giggled a little and some of the tension was eased. One by one the pledges drank the cup of whiskey.

Dana swallowed hers quickly. Jericho saw her face squeeze into a grimace, but she didn't choke or gag. Eddie walked around the group, making sure each cup was empty. He stopped in front of Jericho, who still held the cup of whiskey in his hand.

In one swift movement, Jericho put the cup to his lips and swallowed it all at once. His throat burned like he had swallowed flaming branches. Seconds later he felt a heat in his stomach like nothing he had ever felt. It was as if a fiery tree had grown within him. It began in his gut and expanded to every part of his body. He felt like he was caught in a science fiction movie where the character's guts get invaded and then explode. It was hard to breathe. Eddie laughed.

Eddie then walked around and refilled the cups. Jericho couldn't believe they had to do it again.

"Drink!" Eddie commanded once more.

Jericho noticed that for some reason the pledges drank the second cup much more quickly. Even he had very little difficulty the second time around. The liquid still burned like hot fire, but the shock and the hot reaction was softer and muted.

"Again!" Eddie ordered as he refilled the little cups. Once more the pledges obediently swallowed the liquor. "You like this, don't you?" Eddie taunted as he made them drink a fourth time. The rest of the Warriors, Jericho noticed through hazy observation, had their own bottles and were sipping from them periodically as they laughed at the pledges.

By the fifth round of drinks, Jericho didn't even care. He drank it sloppily, spilling a little in the process. For some reason, that struck him as incredibly funny. *This ain't so bad,* he thought dimly. He noticed that the liquor bottle was now empty.

Jericho watched with blurry vision as Eddie quietly opened another bottle and replaced the small plastic medicine cups with full-sized paper cups. "Let's party!" he heard himself say. He tried to stand up, but fell to the floor in a heap. Josh laughed so hard he fell off his chair, and Luis rolled out of his seat as well. By this time the pledges were voluntarily passing the bottle around, some of them ignoring the paper cups and drinking straight out of the bottle. They laughed, they sang, they told dirty jokes. A couple of them ran to the bathroom where the night before they'd been forced to dip their heads, and vomited. Jericho looked for Dana, and saw she was sitting on Kofi's lap, giggling hysterically at something he'd said.

Jericho knew he was drunk, and he didn't care. Any doubts or worries he'd had about the Warriors disappeared in the bottom of that paper cup.

Eddie and Rick and the rest of the Warriors stood then and started chanting quietly, their voices almost a whisper:

> *You don't know what time it is—*
> *It's time to get live!*
> *It's time to represent!*
> *Warriors rock! Warriors rule!*
> *You don't know what time it is—*
> *It's time to get live!*
> *It's time to represent!*
> *Warriors rock! Warriors rule!*

Gradually the chanting got louder and louder. Louder and louder they repeated the rhythmic words. Slowly, hesitantly, the pledges joined them in the chant. They stood shakily, joining arms and swaying together as they shouted drunkenly with the others the rhythmic beats:

> *You don't know what time it is—*
> *It's time to get live!*
> *It's time to represent!*
> *Warriors rock! Warriors rule!*

The chant gradually slowed and stopped, but Jericho felt excited and anxious to begin whatever awaited. His head seemed as though it was full of cotton wrapped in explosives. He wasn't sure if he felt like curling into a ball and sleeping for a week, or exploding like a grenade and destroying something. All he knew was that whatever they asked him to do, he was ready to do it.

The room was finally completely silent. Jericho glanced at the candle and noticed it had burned out.

In the darkness Madison's strong bass voice broke the silence. "Sit down, please. We will now remind you of the vows you made. Remember, we demand your dedication, your obedience, and your very life, if necessary. Any problems with that? If so, this is your last chance to back out."

"Don't be hatin', man. We with you all the way. Bring it on!" Cleveland's slurred voice answered. He was sitting on the floor, laughing to himself. Jericho tried to remember what was bothering him earlier, but his thoughts were fuzzy and warm, and right now Cleveland sounded like the wisest man in the world.

Madison looked like he was holding back a laugh. "Remember that each pledge holds the responsibility for the other tonight." Jericho looked at the pledges. He felt, for once, like he was part of the big picture. "In addition, you must agree to do *anything* you are asked to do," Madison continued.

"Anything!" Cleveland shouted drunkenly. He burped.

"Anything!" the rest of the pledges cried out as well.

"It's all good."

"Let's get it on!" They had all risen to their feet once more, and Jericho felt like their unsteady legs were his own, their gravelly voices belonged to him, and their thoughts and vows were part of his as well. He'd never felt such power.

"Repeat after me," Eddie demanded. "All of us or none of us!"

"All of us or none of us! All of us or none of us!" Jericho and the other pledges yelled back. "Warriors rock! Warriors rule!" Jericho found himself accepting it, believing it, swallowing it whole.

The room gradually settled into silence. "Follow us," Madison commanded. The Warriors opened the door of the warehouse and headed into the darkness.

JERICHO COULDN'T IMAGINE ANYTHING ELSE they could do to them. The cold slapped his face and bare arms as they left the warehouse, but the night was icy clear. The fifteen pledges followed Mad Madison, Rick Sharp, Eddie Mahoney, and the other Warriors out the door, through the parking lot, and around to the back area where the Dumpster loomed darkly in the distance.

"Give me five laps around the building," Eddie demanded. The pledges shrugged and started to jog. Jericho was a little glad for the run because it seemed to clear the thickness in his head, but he still ran as if he were another person watching himself from a distance. A couple of the pledges vomited between laps. When they returned to the starting point, exhaling hot breaths while inhaling the cold night air, Jericho waited with the others for the next task.

"We are almost finished," Madison called to the anxious

pledges. The wind had increased and was whipping them all.

"The sooner you complete this last task, the sooner you can go to a place of warmth and celebration. Mr. Culligan is back at school, getting everything ready for our party, so let's get this over with!" Madison shouted over the wind. "A warm shower and your black silk jackets await you!" That was enough to get them going.

"March!" Eddie commanded. He and the other Warriors then led the pledges behind the Dumpster, down the broken and crumbling driveway, and into the yard of the deserted house in the back. From a distance the house looked shadowy and forlorn, but up close it was dilapidated and frightening. The wooden porch was almost rotted away, with huge gaping holes looming darkly between the boards that still remained. The windows had been boarded up, but time and weather had loosened many of the wooden coverings so that jagged glass protruded and gleamed in the light of the Warriors' flashlights. The front door, hanging by just one hinge, stood ajar. To Jericho it looked like a scene from one of those horror movies where chain-saw killers lurk in the darkness. He almost wished he had another drink to get rid of his returning feelings of fear and misgiving.

As if he read his mind, Eddie pulled another bottle of liquor from a bag and passed it around to the pledges. "Drink!" he told the pledges. "You will need this."

Jericho didn't even think this time. He swallowed several huge gulps, grateful for the temporary warmth he felt. He searched for that feeling of kinship and peace he'd felt earlier, but it was gone.

"You will enter the house together. Make your way to the second floor, enter the first room on your left, go to the window there, and wait for further instructions. Here is a flashlight."

The pledges walked slowly toward the crumbling porch. Jericho, who had been given the flashlight, placed one foot shakily on the first step. It held but groaned under his weight. The others followed quietly. Jericho reached the front door, cautiously grabbed the handle, and pushed. It took very little effort to open it fully.

Jericho wasn't sure how he ended up first in line, but here he was, so he pressed forward. He peered into the darkness of what had once been a living room. One whole side of the floor had caved in, but the side that led to the staircase seemed to be solid. Heart thudding, he carefully entered the room. The others followed.

"Talk about your haunted houses!" Luis whispered.

"If some freak with a mask or a butcher knife comes around the corner, I'm outta here!" Josh laughed quietly.

"Dana, stay close to me," Kofi called to her.

"I'm right here. Eddie's freaky enough to scare me— don't need no real monsters," she quipped.

"Aw, you just want her to protect *your* tremblin' butt!" Josh teased.

"I bet there're rats in here," Cleveland whispered.

"And spiders—look at all those webs." Jericho pointed them out with a shudder.

The room, heavy with dust and decay, was not as deserted as they thought. In one corner they saw a pile of newspapers that were stacked on what looked like a bed.

The papers were partially covered with an old blanket, and dozens of beer bottles were strewn over the floor. The room smelled of old garbage and urine.

"Looks like somebody else has found this place too."

"Probably some homeless people."

"I hope they're not here hiding or something. I'll freak," Luis admitted.

"Let's get upstairs and get this over with," Jericho suggested.

The fifteen pledges slowly crept up the stairs. The railing had long since fallen down, so they had nothing to hold on to but fear and faith—and each other. At the top of the steps, Jericho breathed slowly and pointed the flashlight beam at the floor and ceiling of the upstairs hall. The hallways had once been decorated by a lovely carpet, but it was ripped, faded, and completely gone in some spots. Several closed doors loomed darkly down the hall, but Jericho concentrated on the first door on the left, where they had been told to go. He turned the knob, pushed open the door, and entered the small bedroom, the other pledges following closely. The door slammed behind them and they all jumped.

The Warriors had obviously been there earlier. Candles had been lit. They flickered from the boxes and crates that had been stacked around the room. The room was well swept and free of cobwebs, Jericho noticed thankfully.

Kofi asked, "So what do we do now?" He held Dana's hand. Some of the pledges swayed a little from the alcohol. Several of them sat gratefully on the boxes, while others slumped to the floor. Jericho felt dizzy and thickheaded, and slightly nauseous. He was chilled, and the cold seemed to have seeped into his skin. He wanted to go home and sleep.

"Is this the window they talked about?" Jericho asked as he walked over to the largest window in the room, the type that opened from the bottom. It reminded him of the windows at home, which on a summer night let in fresh air and thirsty mosquitoes.

Just then the door to the small room swung open and Eddie Mahoney blew into the room like a storm, making the candles flicker and sputter. One candle went out completely.

"Open the window!" he commanded.

Jericho, who was still standing closest to it, lifted the bottom handles. The window rose easily. A cold gust of wind blew through the open window.

"All of us have been where you are tonight," Eddie explained. "It is now time for the Leap of Faith." Jericho thought back vaguely to something Mr. Redstone had mentioned, but he couldn't remember what he had said. "This is how you test your courage," Eddie continued. "It is time to leap into the brotherhood, leap into your future, leap into success. You will jump from this window a lowly piece of Pledge Slime, but you will arise, like a phoenix, as a respected and honored member of the Warriors of Distinction!"

The pledges, eyes wide with fear, glanced at the gaping window. "Just jump?" Jericho asked, a look of disbelief on his face.

"Beneath the window we have arranged a soft landing

for you—old mattresses and pillows, lots of foam rubber, even a mat from the boys' gym," Eddie explained.

"But I don't see anything," Jericho insisted. His voice sounded high and nervous, even to his own ears.

"Of course you don't. We've covered it all with mud. It will be soft, but not pleasant. You scared to get dirty?"

"No, sir." Jericho sullenly said nothing else, but he moved away from the window. He didn't like heights, and he hated the feeling of losing control and falling. He was starting to feel dizzy and nauseous from the alcohol, but the thought of the ground jumping up to grab him was almost too much. He wasn't sure if he could do this.

"Who's first to try the Leap of Faith?" Eddie asked. No one answered. Eddie pulled the gun from his jacket. "I asked," he repeated ominously as he pointed the gun at each of them, "who will be first?"

Ram jumped up. "I'll go first, man. Put that thing away before you hurt somebody."

"Good man," Eddie told him. "The rest of the Warriors await you at the bottom to help you. We do this every year—it's a piece of cake."

Ram took a deep breath, tossed his legs over the ledge of the window, and disappeared. Jericho heard a soft thud, then a whoop of victory. "I'm in, dudes! It's muddy, but it's okay. Come on down!"

Jericho realized he'd been holding his breath. He backed farther away from the window. Cleveland jumped next. "For the rats!" he yelled as he jumped. In a moment came a cheer from below.

Luis volunteered next, but he was frightened, Jericho

could tell. He made the sign of the cross several times, but just sat there, feet dangling over the edge while the wind buffeted him. Eddie pulled out the gun again. "Jump, coward!" he hissed. Luis jumped. Jericho and the others heard him scream as he fell.

"You okay, Luis?" Eddie called out the window.

"Yeah," Luis answered, his voice shaking.

"Congratulations, my brother," Eddie yelled, "and to the rest of you down there as well!"

Eddie pointed the gun then at Arnold, Rudy, and Deshawn. One by one they jumped silently into the darkness. So did several other pledges. But the thuds that signaled their victorious landing only made Jericho more afraid. All of the muddy, successful jumpers screamed encouragement to the remaining pledges above who hovered hesitantly near the window.

Soon only Jericho, Josh, Kofi, and Dana remained. The cold, harsh wind continued to blow mercilessly into the room, making Jericho shiver even more. All the candles had been blown out.

Eddie eased himself close to Dana in the darkened room. "If you don't get away from me," Jericho heard her say, "I swear I'll stick that gun up your butt!"

Eddie backed away, but snarled, "Jump!"

"I'm not scared of you, Eddie," Dana said clearly. "My daddy taught me to skydive when I was little. As a matter of fact, I was just as tall as you are now!" She laughed in his face and walked over to the window. She gave Kofi a hug, climbed onto the windowsill, pulled her long legs over the ledge, and breathed deeply for a few seconds. Then she just slid into the darkness.

Kofi ran to the window to check on her. Jericho, though glad to see Kofi waving to her with a smile on his face, felt dizzy and lightheaded. The walls seems to be wobbling. He stumbled to the back of the room and vomited in a corner.

"You not gonna punk out on us, are you, Jericho?" Eddie sneered. "Even Dana did the Leap of Faith, man."

Jericho didn't answer, but wished the world had a door. He wanted out.

"Don't worry about it, Jericho. I gotta go next," Kofi announced with certainty. "Dana needs me."

"I think it's you who needs Dana," Josh said with a small laugh. Kofi climbed onto the window and gazed at the darkness below. The shouts of the others could be heard from below, but he sat without moving.

"You okay, man?" Jericho pulled himself together and walked over to him.

Kofi didn't reply. Eddie walked over to where Kofi sat in the window and spoke softly. "I knew you were soft when I first saw you. I knew you didn't have the guts to be a Warrior! And you're sure not man enough to handle a woman like Dana."

"Watch me!" Kofi told him fiercely. He turned slowly then, swung his legs back inside the room, and stood up straight and tall. He glared at Eddie, who looked uneasy. Without saying a word, Kofi quickly grabbed a very surprised Eddie Mahoney, picked him up, and tossed him unceremoniously out of the window.

Josh and Jericho ran to the window and cheered as Eddie plopped in the muddy mess below. All of the pledges laughed hysterically. Even some of the Warriors joined in.

Kofi, noticeably more relaxed, laughed as well. He climbed back onto the windowsill, sat on the ledge and dangled his feet, pushed off with his tennis shoes, and jumped. Jericho heard the familiar thud, then sounds of an argument as a furious-sounding Eddie confronted Kofi. The others sounded like they were trying to break it up.

"It's just you and me, Cuz," Josh said to Jericho.

"We better get down there," Jericho said weakly. "Sounds like the brotherhood is fallin' apart."

"I'll go first," Josh offered.

Only Josh knew how scared I am, Jericho thought.

"Naw, I can do this," he told his cousin. His heart pounded. He climbed onto the windowsill and looked down. Everyone looked so small. The filthy, pink-shirted pledges huddled on one side of the mud pit, waving at him in encouragement. The pledge masters stood on the other side, some of them still passing around the bottle of whiskey. Eddie was being restrained by a couple of them. Jericho wondered why Kofi was sitting on the ground, near the pledges. Kofi was the only one not waving him on. The ground looked miles away and the successful pledges stood shivering and muddy below.

"We're freezin' our butts off out here!" Cleveland called. "Come on down, man!"

Jericho felt light-headed and weak. He closed his eyes and tried to bring pleasant, comforting thoughts to his mind—Arielle, his trumpet, jazz music. Eyes squeezed tightly, and with those thoughts surrounding him, he let himself fall.

Faster than he ever imagined, the shock of the wet, thick mud jarred him. Jericho landed on his back, once again thankful for his fatty padding. He lay stunned on the ground for a moment. He was amazed he was still conscious and aware of everything. *He did it!* But that moment of exultation faded quickly as he realized he'd never been so cold and miserable in his life. His head throbbed and his back hurt. He opened his eyes, looked up at the dark sky, and took a deep breath. The landing was not as soft as they had predicted, but it was bearable. And it was over. Luis reached down, offered his arm, and helped Jericho to stand.

Jericho looked around. Eddie, looking angrier than ever, was muddy and nursing a small cut on his head. Kofi sat on his knees in the mud near where Jericho landed, head down, a miserable-looking, muddy creature. His face looked blue and ashen, and his right arm, which he held with his left arm as if to support it, hung stiffly by his side. He shivered uncontrollably.

"Are you okay, Kofi?" Jericho asked with concern.

Kofi replied quietly, "I think I broke my arm." He looked pale, as if he were about to faint. Madison sat in the mud with him, placing his own jacket around him.

Dana sat quietly next to Kofi. "He won't let us help until we've all jumped," she told Jericho. "Come on, Josh!"

Jericho looked up at the window, which looked even higher from the ground, and waved encouragement to Josh.

"Jump! Jump! Jump!" the Warriors shouted. Josh hesitated. Jericho knew he had to be a little scared—the last one up there, and all by himself. "Jump!" the Warriors shouted once more.

"Here I come!" Josh shouted cheerfully. "It's my turn to fly!" He waved to the group below, took a bow like he always did when he was showing off, then, instead of sitting in the window like the rest of them had done, he climbed up, stood on the windowsill, raised both his arms as if they were wings, and let himself go. And for a moment he really did look like a bird in flight.

THEN, SUDDENLY, JOSH TWISTED IN THE AIR.
Jericho gasped in horror as Josh's graceful
dive became a frantic fall. Josh flailed his
arms wildly. He seemed to be trying to regain
control of his body, but the ground swallowed
him before he had the chance.

"Josh!" Jericho screamed desperately. He
wanted to shout out a warning, scream to the sky
to catch Josh, pray for time to stop forever, but
the words wouldn't come fast enough. Josh landed
headfirst, beyond the assorted muddy mats, onto
the dark, cold ground.

It had all happened in seconds, but it seemed like
hours. Jericho rushed to where Josh landed. The others
followed. Jericho stared with incomprehension. Why
wasn't Josh moving?

His cousin lay on the ground in the mud, his face to
the sky. Trembling, Jericho thought it odd how Josh's
head rested unnaturally on his right shoulder. He couldn't

comprehend Josh's face, which instead of his usual easy smile, was contorted into a terrible grimace—a mask of pain and surprise. Even though he was almost afraid to reach out, Jericho gently touched Josh's right hand, which lay open as if he were reaching for something or someone. He couldn't touch Josh's left hand, for it was hidden beneath his body, his left arm twisted at a painfully awkward angle.

"Oh, my God, Josh!" Jericho groaned from a place deep within. Suddenly from the darkness came a scream of terror and agony, and Jericho realized *he* was the one who was screaming. *"Help!"* he shouted. "Oh my God, some-body please! *Help!"* Terror and desperation distorted his voice. "Hurry!" he screamed again. "Call nine-one-one! Call the police! Call somebody!" Rick Sharp fumbled in his pocket for a cell phone and frantically punched the numbers.

Jericho lowered his head so his mouth was close to Josh's ear. He whispered desperately, "Stop playin', man! Quit tryin' to fake us out! Josh, please, talk to me!"

Someone covered Josh with his jacket.

"Oh, my God," Jericho whispered. Then he roared, "We gotta *do* something to help him! Anybody know CPR?"

"Yeah, man, I do," Cleveland answered. "I used to be a lifeguard."

"I don't know if it will help," Jericho admitted, "but we can't just sit here!"

"I don't think we ought to do chest compressions," Cleveland said thoughtfully. "We don't know if he's . . . uh . . . bleeding. Let's just try the breathing part."

Jericho knelt in the mud and prayed while Cleveland attempted the rhythmic breathing. But Josh did not move or respond.

After an excruciating minute or so, Luis said quietly, "It's not working, Jericho. But I hear the sirens. The paramedics will know what to do." The group huddled together, trembling and hoping for a miracle. Josh still had not moved.

Rick ran out to the street to direct the paramedics back to where Josh lay. They ran down with their equipment and told everyone to stand back as they rushed over to Josh and began to assess the situation.

"We'll take over now, son," one of the paramedics said to Cleveland. Cleveland stood up, but Jericho wouldn't move.

He touched Josh again, whose arm felt surprisingly warm in spite of the icy air. *Where are you, Josh? I'm scared, man.* Jericho wept then, holding his cousin's rigid hand in his own. Josh did not move. His eyes, open and unblinking, were turned toward the night sky.

THE INTENSITY OF THE VOICES OF THE
emergency rescue team and the squawking
of their receivers as they radioed in information pierced the night.

"Bring some lights back here, Mac!"

"Is he breathing, Bill?"

"Call for police backup, Joe. What's the kid's
name?"

Dana had placed another jacket around the
shivering Kofi. They sat on the ground not far from
Josh. "His name is Josh," she informed the paramedics. "Oh, please help him!"

"Josh!" the paramedic shouted loudly. "Can you
hear me, Josh?" Jericho thought that was stupid—it
was obvious Josh could not hear him.

"What happened?" another paramedic asked as he
examined Josh.

"He fell," Madison answered meekly. "It was an accident."

"From where?" the paramedic asked sharply.

"That window up there," Madison replied, pointing to the dark hole above.

"Did he fall or was he pushed?" another paramedic asked, as he tried to get a pulse.

"He wasn't pushed," Madison answered quickly. "And he didn't fall, not really. He was the last one to . . . uh . . . jump."

"What you kids doing out here in the middle of the night, jumpin' out of windows? You all crazy?" The paramedic stared at the numerous muddy pink shirts. "What is this, some kind of stupid fraternity hazing?"

Madison opened and closed his mouth several times, but nothing came out. Jericho had never seen him look so frightened.

"All the pledges had jumped except Josh," Rick began. "But . . . but . . . uh . . . he lost his balance somehow, and he didn't land like the others. . . ." His voice faded.

"Why did the pledges have to jump out of the window?" the paramedic asked incredulously.

"To . . . show . . . uh . . . to show that they were brave and loyal." Even to Jericho it sounded juvenile.

"Who was giving him CPR when we got here?" the paramedic asked. Cleveland raised his hand timidly. Jericho wasn't even sure if he could speak. He felt as if he were about to throw up.

"You did good," the paramedic said. "At least you tried."

"Get out of the way, kid!" another paramedic shouted at Kofi, who was still kneeling close to Josh. "We need room here."

"I can't," Kofi responded weakly. "My right arm—I think it's broke."

"Sorry, son," the paramedic replied. "Let me take a look at that." Kofi nodded. "Is anyone else hurt?" The boys all said no. Jericho looked around for Eddie, but it seemed that Eddie had quietly disappeared.

Jericho's attention went back and forth between Josh and Kofi. He watched in horrified fascination as the paramedic named Bill turned Kofi gently on his side and began to examine him. He and another emergency technician checked his pulse and breathing, wrapped his arm so it could not move, and covered him with a blanket, then elevated his legs with another blanket. Kofi, too weak to complain, lay limp as a rag doll as they worked on him. Dana hovered close to Kofi the whole time, a look of quiet horror on her face.

Tears filled Kofi's eyes. Finally he said, "Is my friend gonna be okay?"

"They're working on him right now. Don't you worry. My name is Bill, and I'm gonna get you together, okay? Does your arm feel any better?"

"A little." Kofi was trying to get a glimpse of Josh, but too many people were in the way. "I have a heart murmur," Jericho heard Kofi whisper to Bill.

"That's something we need to know, son. Thank you. Now we need to contact your parents."

"They're not home," Kofi said quietly.

"Mac, bring the stretcher—this one is stable and ready to transport," Bill said.

"What about Josh?" Kofi asked tearfully as they carried him away. No one answered.

"I'm going to follow Kofi's ambulance to the hospital," Dana whispered to Jericho, who barely acknowledged her. She hurried off into the darkness.

The paramedics, talking on their transmitters to the hospital Jericho assumed, placed an IV in Josh's arm. Another medic brought a board to strap him on. The two men who worked on Josh looked grim but determined in the greenish light that had been brought to help them see. Josh, still motionless except for the movements of the men who were trying to get him to breathe, looked so cold and helpless as he lay there in the mud. Jericho continued to sit by his cousin, numb, afraid to think beyond this moment. "Move out of the way now, son, so we can turn him over," they told Jericho.

"Here, let me help," he offered, but the paramedics waved him off.

Jericho had never been so afraid in his life. The mud under Josh made a soft sucking noise as they gently lifted the left side of Josh's body. It was stained a deep, dark red. Jericho looked on in horror. Josh had not fallen on the soft mats, but had managed to hit his head on a large rock just outside the mattress pit. His shirt, no longer pink on the back, but a sickening dark brown, was cut from his body. It was then that Jericho saw the wound. At the back of Josh's skull was a jagged tear, open and oozing bright blood.

Jericho ran to the side of the yard and vomited.

More sirens seared the night. A couple of fire trucks arrived, another ambulance, and several police cars. Jericho looked up and saw his father approaching, his face tenser than Jericho had ever seen. His relief was visible when he spotted Jericho, who ran over to him, hugged him tightly, and let the tears fall.

"We got the call a few minutes ago. I was on the other side of town, but when I heard there was an incident at the warehouse, I knew you and Joshua were involved and I rushed over." Jericho could not stop sobbing. "Jericho, what happened, son? Are you all right? You're freezing!" He took off his jacket and gave it to Jericho, who put it on quickly. He had forgotten how cold he was.

"Dad, it's Josh. He's hurt bad—real bad." Jericho would not let himself think anything worse.

Jericho's father sniffed the air. "You been drinking, son?"

"Yeah, Dad, a little," Jericho admitted. A little didn't begin to cover it, he thought.

"Tell me what happened," his father said quietly.

Between gulps for breath Jericho told him about the night's events. "Pledging was almost over. All of us had done the Leap of Faith except Josh."

"The Leap of Faith?" his father asked with confusion.

"We had to jump out of that window," Jericho confessed, pointing in that general direction. He couldn't bring himself to look at it. "They called it the Leap of Faith, and it was pretty easy, I guess. Kofi got mad at Eddie and threw him out the window because he was messin' with Dana, and he kept threatening us with that stupid gun, and . . ."

"A gun? A gun?" His father looked incredulous as he angrily grabbed Jericho's arm. "What gun?" he asked sharply.

Jericho sighed. "Nobody got shot, Dad. It was part of the ceremony. It wasn't loaded. It was just a trust thing, and Eddie's kinda crazy anyway."

"Are *you* crazy?" his father shouted. "Where is this gun now?"

"I guess Eddie still has it." Jericho bowed his head. He couldn't look his father in the eye.

"So did Joshua get shot?" his father asked, his voice quaking with anger and fear.

"No," Jericho answered weakly. "Kofi jumped out of the window just before me, and I think he broke his arm. Then I jumped next, and even though I was scared, I did it." He knew he was babbling. Again, guilt and fear began to envelop Jericho. "Everything happened so fast. I looked up, I saw Josh up there, lookin' like he could fly, and then he fell. He landed on his head, Dad. He landed right on his head." Jericho began to cry.

His father pulled him close again, then told him, "I have to go check on Joshua. Are you going to be all right for now?"

"Yeah, I'm fine." He sniffed loudly. "Go help them make Josh be okay. Please, Dad. Please, make everything be all right. Do *something*," Jericho pleaded.

"Officer Prescott, we need you down here, sir," one of the paramedics called. His father gave Jericho another quick hug, then ran down to help.

Jericho sat on the wet grass, clutching his father's jacket to him, praying to the dark sky that everything would turn out all right, that when the sun rose in the morning, Josh would show up at his door, laughing and joking about his father or November or Mr. Boston. But Jericho was afraid that nothing would ever be the same again.

JOSH WAS TRANSPORTED TO THE HOSPITAL IN a blaze of sirens and speed. The rest of the Warriors of Distinction sat in the warehouse, in a daze. Most of the former pledges had removed their wet pink T-shirts and changed to the dry clothes they had brought in their gym bags. The pledge masters looked pale and shaken. Several of them were crying openly. On a table in the back of the room the fifteen unopened boxes of coveted black silk jackets sat untouched.

"I don't know what to do," Luis whispered to Jericho. "I'm so scared."

"Me too, man. But he'll be all right. He just has to be." But Jericho didn't believe his own words.

"Did you *see* him?" Cleveland asked them both as they whispered together. "He didn't look real, man. He looked . . . he looked . . ."

"Don't say it!" Jericho cut him off angrily. "Don't you dare say it!"

Police officers went from group to group, talking to them and asking them questions. Jericho thought about how stupid their descriptions of the pledge activities would sound.

Mr. Zucker, the principal, rushed in. His hair was uncombed, and he had on his pajama top and a pair of blue jeans. Mr. Culligan arrived shortly after that, looking confused and guilty, Jericho thought. He and Mr. Zucker stood off to one side, having what looked to be an angry and animated conversation.

Jericho was glad his father was there to handle all the details. Officer Prescott chased out a reporter who arrived a few minutes after everyone got back inside, and he organized the boys into groups so that their parents could be called. Jericho wondered grimly if his father had been the one to call Uncle Brock and Aunt Marlene to tell them about Josh. There was still no word on his condition.

A police officer walked over to Dana, Luis, Cleveland, and Rudy. "May I ask you a few questions?" he said. Jericho sat listlessly in a chair close by. He didn't want to talk to the police. He just wanted to hide in a hole somewhere and make all of this go away.

Cleveland sighed. "I didn't see nothin'," he told the officer.

The officer didn't seem to care. "That's fine," he said. "We're just trying to establish a chain of events here. May I have your names, please?"

"Luis Morales."

"Cleveland Wilson."

"Dana Wolfe."

"Rudy Amadour."

"The four of you were pledges?" the officer asked.

"Yeah," Cleveland said, answering for them.

"They're letting girls in now?" the officer asked with surprise. "When I was in the Warriors . . ." He stopped himself and continued his questions. "What were you doing just before the incident occurred?" the officer asked.

"We were waiting for them to finish the last activity," Luis explained.

"Which was?" the officer queried.

"The Leap of Faith."

The officer looked as if he was about to ask another question, but Dana told him, "Look, it was dark and cold, Josh jumped, and he hit his head when he fell. It was all just a terrible accident."

The officer scribbled notes in his book. "When we did the Leap of Faith," he explained, "it was just jumping off a chair with a blindfold on. When did the Leap of Faith get to be a jump from a second-story window?"

Jericho watched as Rudy shrugged. Then he said, "You'll have to ask the seniors about that."

"What else did they make you do?" the officer asked.

Rudy hesitated and looked at his friends. "Nothing bad—just silly stuff. It's about faith and trust and belief in yourself."

"That's all?" the policeman asked.

"That's all," Rudy answered firmly.

The policeman looked at them, but did not pursue the matter. Jericho didn't think the cop believed much of what they were saying, and probably wanted to ask more, but he stopped then. "Thank you," he said. "I hope your friend pulls through. We'll need to talk some more later—maybe tomorrow."

The policeman moved to another table to talk to another group of boys. Jericho wondered if the stories that each boy told would match the others. He doubted it.

Parents started to arrive, and a few more reporters showed up. The same unanswered questions kept being repeated. A parent yelled out, "What's going on here? What happened tonight? We want some answers!" Anger and agitation filled the room.

Mr. Zucker and Mr. Culligan moved to the center of the room. Mr. Culligan, instead of looking smooth and in control as he usually did, looked distracted and frightened. Mr. Zucker spoke first. His face was rosy pink and puffy—it looked a little like the salmon that Geneva had fixed for dinner last week, Jericho thought.

"These are the facts as we know them," Mr. Zucker began. He adjusted the portable microphone that had been hastily set up. "At approximately eleven thirty P.M., after almost successfully completing pledge activities for the Warriors of Distinction service club, junior student Joshua Prescott fell from a second-story window of the abandoned house behind this warehouse. His fall, or jump—we're not quite sure yet—was apparently the last task of pledge week activities. He has been transported to Mercy Hospital. His condition at this time is unknown."

272

He paused to wait for the onslaught of questions.

"What kind of club forces a child to jump out of a window?" one father demanded angrily.

"Why weren't they supervised?" several other parents wanted to know.

"I want to know why the pledges were outside in this cold, winter weather with just T-shirts on! What were they doing?" a mother asked vehemently.

"I smell liquor on my boy's breath!" a father shouted to the principal. "What's up with that?"

"Who runs this stupid thing anyway? He ought to be arrested for negligence!" another demanded.

Mr. Culligan spoke quietly, his voice barely a croak. "My name is Richard Culligan and I am the sponsor of the Warriors of Distinction club. I've met most of you in person or through the letters we have sent as part of the pledging process. I assure you that what happened tonight was a terrible, tragic accident. We will be conducting a full investigation." Jericho noticed that Mr. Culligan's voice was quivering.

"So did you see it happen?" another parent asked. "Why in heaven's name didn't you stop them? Why did you let them jump out of a second-story window?"

Mr. Culligan hesitated. "I did not see the incident," he replied quietly.

"What do you mean, you 'did not see the incident'? Where were you?" the parent pressured him, his face almost purple with rage.

Mr. Culligan cleared his throat. "I . . . I wasn't here. I was back at school, getting things ready for the party," he admitted. He looked pale and drained, as if he had been sucked dry. His eyes darted everywhere except at the parents who were demanding answers.

"You mean our children are outside in the freezing cold, risking their lives to be in this stupid club, and you weren't even out there with them? This is an outrage!" the parent screamed.

"The Warriors of Distinction have been an important part of this school and the city for over fifty years," Mr. Culligan tried to explain. "The boys who run the pledge activities every night are responsible seniors who know exactly what to do."

"My name is Johnny Madison and my boy is a senior, and he didn't know what to do!" shouted Mad Madison's father. Madison sat next to his dad, looking more like a little boy than an intimidating pledge master. "I bet there's nothing in your pledge book that says what to do when a kid falls two stories out of a building!" his father added angrily.

"I wasn't aware of every single pledge activity," Mr. Culligan admitted. "I trusted the seniors," he said as an afterthought.

"So that's supposed to make it okay?" A mother burst out as though exploding with anger.

Mr. Culligan added weakly, "We've never had a problem before."

"Well, now you do!" she shouted.

Mr. Culligan bowed his head and looked at the floor.

Another mother jumped out of her seat and spoke. "My son wouldn't tell me anything that happened when he got home each night. He mumbled something about some 'code of silence.' I want answers. I want to know what other nasty little secrets this club is hiding."

"They are hiding nothing," Mr. Zucker replied, stepping up to the microphone. "What the boys do, uh, did, up to this point, was all good, clean fun—character-building activities that teach responsibility and integrity."

"What part of their character was built tonight?" a father asked, his deep voice roaring from the back of the room.

It was Mr. Zucker's turn to say nothing.

Jericho noticed that Mr. Zucker never really answered any of the parents' questions. And he wondered whether it was integrity or responsibility he learned from standing in a Dumpster or drinking till he puked or being led around a room like a dog.

The back door opened and Geneva and the boys came in. Todd and Rory, dressed in pajamas under their coats, ran to Jericho, their eyes wide, and hugged him. Geneva gave Jericho a strange look, then she smiled at him with a look of soft love. He was surprised at how glad he was to see her. He returned her genuine smile. Geneva then hurried over to her husband and whispered something to him. Jericho watched his father's face crumple. And then he knew. Josh was dead.

JERICHO COULDN'T BREATHE. HE FELT LIKE HE was watching a terrible, grainy, slow-motion movie, and that he was trapped inside the screen—unable to escape from what was about to be said, unable to change the realities of the plot. He watched his father walk to a corner, take out his cell phone, and make a call. Jericho could not hear the words, but he could tell by the sorrowful expression on his father's face that the world had caved in.

His father then went over to Mr. Zucker and Mr. Culligan. They talked quietly and solemnly, their faces grim and ashen. Then slowly, very slowly, his father walked to the microphone. Jericho couldn't make this horrible movie stop. He couldn't turn it off to a channel with championship wrestling or baseball or even a love story.

"May I have your attention, please?" Jericho's father

said quietly. His voice was cracked and raspy. "I have something to share with all of you."

Jericho could not bear to hear the words, could not let this awful movie run to its conclusion. He jumped from his chair, knocking it over, and screamed, "Noooooooooo! I won't let you say it! I won't let you say it!" as he ran from the warehouse, out of the door, and into the dark parking lot. Light snow had begun to fall, but Jericho didn't notice. He screamed and screamed and screamed.

Then Jericho felt someone's arms around him. It was his father. He held him until the screaming subsided. "He's gone, Jericho," his father said gently.

"No! Don't say it! If you don't say it, he still has a chance!" Jericho begged, sobbing.

"I can't change what's happened, Jericho. I can only try to make this easier for you—for all of us. I can't even imagine what Brock must be going through." It was then that Jericho realized that his father was also weeping.

"He's not just my cousin, Dad—he's like my brother, my very best friend! We've been together since birth!"

"I know, baby boy. This has gotta be so hard for you."

"Hard? It's impossible!" Jericho broke away from his father's grasp and paced angrily on the sidewalk in front of the warehouse. "It just can't be true! I won't let it be true. Why can't they fix him? What's the use of having doctors and hospitals if they can't fix one stupid, fuzzy-headed kid?"

"They tried, Jericho, but it was too late. He was already gone when he got to the hospital," his father told him.

"Gone? What's that supposed to mean?"

His father placed his hand on Jericho's shoulder. "It is so hard to fit all of this into our minds—it just doesn't want to go there."

"Gone! Gone! I can't deal with it. I won't!" Jericho jerked his shoulder away from his father.

"Kofi needs you now, Jericho."

Jericho stopped pacing. He had almost forgotten about Kofi. "What about Kofi? Is he okay?" he asked. "Please tell me *he's* all right. I couldn't take any more bad news tonight."

"He'll be fine," his father assured him. "His parents have been located and they're with him."

"Does he know about . . . Josh?" Jericho asked.

"I don't know—we only just found out. Would you like to go to the hospital to see him?"

"Yeah, Dad, I would. Thanks." Everything still felt completely unreal. He realized he was waiting for someone to tell him it was all a horrible mistake.

"What about Uncle Brock and Aunt Marlene?" Jericho felt a sharp stab in his own chest at the thought of Josh's parents dealing with such pain.

"They know." Jericho's dad sighed. "It's the phone call that all parents dread—and all policemen dread making. I never imagined that I'd ever have to be the one to call my brother and tell him that his precious boy is dead." He choked back more tears.

"We gotta go see them, Dad."

"We will—we will." He touched Jericho on the hand. "You don't know how relieved I was when I got here and saw you standing there—alive and well. Makes me feel so

guilty because Brock won't get to feel that joy and relief—
ever again."

Geneva and the boys walked out of the warehouse then.
Geneva went to Jericho, held out her arms, and hugged
him close. It was the first time she had ever done that,
Jericho realized as he buried himself in her comforting
brown coat.

"Mr. Zucker made the announcement," she said.
"Everyone in there is pretty upset. How are you doing,
Jericho?"

"I want it to be yesterday," he said honestly.

"If only it could be so," she answered softly. She pulled
a couple of tissues from her purse and handed them to
him.

Jericho blew his nose, then looked at Todd and Rory,
who stood quietly, their eyes large and frightened. "It's
gonna be okay, you little scrubs," he said to them in what
he hoped was a reassuring voice. "Go on home with
Geneva and get some sleep, okay? I'm going with Dad to
check on Kofi and then I'll be home." He scooped them
into a hug, then said, "Now, scoot!" He thanked Geneva as
she left with the boys.

"You ready, son?" his dad asked. "We'll get your car in
the morning. You want to go back inside to talk to your
friends first?"

"Not now, Dad. I have a feeling there's a whole lot of
talking that's gonna come after this."

"You're right. There are lots of questions that must be
answered."

"About the Warriors of Distinction?"

"And their pledging activities," his father added.

"Some of it was pretty bad, Dad," Jericho said quietly as they walked to the patrol car.

His father looked at him and asked, "Was it hazing, Jericho?"

"I'm not exactly sure what hazing is, Dad. We just did stuff."

"Dangerous stuff?"

"Not really. Mostly stupid things."

"Were they character-building activities, like Mr. Zucker said?" his father asked as they walked to the car.

"The daytime stuff was pretty straight—like helping teachers and janitors. But some of the nighttime things made me feel uncomfortable."

"Like what?" his father asked.

"Dog collars, paddlings, toilet swirlies—stuff like that." Jericho wasn't sure if he was saying too much, but right now he didn't really care. Remembering it all didn't make him feel proud—he felt ill. He kept thinking back to the phrase that Mr. Redstone had used—feeling 'less than yourself.' That's the way he felt right now.

"Did you know that hazing is illegal in the state of Ohio?" his father asked as they got close to the police cruiser.

"Yeah, but so is parking without putting money in the meter. People still do it."

"It's not exactly the same thing," his father replied gently.

"I guess."

"Right now, Joshua's death seems to be directly related

to hazing activities. You know there will be serious conse-
quences."

"Please don't say the word 'death' out loud," Jericho
pleaded. "It chokes me—I can't stand it." Jericho took
deep, heavy breaths of the wet night air.

His father unlocked the cruiser. "Some words won't go
away, Jericho."

"I'm scared, Dad," Jericho admitted.

"I know, son. I am too. But I'm right here with you."

THE FIRST PEOPLE THEY SAW WHEN THEY GOT to the hospital were Josh's parents. Brock and Cedric met each other's eyes, then Brock collapsed into his brother's arms. Jericho tried to approach his Aunt Marlene, but she would not be touched. She sat in a chair in the hallway of the hospital, eyes bleary with tears, her arms crossed tightly in front of her as if to ward off the reality and finality of what had happened. Jericho sat on the floor in front of her chair.

"It had to hurt," she mumbled. "It had to hurt so bad! My baby boy shouldn't have had to suffer like that!" She put her face in her hands and sobbed. Her shoulders heaved. Jericho wanted to say something to make her feel better, but he didn't know what. So he wept with her.

"How could this be?" Brock asked his brother, pulling away from him. But Jericho could tell he didn't really expect an answer. It was one of those questions that, even if you asked all day, heaven would not send down an answer. "I was so proud of him, Cedric, so very proud." He broke down in tears.

"I know that, Brock. Josh knows it too. He's watching you now, trying to help you through this. Make him proud of you as well." Cedric touched his brother on the shoulder.

"This should *not* have happened—could not have happened," Brock said to the ceilings and walls. He paced up and down the hospital hallway. Finally he turned to Jericho. "What went wrong, Jericho? I just don't understand."

Jericho pushed himself up off the floor and looked at his uncle. "It was the Leap of Faith. We all jumped, Uncle Brock, but it seemed like Josh tried to fly. He was happy, having fun, in a really mellow mood. It shouldn't have happened, but it did. It was a horrible, horrible accident." Jericho hung his head.

"When we did the Leap of Faith, we jumped from a chair, Jericho," Uncle Brock said, his voice choking with grief. "There was *never* any danger involved."

"Nobody thought . . ." Jericho stopped, unable to put his jumbled thoughts into words.

"It's clear no one was thinking," Uncle Brock said angrily. "Where were the pledge masters, Jericho?"

"On the ground, waiting for everybody to finish the jump. Josh was the last one."

"And where was Mr. Culligan?"

"He . . . he wasn't there." Jericho wasn't sure if he saw anger or sorrow in his uncle's eyes. Probably both.

His uncle started crying once more. "At least you were

there with him, Jericho," he said finally. "There's so much more I need to know, but right now, my brain is full of explosions."

Jericho knew exactly what he meant. His head felt full and his heart felt empty. He said weakly, "I'm so sorry, Uncle Brock."

"It wasn't your fault, Jericho. Joshua would have been the first to tell you that," his uncle whispered. Tears streaming down his face, he walked over to his wife and gently took her arm. "C'mon, Marlene. We have to go home now," he told her softly.

"I can't leave my baby here," she moaned. She grasped the arms of the chair and refused to get up.

"He's not here, sweetheart. He's in a better place—he's with God."

Marlene sat trembling for several minutes. Finally she nodded and he took her hand. They walked slowly down the hall together, leaning on each other for support.

Jericho took a deep breath as he watched them leave. He wiped his nose, then said to his father, "Can we go find Kofi, Dad?" They went to the information desk and found his room. Kofi's parents, looking confused and distressed, paced in the hall outside his room.

"How is Kofi?" Jericho asked.

Kofi's mother had been crying. "You're Jericho, right? Kofi talks about you all the time." She took out a tissue and blew her nose.

"The doctor said he'll be all right," Kofi's father told Jericho. "He has a broken arm, but they're going to keep him overnight to keep an eye on him."

Kofi's mother added, "They said he had a heart condition." She shook her head. "You know, the doctors told me they heard something unusual in his heartbeat when he was just a baby. I figured he'd outgrown it." Jericho didn't know how to respond. "They also told us he was really lucky not to have had something worse happen because of all the physical activity and the alcohol." She continued to pace restlessly in the corridor.

"Jericho, how much alcohol?" his father asked.

"A lot, Dad. It got easier with every drink." He looked up at the bright, fluorescent hospital lights. "I'll tell you everything when we get home. Everything." Jericho felt overwhelmed. "May I go in and see him?" he asked Kofi's parents.

"Sure," Kofi's mother replied, "but I think he's sleeping now. And Jericho," she added, "things are gonna change at our place. When Kofi gets out of the hospital, I want you to stop by sometime. I used to be a pretty good cook— maybe I'll throw together some burgers or something."

"Yeah, I'd like that," Jericho answered quietly.

Kofi's mother began to pace again, then she stopped and looked at Jericho. "I coulda lost my boy tonight. I'm gonna do right by him, you hear?"

Jericho wasn't sure what to say, so he asked, "Can I see him now?"

Kofi's father, tall and skinny like his son, put his arm around his wife and nodded. He said. "Go on in. He already has one friend in there with him. We'll be right here if you need us."

Jericho asked his father to wait for him, then he opened the heavy hospital room door. The lights were dim and Kofi lay in the bed, an IV running into one arm, plastic tubing running oxygen into his nose, and a heart monitor beeping faintly in the background. His right arm was wrapped in a huge white cast. Sleeping soundly, he looked more pale, more slender, than usual. Dana sat in a chair next to him.

"Hi, Dana," Jericho said quietly. "How're you handling this?"

"Oh, Jericho, what are we gonna do? How will we make it without Josh?"

"How'd you find out?"

"I saw Josh's parents in the hall a little while ago. Jericho, this is like some kind of nightmare!"

Jericho just shook his head. It felt like the room was closing in on him and swallowing him up. He knew he wouldn't be able to stay much longer. "Does Kofi know?" he asked finally.

"I told him a few minutes ago. He was so upset that they had to give him a sedative."

Jericho touched Kofi's cool, slim hand, then turned to leave the room. "I gotta get out of here. Take care of him, Dana."

"Fiercely," she told him. "Jericho?" she called as he reached the door.

"Yeah?" He turned to face her.

"It wasn't worth it."

"I know." He left the room and took several deep breaths, but even the air in the hall was suffocating. He gave Kofi's mother a quick hug and nodded to Kofi's dad. He then turned to his own father. "Can we go, Dad?" he asked.

"Sure, son. Let's go home." Large heavy flakes of snow began to blanket the city as they drove.

As soon as he got home, even though it was almost five o'clock in the morning, Jericho called Arielle. She answered on the first ring. He could tell she had been crying.

"Are you okay?" she asked. Jericho thought she sounded really concerned.

"I didn't get hurt, if that's what you mean," he told her, "but I don't think I'm gonna be okay for a long time." He sighed. "Have you talked to November?"

"She's right here," Arielle said. "Her mother brought her to my house right after they got the news. She said November could stay the rest of the night."

"How's she doing?" Jericho asked.

"Not good. Her voice is almost gone from screaming and crying. She was hysterical for a while, but my mother and her mother were pretty cool and helped to calm her down."

"Can I talk to her?" Jericho asked.

"She finally fell asleep. Let her get some rest. The next few days aren't gonna be easy."

"For real. My dad said there's going to be a police investigation, and a school board investigation too. Plus there's already talk about lawsuits. Looks like the Warriors of Distinction are in big trouble—probably gone for good."

"I heard all the Warriors—even the pledges—are going to be brought to the police station and questioned, maybe even arrested," Arielle told him. "I have a feeling this is going to blow up into a real mess. You've got some serious trouble ahead. Are you going to be able to handle this?"

"I guess I have to. I know I can if I've got you with me," he told her earnestly. He suddenly felt dizzy with emotion—Josh's death, his own fear, anger, guilt, grief, and lack of sleep swirled together in his mind and he blurted out, "I think I love you, Arielle." He gulped. What had he said? The words somehow slipped right out. He waited for her response. At this moment he needed to hear her soft, sweet voice tell him he was loved.

Arielle was strangely silent on the other end of the line. "I don't think this is the right time for talk like that," she said slowly.

Jericho felt suddenly mortified. He wished he could suck the words back in. "I'm sorry. It's just I, uh, I'm so filled up with all these heavy feelings and stuff, I guess I said too much." He felt like kicking himself.

"I know this is a hard time for you," she replied. She paused for a moment, then said, "But I think maybe we better not see so much of each other. You need time to deal with the grief, and my friends need me now." She offered no other explanation.

What? Jericho couldn't believe what he was hearing. She was dumping him? Now, when he needed her most? "I don't understand, Arielle," he said helplessly.

"It was fun while it lasted, Jericho, but it's gotten too crazy. I don't think you should call me for a while, okay? I'm sure you understand." She hung up the phone.

Jericho sat there, stunned. He felt as if he were falling from that window once more, only this time, there was no ground below to catch him.

THE NEXT FEW DAYS SEEMED TO MOVE LIKE mud. Even Jericho's arms and legs felt heavy and sluggish, unable to work properly. His thoughts, thick and confused, swirled around the void where Josh should be. He knew that Josh was gone forever, but the reality of it kept slipping through his fingers like wet sand. He couldn't sleep. He ate very little.

Nothing was as it should have been. Instead of the party on Saturday night to celebrate their membership in the Warriors of Distinction, a memorial service for Josh was held in the school auditorium. Instead of strutting proudly to school on Monday morning wearing their new Warrior jackets, Jericho and his friends sadly wore their best church clothes to attend Josh's funeral. Classes had been cancelled for the day so that students could attend. And instead of being comforted by Arielle's warmth and smiles, Jericho drifted through all of it alone.

Jericho's mother had flown in from Alaska to be with them for the day of the funeral. He buried himself in her arms. Her smile made him remember when he and Josh were little—picnics, dressing up for Halloween, swimming lessons, Little League baseball games, all with his mom and Aunt Marlene making sure they were safe and happy. *Where was safe and happy now?*

The weather turned colder and a freezing rain turned to snow, which fell like a soft blanket over all the raw pain. But Jericho couldn't stop the memories. He remembered building snowmen with Josh when they were seven, snowball fights when they were ten, sledding at French Park just last year. The city looked frosty and full of sparkles, but Jericho's thoughts were dark and muddy.

It was the little things that Jericho would remember about the day of Josh's funeral. He couldn't remember one word of what the minister had said, but he would never forget the tilt of the single yellow lily that had been sent by Mr. Boston, the cool metallic feeling of the handle of the casket as he helped as a pallbearer at the end of the ceremony, or the fluttering of the little purple flag that the funeral directors placed on his father's car as they headed for the cemetery. He would never forget the mask of grief and disbelief that now seemed a permanent part of his uncle's face, or the unending silent tears of his Aunt Marlene. And he'd never forget the expressions of surprise, fear, and humility on the faces of his friends, many of whom looked at death up close for the first time.

November sat between Arielle and Dana, who each grasped one of her hands and held her when she was wracked with dry, heaving sobs. Her eyes were swollen and red. Jericho caught Arielle's eye once, but she looked at him as if he were a stranger. Kofi was there, but Jericho wondered if he was really up to it—he looked awfully pale and weak as he stood next to the casket as a pallbearer, his arm in a sling. Eric Bell, who also had been asked to be a pallbearer, rolled with dignity as an honor guard behind the casket as it was carried out of the church.

All of the Warriors of Distinction except for Eddie Mahoney attended the funeral, but they did not sit together as a group and they didn't wear their jackets. Most of them looked scared, Jericho thought. No decision had been made yet as to what would happen to the club. None of them had been asked to be pallbearers.

Jericho was surprised at the number of teachers who attended—Mr. Boston, Miss Hathaway, Mr. Zucker, Mr. Tambori, even Mr. Redstone was there. Mr. Culligan was noticeably absent. Many of them hugged Jericho after the service.

When it was all over—the last of the flowers placed at the snowy gravesite, the last of the tears shed for the day—Jericho and his friends gathered at Josh's house, the only place they knew to go. It was as if they needed to be close to his spirit.

Marlene, shaken and weepy, welcomed the young people. Miscellaneous sofa cushions and chairs filled the living room, which was warm and cozy from the roaring fire in the fireplace.

Dana brought November and Kofi. Luis, Rudy, Ram, and Cleveland from the pledge group arrived, but Rick and

Madison were the only old Warriors who showed up. Even Eric Bell rolled into the room—Jericho had made sure that he'd been invited. Jericho came alone. Arielle, though she had been asked, chose not to come. Josh's parents disappeared upstairs.

"So what do we do now?" Jericho asked the subdued group of young people.

"We cry some more," November said sadly.

"Then what?" Dana wondered.

"We try to see who's to blame," sighed Kofi. His voice could be barely heard.

"Mr. Culligan's been arrested," Jericho informed them. "My dad told me."

"I heard he got fired, too," Rudy offered.

"Yeah, but Mr. Culligan didn't make Josh fall," Madison reasoned.

"No, you and the rest of the seniors get to take the blame for that! " Cleveland declared fiercely.

Madison hung his head. "I know. I'm not tryin' to hide from responsibility. They may be pickin' me up next."

Rick reported, "We're all gonna be questioned in the next few days—pledge masters and pledges, too." Jericho closed his eyes.

"Is there still going to *be* a club?" Eric asked. "I heard they were going to shut it down."

"I guess that's out of our hands—the school board meets with the police tomorrow," Kofi told him.

"Eddie got arrested too," Rick announced.

"Eddie's got some serious issues," Dana replied tersely.

Madison sighed. "Yeah, I know."

"He's been arrested for illegal possession of a firearm, threatening bodily harm, and a couple of other charges as well," Rick told them.

"Eddie is also going to be charged with several counts of assault," Dana said quietly. "My parents have talked to the police about what he did to me."

"Good, 'cause I was gonna have to kick his butt," Kofi said with more energy than he'd shown all day. "Good thing I only got one good arm!" He smiled slightly and held on to Dana with his good hand.

"What was the deal with the gun?" November asked angrily.

Rick lifted his head from his hands. His face looked ragged and worn. "We'd never included a gun in the pledge stuff before. Eddie found it and thought it would be a good addition," he admitted. "It was just to scare you. There were never even any bullets."

"What an idiot!" Dana snapped.

"What happened to it?" Ram asked.

"My dad says the police have it," Jericho told the group. "It's evidence for a criminal investigation."

"Why'd you let Eddie get away with all that stuff?" Kofi asked angrily. "There's something seriously wrong with that dude!"

Rick and Madison had no reply.

"Are you sorry you pledged, Jericho?" Eric asked quietly.

"How was I supposed to know this would happen?" he answered sadly. "It seemed like such a good idea at the time."

Eric looked down at his wheelchair. "That's the same

thing I thought when I fell and broke my back."

"What about you, Dana?" Madison asked. "Are you sorry you tried to pledge?"

"I didn't *try* to pledge, Madison. I *did* pledge. I succeeded in every single task, in spite of Eddie. I'm glad I proved I could do it." Then she admitted, "But I'd erase it all if it would bring Josh back."

"How can he be dead?" Jericho whispered. The crackling of the fire in the fireplace was the only sound. "Who's to blame?" he asked the silent room.

"Josh's death is nobody's fault, really . . . ," Rick started to say. But November interrupted him.

"That's a lie! It's the Warriors fault!" she shouted angrily, standing up and rushing over to where Rick sat. Then she sat down again as the enormity of it all seemed to hit her once more. She mumbled through more tears, "Stupid club with their stupid rules and shirts and jackets and parties." Rick had no answer.

"They've been doing this for fifty years. It was supposed to be tough, but fun—just a buncha dudes foolin' around and gettin' to know each other," Madison tried to explain.

"Josh isn't laughing," Jericho replied quietly. The room was silent once again. The only sound that could be heard was November's soft sobbing.

"I could be dead too," Kofi said quietly. "Maybe I should be. I feel so, you know, like guilty." He hung his head.

Jericho nodded his head in agreement. "I know what you're talkin' about. It's like I feel like I shouldn't be able to see the sky or hear a dog bark—you see what I'm sayin'? It's not fair that I can do that and Josh can't." He was not afraid to weep in front of them.

November took Jericho's hand and gave it a squeeze of encouragement. "I think Josh would have enjoyed sittin' in on this little meeting," she said in a small voice.

"He would have made jokes about how puffy your eyes look, November," Jericho told her. She sniffed and smiled in spite of herself.

"And how Jericho looks like a lost teddy bear without him," Eric said.

Kofi added, "Josh would have been amazed at all the attention he's getting."

"He woulda loved it—he sure liked attention." Jericho finally smiled a little.

"I wonder," November mused, "what would he have to say about the Warriors of Distinction now?"

Eric responded quietly. "He would have said that there's nothing very distinguished about death." The mood went somber once more.

Into the silence that followed November whispered plaintively, "I miss Josh."

There was nothing else to say.

"Are you coming to school tomorrow?" Kofi finally asked Jericho.

Jericho sighed. "I guess. It will be hard, though."

"I'll be there," Dana said. Most of the others also agreed to show up.

"Mr. Zucker said he would have a moment of silence in

the morning so that everyone could remember Josh," November said.

"Is that all he gets? A moment?" Jericho asked outraged. "Seems like he oughta get a band concert or a choir of screamers—something more than silence!"

Kofi said softly, "Maybe the silence is so everyone can think quietly—private thoughts, you know."

Jericho's grief and anger seemed to be all mixed up inside him. "Silence is like, you know, nothing. Just air," he said, shaking his head. "Nothing just isn't enough. Josh deserves shout outs, not silence."

"Did Josh die for nothing?" November finally asked.

"It had to mean something," Cleveland whispered.

"Then what was it?" November wanted to know.

No one had an answer. The question hung in the air like smoke.

Jericho took Zora out of the trumpet case then, and slowly began to play. The tones, sweet and mellow, floated above the young people in the room. He began with soft, clear notes, bright like jewels, followed by a series of trills that swelled with power. He played the loss of yesterday and tomorrow, of friendship and love. He remembered childhood laughter as he played, and teenage troubles as well. One series of notes, high and delicate, sang of a sweet moonlight kiss gone sour; another line of music rippled with regret over opportunities forever lost.

And Jericho played fierce, sharp combinations he'd never even conceived of before, giving voice to his anger and frustration at death. Josh, his quick wit, and his swift, final leap into forever, exploded from Jericho's trumpet in notes that erupted hot like painted steam. The tones from the trumpet replaced his tears and captured his grief. He then slowed down and played a sweet, gentle melody that made him remember Josh's laughter and spirit. The music flowed quietly to just a whisper. It ended as Josh did, in silence.

Turn the page for a peek at the next book in the Jericho Trilogy, *November Blues*.

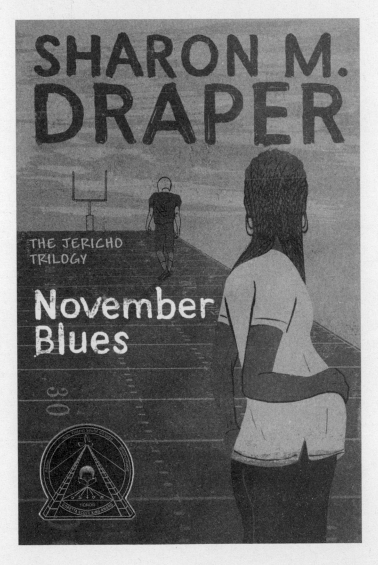

NOVEMBER NELSON LURCHED TO THE bathroom, feeling faint and not quite in control of her suddenly unsteady legs. She touched her forehead and found it warm and glazed with sweat. Sinking down on the soft blue rug in front of the toilet, she was grateful for the momentary stability of the floor. But her head continued to spin, and her stomach churned. She lifted the toilet lid, gazed into the water, and wished she could disappear into its depths. Her breath became more shallow, and her nausea more intense. Finally, uncontrollably, and forcefully, all her distress erupted and she lost her lunch in heaves and waves of vomiting. Pepperoni pizza.

She flushed the toilet several times as she sat on the floor waiting to feel normal again. Finally she stood up shakily, gargled with peppermint mouth-wash, and peered at herself in the mirror.

"You look like a hot mess," she whispered to her reflection. Her skin, instead of its usual coppery brown, looked gray and mottled. She hadn't combed her hair all day, so it was a halo of tangles.

November knew her mother would be home soon and would be angry to find out she'd skipped school. She didn't care. Her thoughts were focused on the package in her backpack. Even though she knew the house was empty, she made sure the bathroom door was locked. She dug the little purple and pink box out of her book bag and placed it on the sink. It seemed out of place in her mother's perfectly coordinated powder blue bathroom.

With trembling hands she unwrapped the plastic and opened the box. She read the directions carefully. She looked out of the small bathroom window and watched the last of the early spring snow melting on the grass. Everything looked the same, but she knew in her heart that it was all different now.

November finally turned back to the little white tube in the box and followed the instructions, which were written, she noticed, in Spanish and French as well. Three minutes later the indicator silently screamed the news that she already suspected. She was pregnant.

"I BROUGHT YOUR HOMEWORK, GIRL," Dana announced as she bounded through the front door. "Whew! It's cold out there. Calendar says spring, but the weather doesn't seem to know that." She shivered and tossed her coat on the sofa.

"Thanks," said November quietly. "Did I miss much?"

"Same old junk. Busywork. The chemistry might kick your butt, but everything else is pretty easy. You got anything to eat? I just left the library and I'm starved."

The thought of food made November instantly queasy, but she heated up a bowl of her mother's spaghetti in the microwave for Dana. "Dig in," November said as she fished for a spoon in the silverware drawer and slid the bowl across the table.

"Aren't you gonna eat?" asked Dana. "Your mom makes the best pasta in the world!"

"I already ate," November lied. She picked at a crumb on the table.

"What's wrong, November?" her friend asked, cocking her head.

"Nothing. Just thinking about Josh, I guess."

"Still hurts deep, doesn't it?" Dana said, reaching for November's arm.

"You don't know the half of it," replied November.

"Well, let's see what we can do to make you feel better. You ever heard of a brush and comb?" Dana teased.

November chuckled and ran her hands through her hair. "I didn't feel like messing with it today. I stayed in bed and watched game shows and soap operas. Talk about depressing!"

Dana finished her spaghetti, put her bowl in the sink, and said, "Let me braid your hair for you. That'll make you feel better."

November grinned, went to get her hair stuff from her bedroom, and returned to sit on a pillow in front of the sofa. "You're gonna need magic fingers," she said, handing Dana a comb.

Dana turned on the CD player, and the two girls sat in silence in the living room, while Dana deftly combed November's hair. November could feel some of the tension leave her back and neck as her friend worked.

"Josh used to like your hair braided, remember? He'd call you his African queen," Dana said softly.

"Yeah, he was always makin' up stuff like that." November sighed. She shifted her weight on the cushion.

"It's gotta be hard to lose somebody you love," said Dana. "I don't know how you deal with it, girlfriend. I'd go crazy if anything ever happened to Kofi."

Despite the music, silence filled the room. "I never really loved Josh," November whispered to the floor.

Dana stopped in midbraid. "What did you say, girl?"

"I never really loved Josh," November repeated, her voice full of regret. "I know I *said* I loved him. Isn't that what you're supposed to say when you're going out with somebody?" And then she started to cry.

"Girl, you trippin'," Dana said as she put the comb and brush on the table. Fine strands of dark brown fuzzy hair laced the teeth of the comb. She sat down next to November and put her arm around her friend's shaking shoulders.

November pulled a tissue out of her pocket and blew her nose. "I'm for real. I never told anybody this before."

"But . . . but you two always seemed to be so happy together," Dana exclaimed. "Lots of kids at school envied the two of you because it seemed so deep, so real."

"Josh made me laugh. He was so much fun to be with—always cracking jokes and acting silly. But I don't know if that's enough to be called love."

"He was the most lovable, craziest kid I ever met, that's for sure," Dana said with a smile. "Remember when he rode on all the kiddie rides at Kings Island? His legs were sticking way up over the edge, and he kept telling the ride operator that he never wanted to forget what it felt like to be six."

"That's what I mean," November said, her face a frown of confusion. "I'm all about helping disabled kids learn to walk, or teaching a second grader how to read. Josh was always just looking for the next joke, the next laugh. He didn't have a serious bone in his body."

Dana looked November in the eye. "So why did you stay with him?"

"Be for real! Josh was fine and he was fun. But I'm sixteen years old! I just wanted to have a good time—I didn't want to marry him or anything." She sighed. "Isn't having a boyfriend just what happens in high school—like doing math homework or going to dances or buying new shoes?"

"I don't know. I never really thought about it. Kofi makes me tingle when he touches me. I guess that's love."

November tried again to explain herself. "The girls at school say they love somebody until he makes them mad, or they find somebody better to love, and then they move on. You don't plan to marry the dudes or have them in your life forever. You just say 'I love you,' enjoy the juicy feelings while they last, then you go your separate ways. Sometimes it hurts, and sometimes you're just glad it's over."

"This is heavy, November," Dana said quietly. "Maybe you're just overreacting to all that's happened. Maybe you miss him so much that you're just saying this to help you get over all the hurt—you know—'cause he's gone." She looked at her friend with concern.

"No, it's more than that." November picked up the comb and began slapping it in her hand. "Don't get me wrong—for a while I really did think I loved him. I figured that love meant going out on dates and getting dressed up and making out in the backseat of somebody's car."

"That's what me and Kofi do," Dana admitted.

"I loved being with him. But I didn't love him—not deep down inside where those feelings are supposed to be."

"But that's okay, November. That's no reason for you to feel guilty."

"Josh died exactly two months ago today," said November sadly.

"I know. It seems like his funeral was just yester-day. I miss him so much."

"I do too. But everybody treats me like the broken-hearted girlfriend. I feel like . . . a fake."

"You two had been together for a couple of years, right?"

November nodded. "But now that he's gone, every-body seems to be expecting me to feel something that just isn't there—at least the ones who still talk to me."

"What're you sayin'?"

"Kids treat me funny—like they don't know what to say or something. It's like death is a bad word, so they pretend like they're in a hurry and book out of there instead of talkin' to me."

"Don't let them stress you, November. Soon enough, when more time's gone by, people will start to treat you like before, and let you get on with your life."

"Somehow I have a feeling that's not going to hap-pen." November began pulling hairs from the comb, tears spilling down her cheeks.

"Girl, what's wrong with you? What do you care about what people think about you and Josh? It's none of their business, anyway!"

"My life is a mess, Dana," November said delib-erately.

"You flunk that chemistry test that O'Brian gave us last week?"

"No. I'm pretty sure I got most of the questions right."

"Your mother sweatin' you about your clothes?"

"No. Actually, she gave me some money to buy clothes just last week. Mama deals with stress—my problems and hers, too—by spending money."

"I'll switch mothers with you any day!" Dana said with a grin. "So what's wrong? You look like you just found out they're gonna quit making chocolate chip ice cream."

November took a deep breath and looked directly at her friend. "I'm pregnant."

DANA GASPED. "SHUT UP!" THEN SHE whispered, "Are you *sure*?"

November nodded, her eyes welling again. "I bought one of those home pregnancy tests, and it came out positive. I didn't want to believe it, but there's no mistake."

Neither girl spoke for a moment. The CD played in the background—pounding bass rhythms and a soulful singer wailing about hot love. Finally Dana asked quietly, "Josh?"

November stared at her. "Dana! Who else?"

"Oh, girl, this is so messed up. You wanna talk about it?" Dana hugged November tightly.

November began slowly. "I'm pretty sure it happened the night before he died. It had been a while since we had, like, you know, fooled around." She kept her head down. "Josh was so excited about finally getting into the Warriors of Distinction. We decided to celebrate that Thursday night, even though the formal induction wasn't until Friday."

"You must have really partied hard," Dana said carefully.

"Not really. We talked and laughed and ate pizza and chicken wings until three in the morning—right there in his basement—in the rec room of his house. Then we stopped talking and started kissing, and . . . well, usually we're better prepared, but this time things just got out of hand. It wasn't anything either of us planned. Everything just started feeling really mellow and we just rode the wave."

"Did you think about . . . ," Dana began.

"I didn't think at all. It was like everything was swirled with color and I was, like, seeing all these different shades dazzling around me."

"You make it sound like it was pretty cool that night."

November shrugged. "You know what?"

"What, girl?"

November looked away from her friend. "I think it's overrated," she admitted quietly. "When the colors faded and reality came back, I felt, I don't know, like, disappointed or something, like it didn't really mean anything."

"What do you mean?" Dana asked gently.

November frowned, trying to make sense of her jumbled thoughts. "You know when you're a kid and you put together those jigsaw puzzles?"

"Yeah."

"Well, I always felt like a piece was missing—that big crooked one in the front that all the others connect to. You feel me?"

Dana nodded.

"When you look at movies, it seems like the actors feel some kind of magic when they make love—with violins and pretty music playing. All I ever heard was creaking springs. It was really pretty pathetic."

"What does 'make love' mean, anyway?" Dana asked, frowning. "Seems to me love is something you ought to feel, not make."

"Would loving him have made a difference?" November asked bleakly.

Dana had no answer.

November put her hands to her face and wept again. "What am I supposed to do with a baby?"

Dana let her cry for a few minutes. Then, when November seemed to have calmed down a little, Dana began brushing her friend's hair again in the uncomfortable silence that followed.

"Have you told your mother?" she asked finally.

"No. Just you."

"What will she say?"

"She scheduled me to go on the Black College Tour in a couple of months. That's all she talks about these days—college and majors and tuition and stuff. This is gonna kill her. And then she's gonna kill me!"

"That didn't make any sense, but I'm not gonna argue with a pregnant woman!" Dana said in a teasing tone.

But the words seemed to sober November. "I'm no woman, Dana. I'm just a kid. I don't know how to raise a child. I don't think I can!"

"So you think you're going to keep the baby?"

November looked up. "I guess. What else can I do?"

"There are lots of options, you know," Dana said tentatively.

"No. I can't go there. But the kid deserves better than me," November replied.

"What do you think Josh's parents will say when they find out?" Dana suddenly asked.

November looked startled. "I never even thought about them! What would they care?"

"November, Josh was their only child! I have a feeling they would be real interested in a potential grandchild."

"It's none of their business," November said, her

jaw set. "This is my problem. I'll figure it out somehow." But she knew she was just spouting words. She had no idea what that meant.

That night November shivered as she curled up in bed with her Big Bird stuffed toy that she'd gotten when she was five. She would never let her friends know she still slept with a stuffed animal, but Josh had known. He'd even bought her a little green Kermit the Frog for her birthday last year. When she'd asked him why Kermit, Josh had said, "The frog can keep the bird company while you're at school, and besides, it will drive Miss Piggy crazy with jealousy!"

They'd giggled and pretended and figured they'd have forever to laugh together. But they didn't. Kermit was still around to keep Big Bird company, but November knew *she* was now on her own. She cuddled the well-worn toy and cried herself to sleep.